D1006080

BILOXI

Also by **Mary Miller**

Always Happy Hour: Stories

The Last Days of California: A Novel

Big World

BILOXI

A NOVEL

MARY MILLER

LIVERIGHT PUBLISHING CORPORATION

A Division of W. W. Norton & Company

Independent Publishers Since 1923

NEW YORK · LONDON

Copyright © 2019 by Mary Miller

All rights reserved
Printed in the United States of America
First Edition

For information about permission to reproduce selections from this book, write to Permissions, Liveright Publishing Corporation, a division of W. W. Norton & Company, Inc., 500 Fifth Avenue, New York, NY 10110

For information about special discounts for bulk purchases, please contact W. W. Norton Special Sales at specialsales@wwnorton.com or 800-233-4830

Manufacturing by Lake Book Manufacturing
Book design by Fearn Cutler de Vicq
Production manager: Beth Steidle

Library of Congress Cataloging-in-Publication Data

Names: Miller, Mary, 1977– author.
Title: Biloxi : a novel / Mary Miller.
Description: First edition. | New York ; London : Liveright Publishing Corporation, a division of W. W. Norton & Company, [2019]
Identifiers: LCCN 2018056974 | ISBN 9781631492167 (hardcover)
Classification: LCC PS3613.I5446 B55 2019 | DDC 813/.6—dc23
LC record available at https://lccn.loc.gov/2018056974

Liveright Publishing Corporation, 500 Fifth Avenue, New York, N.Y. 10110
www.wwnorton.com

W. W. Norton & Company Ltd., 15 Carlisle Street, London W1D 3BS

1 2 3 4 5 6 7 8 9 0

For Winter,
who also happens to be
a slightly overweight mixed-breed
who gags a lot

The moment I decided to quit,
I felt much better.

—Charles Bukowski, *Post Office*

BILOXI

CHAPTER 1

I WAS ON MY way to Walgreens when I saw Ellen's car—a Buick Regal in a dark blue color she called "sparkling sapphire"—and panicked, turning left instead of right, which took me to the beach. It wasn't a detour, exactly, but I never took the beach. As I wound my way back up to Pass Road, I saw a house with a sign that said FREE DOGS on the mailbox alongside a couple of drowsy balloons. Next thing I knew I was parked and getting out of my car as an obese man shuffled down his driveway to greet me.

"Harry Davidson, LPN," the man said, his hand extended ten feet in advance.

"Louis McDonald, Jr." It was the first time I'd ever introduced myself in this way, with the suffix. I liked it. Made me sound like I'd inherited something.

"You related to Myrtle McDonald?"

"I don't know a Myrtle."

"Nice lady, goes to my church," he said. "Makes a good carrot cake. You like carrot cake?"

"Sure," I said.

"I've found that all men like carrot cake."

"Is that so?" I wanted to take it back, tell him I didn't like carrot cake that much, that it was just okay.

And then he went into his spiel: he had too many dogs and some of them were going to get turned into dog meat. He hated it, but what could he do? Such was life. His new wife, turned out, was allergic. And then he said nobody'd been by to look at Layla yet, followed by a series of shrugs and oddball faces, which I took to mean it was all up to me.

He didn't say, "It's all up to you." If he had said, "It's all up to you," I wouldn't have been able to take her. I was curious about this new wife and found myself looking into the darkened windows of the house. It was hard to believe someone had recently married this man.

"She's obedient, too," he said, yanking up his pants. Britches, I thought, yanking up his britches—pants were too nice a word for what he was wearing. "Border Collies are known for their obedience. You could probably train her to get your morning paper."

"I can get my own damn paper," I said. I felt manipulated, aggrieved.

Harry Davidson chuckled. "You probably want to see her—of course you want to see her. Let me go get her for you." He pointed at me as if we were in on a joke and shuffled back up his driveway. I looked at my car. I could just get in my car and drive to Walgreens to pick up my diabetes medicine and a two-liter bottle of Pepsi as I'd intended. Maybe I'd even get some of those bite-sized white-chocolate Kit Kats I liked so much. They were new—they were always coming out with new candy and they always would.

He returned with a slightly overweight dog, bright white with a black patch over her right eye. One black ear and one white one. Two of her paws were also black, one in the front and one in the back.

"Check out the coat on this girl—snow white," he said, "beautiful! Go ahead and pet her."

I petted her, hair coming off on my fingers. "She doesn't look all that bright."

"Oh, she'll surprise you. She's complicated—more like a person than a dog, really. Complex emotions and all that."

"Like a person," I repeated. I wasn't in the right state of mind to make a decision of this magnitude. My blood sugar was low. I was getting shaky. "How old is she?"

"Hard to say—young. Maybe a year? Two?" He lifted her lip so I could see her teeth. "Never had a single accident, though she's thrown up a few times. Looked like bile, mostly. Sometimes she gets this gagging thing going." Harry Davidson put his hand up to his throat and flitted it about.

"She gags a lot?"

"Not too bad—I think it's just nerves. I have to tell you," he said, leaning in so I could smell the coffee on his breath, "Layla's always been my favorite."

"What's your wife's name?" I asked.

"What?"

"Your wife."

He took a step toward me and I took one back. "What do you want to know about my wife for?" He turned and looked at the house.

"I was just making conversation."

"That's a strange way to make conversation, buddy," he said, "asking the name of somebody's wife like that, out of the blue."

"I know a Davidson."

"Uh huh," he said.

"Her name's Sally."

"My wife isn't *Sally*. There's no Sally here. So, about the dog," he said. "Let's get back to dogs."

"How many do you have?"

"Fourteen before I started downsizing—mostly small ones. I've got to get rid of all but the hypoallergenic." He was speaking slowly now, looking at me like he had no idea what I might do. He wouldn't be surprised if I started jumping up and down on one foot or took out a knife and jabbed at him.

We continued talking about his dogs and how he'd come to have so many—a litter here, a stray there—until Harry Davidson wasn't bristled any longer. He was smiling when he said, "Oh, yeah, she's really taken to you." There was nothing in the dog's behavior to substantiate this. "I named her after the song. Eric Clapton was in love with George Harrison's wife and it's about this woman, I think her name was Pattie—or was it Debbie?—it wasn't Layla, anyhow. He ended up marrying the girl, though Harrison wasn't too broke up about it. He even went to the wedding. It didn't last, though. . . ." He shook his head and I waited for him to say something like *they never do*, but he spared me that.

After that we stood there and observed Layla together. She didn't look particularly smart or energetic or interested in me. In other words, she wasn't anything you might want in a dog. I thought about the dogs I'd had as a boy: a pack of wild animals that weren't allowed inside the house. Occasionally, if the mood struck, if my mother had made pancakes that morning, I'd toss them into the air to watch them jump. Then I'd close the door and forget about them. And then I thought about Ellen's dog, a small, nervous thing with wiry hair in a burnt caramel color.

"She's a good one," he said. "One of the best!"

That was a stupid thing to say and I felt like pointing out how stupid it was. I didn't care for this man. I liked the idea of training his dog, though, the things I might teach her to do. Perhaps she really could get my paper in the mornings. That would be something for the neighbors to see.

"I don't want to pressure you," he said, "but I've got some burgers I need to flip."

"Oh, I doubt that."

"It's something people say," he said, "a figure of speech. I have things to do."

I wanted the dog but I didn't like the idea of doing him any favors, and I certainly didn't want him to think he'd talked me into it.

"Well," I said, and I paused for much longer than either of us was comfortable with. I opened my mouth and closed it again, really challenging myself. Harry Davidson coughed. Then he narrowed his eyes and started shaking his head. Finally I said, "I think this is the one for me."

"Oh yeah?"

"I believe it is."

"I can't take her back now. This is a one-time deal."

He had the kind of eyes where you could see the whites all the way around—the entire iris on display, exposed and naked-looking. "There'll be no reason for that," I said.

Harry Davidson, LPN, stuck out his hand and I shook it—a firm, dry shake. Then I opened the door and told her to get in and she surprised me by doing just that. We drove home the beach way. The beach pleased me and I didn't regret it even though I was catching every light and there were a lot of people out cruising, driving too slow with their windows rolled down like they had no place in the world to be. I didn't have anyplace to be, either. I had left the house to pick up a Pepsi and look what happened because I'd turned one way instead of the other. Life really was something.

I was feeling better. Decisions had been made. I'd known what I'd wanted and I'd gone after it. The day was sunny and warm but not too warm. I turned to look at her, sitting calmly and staring out the window like a person. It gave me a nice feeling so I kept turning my head to look at her, nearly running off the road every time. She looked happy, like she was smiling, but maybe she was only hot.

"Whatcha see out there, girl?"

I rolled down the window, not too far, I didn't want her to jump out, and she raised her nose to get a good sniff.

"That's the ocean," I said, though it wasn't the ocean. It was the Mississippi Sound. And past that was the Gulf of Mexico, which was an ocean basin connected to the Atlantic. I didn't think I needed to get into all that, though I could and she would listen. I pointed out the sights: the casinos—the Beau Rivage where all the old people gambled and the Hard Rock where they had a Ben & Jerry's and a good steakhouse—the Biloxi lighthouse and Jefferson Davis's home, Beauvoir, which was advertising its 30th Annual Fall Muster. I thought I might like to see that, all the people in costumes reenacting the war. I imagined myself standing over a man pretending to be dead and nosing him with my shoe to see if he moved. Kicking him a bit. They were very serious, I'd heard, and tried to re-create everything exactly as it had happened.

"Not sure why it's called a muster, though, what a funny word. My brother was in a war once, but that was a long time ago. He didn't make it so you won't get to meet him. They lost that war . . . that war was not a success. And there are the trash birds, also called seagulls, and some trash people feeding the trash birds. They love to do that. For the life of me I don't know why. And that's one of the dead trees that the "chainsaw artist" carved into a dolphin after the storm. The storm to which I am referring, of course, is Katrina. But that was also before your time." I talked and talked and didn't feel silly for talking to a dog, which was surprising.

I turned to see if she was following along and she was, steadily gazing out the window. I imagined her running headlong into a pack of seagulls, the way they'd scatter.

"We'll go to the beach soon," I said. "Oh, I bet you'd like that—lots of smells, all sorts of new smells, and you can find some chicken bones and fish carcasses to eat."

There we'd be, smiling at the other dog walkers, the bike riders and joggers. Even the few homeless men on benches, dropping some change into their cups. Looking out at the water with the breeze in my hair. I had been living a very small and quiet life, but no longer! No longer would I live a small life; it might still be quiet—I had yet to hear Layla bark—but it wouldn't be so small.

I parked in the garage and opened the door for her. She hopped out. She'd shed all over the place, a real mess. There was also a strong smell about her and something about the smell reminded me of Harry Davidson and his coffee breath. I really would've liked to see his wife. Sometimes an ugly man—sometimes even an ugly *and* poor man—managed to get himself a nice-looking wife and I suspected Harry Davidson was one of them, though I had no idea why.

I started the water in the guest bathroom and then went to find Layla, slunk down by the couch.

"It's just a bath," I said. "I'm just gonna clean you up a bit."

She wouldn't follow me so I picked her up. She was heavier than I'd expected. It reminded me of my daughter, Maxine, and how stubborn she'd been as a child. Whenever I had to pick her up and move her somewhere, she made her body stiff and heavy as she tried to stay firmly on the ground. She would yell, too. She had dense bones, came by it honest.

I took Layla to the bathroom and closed us in, knelt and tested out the water, impressing myself, and then we waited for the tub to fill. I had brought her into the room too early, like I was purposefully trying to torture her.

"Okay," I said, "it's time." I looked at her and she looked at me and then she walked over to the tub and tried to climb in. Oh, how she pleased me already. Takes it like a dog, I thought, smarter than she seems, rather like a person, really.

I lathered her up with Head & Shoulders and she turned blue in a way I liked. I considered taking a picture of her with the phone on my camera. I only had two pictures on there that Maxine had taken. They were of my granddaughter, her daughter, and they were not good pictures: both blurry, in one of them the girl's eyes had caught the light in a way that made her look possessed. Children could be oddly sinister. It was a lot of work to get the shampoo out but she was cooperative. After that, I rubbed her down with a towel and brushed her with Ellen's purple hairbrush, which I had moved from the master bathroom to the guest bathroom along with the various other toiletries she'd left behind, so I wouldn't have to see them. I couldn't bring myself to throw them away. The remains of a woman, the remnants of a woman I had once loved. Women still existed in the world and so did Ellen. They didn't remind me of her so much except the hairbrush. I recalled the sound it made, how loud it was when she pulled the brush through to the tips of her hair, like something that hurt.

I told her that Ellen was the reason I'd found her, or more accurately, the fear of seeing Ellen behind the wheel of her car, driving along the road, had prompted her unexpected arrival into my life. As I explained it, it didn't seem like any reason to be fearful. What if I'd seen her? There she'd be, behind the wheel of her car, driving. And there I'd be, doing the same. But the terror was there as I imagined her slowly turning her neck to look at me, our eyes meeting.

Layla was still wet so I looked for a hair dryer but couldn't find one. This is a damn load of trouble, I thought. She licked my hand like she knew it was a lot of trouble and she was sorry about it. Then she started gagging but it was more like she was having a hard time swallowing, or she was throwing up in her mouth and choking it back down.

"You okay?"

It went on and on and she was looking at me, sorry and worried and I was sorry about it, too, but mostly I found it very annoying. Extraordinarily annoying. I wanted to put her outside but she was still wet and it was getting cool out. I took another towel from the closet and rubbed her down again, hoping that if we both ignored it the gagging or whatever it was would stop. I dried each of her paws and told her it was alright and I'd take her to the vet if it continued, unlike Harry Davidson who had probably never taken any of his animals to the vet. Finally it stopped and everything was okay. I threw her a piece of bologna and we were back on.

It was five-thirty, the best time of day. Soon I'd eat dinner, maybe fix myself a drink first. And then it would be dark and I could go to sleep at any time after that. I liked to fall asleep in my chair until I woke up—sometimes it was two o'clock in the morning before I got into bed. Ellen had never let me sleep in my chair but would call my name and shake my shoulder until I got up because she liked to be in the living room alone. What would she do after that? It was her special alone time, she called it. She drank wine and watched TV or played games on her phone. I watched the news while the dog crouched at my feet and licked them, not unpleasant. I figured Ellen sat in my chair after I went to bed because it was nice and warm. The most comfortable spot in the house.

"Hold on, I've got something for you."

I went to the closet, unfolded a baby blanket that had belonged to Maxine—yellow because Ellen hadn't wanted to do the whole pink thing—and put it down for her. Bunched it up. I made a mental note to get her a bed and a few bones, some expensive, high-protein dog food because I'd heard that was best. Until then she could eat lunch meat.

"What kind of toys do you like?" I asked. "You like toys? I'll get you one of those things you put treats in and you have to figure out how to get the treat out. I bet you'd like that. It's a puzzle with a reward for all your hard work. Ellen had one of those for her little shiteater—she'd put peanut butter in there and make a real goddamn mess. I forget what it's called but it looks kinda like a snowman."

She didn't know what I was talking about but I didn't have to explain. I was her master. She licked my feet some more. I'd saved her and we both knew it. She was shy, though, and wouldn't look at me straight on.

"Do you know how to use a doggy door?" I asked. "You probably have to go to the bathroom." I should've thought of that. Jesus, how long had she been holding it?

We'd installed the doggy door a few years back when Ellen bought the Chihuahua. The dog had a skin condition and all sorts of other ailments, which seemed to make her love it more. She took great care in giving the dog its shots every day and feeling sorry for it when its eyes went all filmy after. It was funny how that worked. Ellen didn't want anything to do with me when I was sick. She'd hardly wanted anything to do with me at all once Maxine left the house. And she got lazy, too, was always claiming she was tired even though she just watched HGTV and played casino games on her phone, the kind where the money you won or lost was fake, or she met groups of ladies for lunch or bridge and told me all about the renovations they were making to their houses. What she wanted to do with ours. She seemed to think she'd done something amazing when she picked me up a hamburger.

I took the bacon left over from breakfast and went outside, knelt on the concrete. It hurt my knees. Jesus Christ, my knees. The right one in particular. I cursed God, apologized; it wasn't because I believed in him—I didn't, hadn't ever believed, though that was harder to admit—to have lost one's faith is different from never having had it at all—but I was still afraid of a man called God.

I pushed open the flap and called to her.

"Layla! Girl!" I said. "Dog! Come here, girl. I got bacon for you." I held the flap open and she stood on the other side: a standoff. "Come on out." I stuck my hand through and gave her a piece, which she swallowed without chewing.

"This is a doggy door," I said, flapping it back and forth. "Now come on out and see your new yard."

"It's a nice yard. It's real nice out here." The bugs were swarming. It was lovebug season.

She stayed safely within the yellow light of the kitchen, looking unperturbed.

"Come on out and try it. Just step your foot over, like this." I grabbed her black foot and pulled but she backed up. I gave her another piece of bacon and she extended her neck to get it. I closed the flap and opened it, closed and opened it. "You step right through here," I said. "I guess it's for a smallish dog but you'll fit."

Her eyes said she loved me, that she heard everything I said and understood, but she had her reasons.

CHAPTER 2

MUCH AS I liked the dog, she wasn't very bright and didn't make a peep unless she was gagging. The gagging annoyed the hell out of me, but it usually only lasted a couple of minutes and when it was over we'd pretend it hadn't happened and never would again. So much of life seemed to be this way.

As it turned out, I had no idea how to train a dog. She would sit and lie down and roll over, a little bit of everything when I opened the refrigerator to take out the bologna, but she didn't know the difference between *sit* or *lie down* or *roll over*, only that I wanted her to do something. I didn't need her to sit or lie down or roll over, anyhow. What good were these things? This ain't no dog-and-pony show. But she couldn't catch, either, which was unfortunate. When I tossed the bologna into the air, it landed flat on the tile. Every time I tossed a slice I thought of my old dogs and how high they'd jumped when the pancakes flew. It didn't matter how badly I tossed them; they never missed. Because the floor was seasoned with bologna, she spent a lot of her time licking it, and my feet stuck to the tile in a way I found highly unpleasant.

On top of it all, she didn't take to the doggy door despite numerous demonstrations. She was smart enough to know I'd give her the bacon, anyhow. And she didn't whimper or scratch or give me the cold-nose so I had no idea when she needed to use the bathroom. I let her out every couple of hours, just to be sure; when I opened the door five or ten minutes later, there she'd be, calm and patient as a stone, and walk back inside to resume her floor or foot licking.

It was tough but I tried not to be irritated because I didn't want her to feel bad about irritating me. She must have been abused. I repeated this to myself and it made me want to rise to the challenge. I imagined her chained to a pole in a dirt backyard, her bowl of food turned to mush in the rain. I conjured a picture I'd seen of a dog with the saddest eyes in the world, the saddest eyes in the whole goddamn world: *When Bruno realizes he's been abandoned and his family isn't coming back for him.* That dog's eyes haunted me. I felt like someone—perhaps Maxine—had shown this to me on purpose. I told myself I would do right by Layla if it killed me. I also felt a strange need to entertain her, be interesting. Lucky for her I was an interesting man.

She was sensitive, just as Harry Davidson said. I was sorry I'd never see him again, though I'd disliked him on sight. I could conjure the smell of his breath and his eyes with the whites all the way around, the way his body shuffled as he walked.

I thought I might drive by his house to see if the sign and the balloons were still there. What other dogs did he have? Had he given me the lemon? Had he spotted me pulling up and pegged me for the sort of man who would agree to take the lemon? I felt sure I'd gotten the lemon and yet I didn't think I'd have taken a different one. No, she was the right dog. I'd known it immediately. There had been a reason I'd taken that route and it wasn't because of Ellen, who had not, so far as I knew, put a Salt Life bumper sticker on her car. And it wasn't Harry Davidson I wanted to see but his wife, a woman I had never laid eyes on and who might not even exist. That had just occurred to me—Harry Davidson had made up his wife in order to have someone to blame, a story to tell. The new wife, allergic, had to get rid of them. It would've made more sense if he'd been asking for money but he hadn't asked for any money. Maybe I should have offered him some and he'd have brought out other, better dogs. I supposed I didn't look like the kind of man who had much. If I had reached for my wallet, he might've brought me a dog that could catch a goddamn slice of bologna.

There was a knock at the door and Layla trotted over to it. It was the quickest I'd seen her move yet. She sniffed the UPS man's leg and went back to her blanket.

After he left the box, I tried to teach her how to bark, show her how it was done. I thought I had a pretty good bark, reasonably authentic. "Ruff!" I tried it an octave higher and then an octave lower to see if anything registered. I attempted a growl but wasn't as impressed with my abilities there and the dog seemed confused, like she hadn't realized I was also a dog.

"I'm just going to have to accept you the way you are," I said. "It'll be a lesson for me." I cursed at her a while, but she had no idea what I was saying. I could call her all manner of names so long as I used my nice voice.

I opened the box: a six-month membership to the cheese-of-the-month club along with a wedge called Ossau Iraty. I picked up a flyer that said IN PURSUIT OF CHEESE in enormous letters at the top that told me about this month's selection: *Ossau Iraty is made from 100% sheep's milk from the famed brebis sheep that graze in the valleys of Ossau and Iraty. These small creamy-brown sheep have helped make several well-known cheeses, including the famed Roquefort.*

I hope you enjoy this early birthday gift! the card said. *Love, Maxine.*

"Small creamy-brown sheep. I'd like to eat one of those, instead." I liked cheddar and mozzarella and those were the only cheeses I'd ever liked.

"What's that girl thinking?" I set the box on the floor. The dog sniffed it and turned up her nose. I would have to call Maxine and thank her, but I wasn't going to do it today.

The newswoman I liked, Christy Something-or-other, blond, large-chested, was interviewing a woman from the local animal shelter. This had to be a sign. Sometimes you were humming a song and it came on the radio. One day you accidentally adopted a dog and then your favorite TV girl was talking about the importance of adopting unwanted animals, and Layla was nothing if not unwanted. With my newfound riches—my inheritance would arrive any day—I might be able to get a nice young girl like Christy to give me half a chance. She could teach me a few things. I'd give her a credit card with an unlimited balance and let her show me what life could be like.

The other woman patted her lap and out trotted a scrawny brown animal barking its head off. Layla sat up and let out a single bark.

"Good girl!" I said, "good dog!" But she looked as surprised and humiliated as a person jolted out of sleep by their own fart.

"Try it one more time," I said. "You just gotta get used to it. For some it don't come natural." And then I petted her head and rubbed her belly, which was starting to smell like a Frito, and what popped out of me was a corn chip song I made up on the spot. It was repetitive and catchy. She loved this corn chip song, watched me straight on and wagged her tail. Right after I stopped singing it, though, I had no idea how it had gone, couldn't remember it at all. *Oh, a corn chip! You smell like a corn chip!* I sang, but I couldn't recapture the glory of the corn chip song for the life of me. I picked my nose for a while and fell asleep. When I woke up, she was licking my shoe. I was wearing shoes inside, which was unusual. I took them off so she could lick my feet. Her tongue was wet but not too wet and it excited me, in a way. I figure the dog wouldn't mind if I got a bit excited; I wasn't going to do anything untoward.

I had never been anybody's whole world before. There had been people in my life—first one family and then another—but there had been so many problems among the individual members that it had never felt much like a group, just a bunch of people trying to redirect their issues by pointing out the shortcomings and faults of the others. That worked alright until they caught up with you.

I had some eggs boiling and was opening a can of tuna when I heard my former brother-in-law pull up.

Frank lived a few streets over and had taken it upon himself to check in on me every now and again. He'd stay for ten minutes and hold a beer, but he never finished it. Sometimes he brought his leftovers from Chili's. The man loved Chili's better than anybody I'd ever seen and he'd made me a fan. Steak fajitas or a Fresh Mex Bowl, occasionally there'd be half a burger and some fries gone cold. I always took them begrudgingly but ate everything the minute he left. There was something about leftovers that made them easy to eat. In the restaurant, what might seem like an overwhelming amount of food was a mere snack once you got it home.

Frank was a fine man, dull and fine. He liked to paint pictures of landscapes—trees and barns, sometimes a lake with some ducks on it but ducks weren't his specialty. The pictures weren't half bad. I had a couple hanging on the walls in my study. They were the kind of pictures that were simply pictures; they never caught your eye, you never noticed them.

I opened the door for him and went to turn off the burner. And then I heard a lot of barking and Frank yelling and I thought a dog must've attacked Layla and Frank didn't know what was happening because he didn't even know I had a dog. But that's not what happened. It was Layla snarling and shaking Frank's pant leg.

He was still yelling as I called her off.

"Down, girl! Down! It's okay," I told her. "It's just Frank. Frank's our friend." I was so proud I couldn't stop myself from grinning.

I touched him on the arm and said, "This is Frank," and she stopped snarling and let go. She was a guard dog, after all. She knew how to bark but only when she needed to. She wasn't going to bark at every bird or cat like some kind of animal.

Frank was understandably upset. His pants had been torn and she'd bitten him.

"Did she break the skin?"

"I don't think so," he said, "but she got me pretty good," which meant he was going to be upset about it anyway. "Look at those teeth marks," he said. "Do you see 'em?"

"I see 'em," I said. His ankle was a little red but I didn't see any marks.

"Whose dog is that?"

"It's my dog, Layla." I tried to explain that she was a humble, docile creature, and I'd thought the commotion had come from a stray or a neighbor dog attacking her. "I'm sorry, Frank," I said. "She must've thought you were dangerous."

"You ought to put that thing down." He was shaking he was so angry. I'd never seen him angry before, not even after the time Ellen and I had had a fight and she'd fallen and hit her head—an accident. It really had been an accident and Frank had understood, though the police hadn't. That was a long time ago, decades, the single night I'd spent in jail. You didn't forget something like that. I could still feel the helplessness that comes when you put your hands in your pockets and find them empty. As drunk as I'd been, I knew exactly what had happened: what I'd done, what Ellen had done, the officers at the door—I could have written a transcript, drawn diagrams—but it still felt like a dream. I resented Frank for reminding me of it. It had all been Ellen's fault, anyhow. She'd fallen without any assistance from me.

"Bad dog!" I said to Layla. "Bad!" I said it a few more times for Frank's benefit and felt terrible—when he left, I'd give her two pieces of bologna. A whole pack.

"I'm real sorry, Frank." I wasn't going to apologize a third time and hoped it would be enough.

"That dog is dangerous," he said.

I made some neutral-sounding noises to let him know I'd heard him and was considering what he had to say. The whole thing *was* curious. Layla had seen me open the door and should've been able to figure out that he was okay. Frank was the least dangerous man I'd ever known. He didn't like dogs, though, and maybe Layla had sensed this, or maybe Frank was a real asshole, a psychopath, and the dull and sober routine was just there to throw everybody off. How better to escape notice than to be as calm and nonthreatening as possible? To visit shut-ins and paint landscapes? I made a mental note to do some research after he left—how to tell if someone is a psychopath, the difference between a psychopath and a sociopath. I'd get out the iPad Maxine had given me for my last birthday and charge it, hope it still worked. An iPad one year and a cheese-of-the-month club the next!

"I dropped your dinner," he said.

I went to the door and looked at the box face down on the walkway. "That's a shame," I said. "What was it?"

"Fajitas. There was a lot left, too."

"What kind?" Tuna was a nonalternative now. I'd have to call Domino's.

He looked at me funny. Then he said, "The combo—chicken and steak. It was really good."

"That's a shame."

"The steak wasn't chewy at all. Sometimes it's too chewy."

I sat in my chair with Layla at my feet. Frank sat on the couch and bent down to examine his ankle, asked me to turn on the overhead.

I got up and turned on the light and then, since I was up,

went into the kitchen. The dog followed. I had this thing I liked to do with her ears, flap them fast as I could like she was gonna take off and fly. I did that for a minute and quietly fed her a piece of bologna.

"Hey, Frank!" I called. "Can I get you anything?"

"Do you have any frozen vegetables?"

"I don't have any vegetables. But there's an eye mask I use for my neck sometimes. It was Ellen's."

He didn't say anything so I said I'd bring it. "You want a beer?"

"Do you have Coke?" he asked. We were both talking in overly loud voices—shouting practically.

"I have Pepsi or Dr Pepper. The Pepsi's flat." I wanted to tell him I'd been on my way to get a fresh two-liter when I'd gone rogue and gotten the dog but decided against it.

"I guess I'll have a beer," he said. "I don't need any caffeine, anyway. I've been having trouble sleeping."

"You?" I said. "Trouble sleeping?" I handed him the beer and the eye mask. "I would've figured you slept like a baby."

I watched as Frank attempted to secure the mask around his ankle but it was awkward so I stopped watching. He propped his ankle on his knee and held the mask in place like that.

"Just keep that thing away from me," he said.

"Layla," I said, using my serious voice. "Get on your blanket." The dog looked at me; she knew I was putting on. The dog and I were strangers to each other and yet I felt like we were together in this thing, partners. That no one had ever known me better.

He continued looking at her warily. No, he could never be a serial killer. A dangerous man wouldn't be so afraid of a thirty-five-pound dog. I wasn't sure how much she weighed, though. When Frank left I'd have to weigh myself and then pick her up and get back on the scale and subtract the difference. She might be forty-three or even forty-six pounds. It was hard to tell, and I'd never been good at eyeballing things. I was reminded of how Ellen and I had gone to the fair every year—first to take Maxine and then, after Maxine left, we continued going just the two of us—and Ellen would have the man guess her weight. She always won. She was compact in a way you couldn't predict unless you tried to lift her; to lift her was to move mountains, same as Maxine. He'd guess twelve, fifteen pounds less than her actual weight and she'd gloat and eat a funnel cake and a corn dog and free biscuit after free biscuit topped with molasses. One year, she'd eaten so many they stopped serving her and she'd gotten a kick out of that. It had been her goal: *How many do you think they'll give me before they refuse?*

So many years we'd gone to the fair and this was the first time I'd miss it. So many biscuits we'd eaten. The biscuits, light and fluffy, were easy to swallow, and my wife and the biscuits—the perfection of those biscuits—were all tangled up together.

"You want me to put her in the bathroom?"

"That's alright," he said. I knew he wanted me to put her somewhere and I should have done it but it was my house and the dog wasn't going to bother him again.

After that, we sat in silence. I was grateful he wasn't asking me the usual questions, at least. Had I heard anything from Maxine? What was going on with my father's estate, and had I talked to that lawyer, Lucky? The lawyer was a child with the name of a child—nothing more than a kid who thought he was better than me. And then he'd ask if I was keeping myself busy, and how, always the same series of questions that I didn't want to answer because he didn't really want to know. The only question he might've wanted to know was whether my inheritance had come through, if it had all been settled and how much I'd netted, and I was never going to give him that information. And what if I told him the truth about the rest of it? That I'd spent the day in my chair napping, watching back-to-back episodes of *Naked and Afraid? What happens when you put two complete strangers, sans clothes, in some of the most extreme environments on Earth?* I could tell him what happened—no sex, no romance, all of the good parts covered up, and yet I held out hope. For what, I wasn't sure. Why did these people, who were often married, who had families and jobs, go on this show? And the women lost weight but they never looked any better, bit up as they were, hair a mess. I didn't know why I liked it so much, though watching them struggle reminded me of my relative comfort—a/c on full blast, plenty of beer in the refrigerator—but Frank didn't want to hear about that, or how often I thought about the guns locked up in my study. How I'd take them out and clean them and consider putting an end to it all.

After his questions, we'd talk about the news and commiserate over the farce that was the government of the United States of America. Ha! What a farce it all was! The right and the left and the people in between. The gays and the transgenders and where they might take a shit. And Frank would say we ought to secede again and I'd agree even though the state was so broke that we needed the federal government a lot more than they needed us, and then he'd go home where he lived with his wife, who was nearly as dull but not quite. Claudia was red-haired and nice-looking for a woman of her age, and when I was feeling generous I liked to believe they were happy. She didn't have much to say, though I suspected she had a lot of thoughts in her head and maybe she even shared some of them with Frank. Perhaps they had a whole world full of fluffy biscuits that I couldn't imagine even in my most generous and agreeable moments.

I petted Layla with my foot, really gave her a good rub. When my foot came close to her head, she licked it.

Besides deliverymen, Frank was the only person who ever stopped by. Maxine called but didn't come by. Ellen called on occasion, as well, though not in several weeks, a month. She had questions about taxes or insurance and the last time she phoned she told me she'd sold her burial plot on Craigslist so I'd be next to a stranger for all eternity. She'd left me but she was the one who was angry about it. I supposed I'd been angry for a time, too: first disbelief, then anger, and then I'd skipped over whatever the other stages were and there had just been nothing, or almost nothing, except for the occasional stab-like pain when I was reminded of something nice, which was followed by a wave of nausea before a return to blankness, nearly pleasant, or at least not unpleasant. Mostly I was fine alone, and having Frank around reminded me what it was like with other people in the house. How I'd never really gotten used to it. There was always tension, though I hadn't realized it until Ellen was gone and I knew for sure she wasn't coming back. When Ellen was at the store or lunch, she might as well have been in the house—anticipating her arrival was even worse than having her around. What if I was doing something she disapproved of? There had been so many things she'd disapproved of. Every moment was an all-too-brief reprieve from her judgment, her accusation that I was lazy, even though I only retired after she left, after my father died and I knew my inheritance was coming. Back then I'd gone to work five days a week selling insurance—a job I was ill-suited for and hated every single day—and on weekends I'd done yard work and small tasks around the house, whatever Ellen asked. But I'd heard people liked to accuse you of the traits they disliked in themselves, and Ellen was one of the laziest people I'd ever known. She was also dirty, hated the water, never even learned how to swim. In the end, I suppose what she'd disapproved of was my presence, and I suppose I'd felt the same.

I never thought I'd live to see sixty-three, or have the money to retire early. It was incredible, preposterous. I hadn't wanted to live this long, and yet there was little to be done about it. I wouldn't put a bullet in my head—the mess of it, what people would say about me once the deed had been done, as if they'd been waiting for it all along.

Frank finished his beer and surprised me by asking for another.

"All the beer you can hold," I said. "I keep a good stock." I went back to the kitchen, the dog hot on my trail. I gave her another piece of bologna and did the flyaway ears before rejoining him.

We sipped our beers while his ankle cooled. When the local news was over, I turned it to Fox and we took turns grunting at the appropriate times. The dog sat on her blanket with her eyes closed. Picks up on social cues, I thought. I needed to go to the store pretty soon. I hadn't gotten my medicine and Layla didn't have any food. She'd been eating bologna and tuna, the occasional saltine or spoonful of peanut butter, and I hoped she'd transition to dog food okay, but my next thought was that she was my dog and I could feed her whatever the hell I wanted. I could make a stack of pancakes and toss them to her and she'd eat them off the tile, same as the bologna. If I made them big enough, she might even catch one.

"Have you heard from Maxine?" Frank asked.

Dammit, Frank, I thought we weren't going to do that. I thought we were past all that. He lowered his eyes to examine his ankle again and touched it in a girlish way.

"I got a present from her in the mail, a cheese-of-the-month-club sort of thing. For my birthday."

"Happy birthday," he said.

"It isn't for another week. I don't know why she sent it this early."

"I like a good cheese," he said. "What kind is it?"

"Something foreign. There's a whole story behind it."

After that I tried to mentally send him messages that it was time to go. *Leave*, I thought. *Go home.* I pictured him standing and walking to the door, raising his hand to wave goodbye. Shortly thereafter, Frank said he'd better be getting home to Claudia. Layla sat up and the two of us watched him hobble over to the door like a cripple.

"Jesus, Frank. You gonna be okay?"

"Yeah," he said. "She really got me. That's a terrible dog."

"I know it is."

"You should take that dog back to the pound."

"It was a one-time deal. Hold on," I said, and I handed him the box of cheese, which was still on the floor. "It's European, you can read all about it."

"I'll see you soon, Louis."

"Not if I see you first," I said, and pointed at him and chuckled like Harry Davidson. He looked at me strangely. I'd never seen that look on his face before and I felt the shame of saying the wrong thing, such a small thing to feel shame over, a joke, nothing. I watched him walk to his truck, hoping he never came back.

"Layla," I called. She was right by my side, focused on the fajitas. I asked her some questions: Was she happy? Did she love me? Was I the most handsome man she'd ever seen? Would we love each other forever? I liked the way her ears went up simply because whatever silly thing I'd said had been phrased as a question. She would accept my faults and ask for nothing in return besides some bologna and a bit of attention whenever I felt up to giving it to her. She didn't need me to tell her I would never love anyone else or that I'd die for her. But I could tell her those things and they'd be true. It was easy with a dog. I didn't have to give her flowers or remember her birthday, didn't even know her birthday. She would never be disappointed in me. I felt like I'd never loved anyone more.

I let her eat the fajitas as she wagged her tail. Then I went out there and picked up the foil-wrapped tortillas. I never bought tortillas at the store, but I could. I could buy whatever I wanted. I had to remind myself. I could spend fifty dollars on a couple of steaks, live lobster if it struck my fancy. Sausage links and pounds of apple-smoked bacon, whole pies from the freezer section. A couple of lovebugs, attached, set down on my arm. I considered squashing them but only brushed them off and they went on to do their business elsewhere. They were harmless; all they wanted to do was love each other before they died.

"Alright, girl," I said, "it's gone." We left the white box splayed for the neighbors to see, and I thought maybe I'd just let everything go to hell.

Layla followed me around the house as we locked the doors— one, two, three—and then checked again to be certain. It was an enormous relief to be alone. I thanked God no one cared about me, hoped no one ever did again.

But a bag of chips and four additional beers later, I was wide awake in the dark.

The bed was old and uncomfortable yet I couldn't seem to replace it. Would I drive to the mattress store and lie down on mattresses while some guy watched, asked me how they felt? I imagined Harry Davidson hiking up his britches, smiling and pointing. I imagined myself in the center of a mattress with my arms at my sides and my legs together, looking straight up at the ceiling, in a position I had never slept in in my life. The store cold and silent and white. Climbing off one bed and onto another. There was no way I'd be able to make a decision under those conditions, or would inevitably make the wrong one—decide I wanted a soft mattress when I wanted a firm one. Did they still make waterbeds? It was possible I'd walk out of there with one of those. Maxine told me I should order a bed in a box but I had no idea what that was. She said she could send me a bed in a box and it would arrive within two days and I told her please don't and then I was thinking about my inheritance. I would call the lawyer in the morning even though he hardly ever took my calls, and when he did I couldn't understand half of what he said. The last time, I lost my patience, asked him to use goddamn layman's terms.

I got out of bed. Layla looked at me as I left the room but it was a look that said, *it's late and I'm sleeping. You're on your own.*

In the kitchen I poured myself a glass of water and stared into the backyard. I wouldn't have been surprised to see someone out there, dressed in black, hunched over as he made his way from shadow to shadow. Living alone was terrifying. There were no witnesses, no one to call. I was afraid of my own voice.

I resumed my tossing and turning, Layla opening her eyes every time I moved a muscle. Judging me.

"Ole Judgy McJudger," I whispered into the dark. "Judgy McJudgerson. You think you know me?" No doubt she thought I was a piece of shit. I apologized. She was unmoved. I shouldn't have had that last beer or eaten all of the Doritos. I was a piece of shit and she knew it and I knew it. I situated pillows on either side of my body, curled my hand into my chest like a baby hand. I had no idea how anyone had ever slept through the night before, how it was even possible. And then I was fast asleep and it was fine. Everything was fine again.

CHAPTER 3

THE FOLLOWING MORNING I awoke to a bird banging against the big window in the den. I knew which bird it was—an ugly one, brown and white with some faded orange on its belly— an oriole that liked to start its activities around six o'clock. I could hear it from my bedroom, could hear it from anywhere in the house. Every few seconds it charged into the glass at a good speed, a good clip. Sometimes it went around to another window and banged into it, too.

After I let Layla out to use the bathroom and tossed a few slices of bologna to the floor, I dressed in yesterday's clothes and drove to the big pet store by the mall. Before getting down to business, I wandered the aisles looking at the fish and guinea pigs and hamsters. They were dull and unimpressive, like the kinds of things you fed other, better things. I stopped to observe some ferrets piled on top of each other, waited to see if one of them moved or if I could see their tiny chests expanding. They looked dead. Limp and boneless. I looked around for someone who might check but there were only a handful of other shoppers, all women, most of them with small, well-groomed dogs. I wished I'd brought

Layla with me but it had seemed like a lot of trouble and there was the whole Frank situation.

I imagined her sniffing the other dogs while their owners and I smiled at each other, just a couple of pet owners running errands on a weekday morning. They would tell me how pretty she was— she really was a pretty dog despite her heft—like people used to do when Maxine was a baby. Ellen had been sick a lot with migraines and the two of us had gone everywhere together, doing all of the things I liked to do and Maxine had come to like them as well.

We fished and ate cheeseburgers and took long drives, looking for deer and turkey and whatever else we might see. Sometimes we'd sit in the woods and do nothing but listen. For a child, she became very good at doing nothing, which impressed me. She never fell asleep and hardly complained as we listened to the birds and the turkeys calling to each other, identifying the sounds different animals made when threatened or trying to attract a mate. This was in Stone County, on the eighty acres my grandfather left me, but I'd sold it years ago to pay for her college.

It wasn't her fault, she'd never asked me to do it, but I'd never forgiven her for it. Ellen hadn't asked me to do it, either. She'd even offered to sell some of the stock her mother left her, said we could take out a second mortgage on the house, but for some reason I can't figure, I insisted. I sold it too cheap, to a neighbor who had wanted it for years. I guessed at the time it felt like a sacrifice I could give Maxine. When she was no longer a child, I had stopped liking her before there was anything to dislike. One day she didn't need me anymore; we had nothing to say to each other.

She hadn't known I'd sold the land until later and had cried when her mother told her.

The women didn't look at me and reined their dogs in more tightly as I neared. Was I imagining it? Was my face doing something funny? I checked my zipper and pushed the cart faster, tossing in dog treats, an assortment of squeaky toys, a large "busy" bone, oatmeal shampoo, flea and tick medicine, but got stuck in the leash-and-collar aisle. I decided I wanted a solid color—that part was easy—but choosing between red and blue and black was tougher. I touched each one, spaced out, and lost track of time. I'd been having the spells for a while, since the sleeping troubles began. The worst ones left me disoriented, turned around in the most familiar places. I selected a red collar and a matching leash and put them in the cart. I also had a hard time with the bed. It needed to be soft and not too big and not too small and maybe have some sides so she'd have something to lean against. I wished she could test them out. I threw one into the cart; it was ugly with triangular shapes in a brown-and-orange pattern but it looked comfortable enough and was on sale. I remembered the red snowman at the last minute—a Kong, the large classic, she didn't need a wobbler—and then went back for the biggest bag of dog food I could buy, as it was the most economical.

In the checkout line, I second-guessed my decision on the bed but there was a lady behind me and then another and I wasn't going to give up my spot.

"My dog doesn't like these bones," the checkout girl said, holding up the busy bone.

"I never bought one before."

"Maybe yours'll like it but not mine."

"Huh," I said.

The girl held up the oatmeal shampoo and said, "There's better shampoo than this, too. This kind doesn't have much scent so your dog won't smell fresh. I prefer something fruitier—there's one called coconut and papaya I really like." She was young and overly confident for someone of her size, with her face. What would happen if I called her a fathead-know-it-all bitch? Would I be thrown out of the store? It was possible. The idea excited me.

The total came to one-hundred-and-eighty-four dollars and fourteen cents.

"A dog's not cheap," I said to the girl, smiling in what I hoped was a good-natured way.

"Are you a member?" she asked. "You could save ten percent right now if you sign up."

"I'm not interested."

"It's a good deal. You could save a lot of money," she said, her whole face scrunched up as she bagged my purchases. Perhaps I'd been too brusque, but surely it didn't deserve such an unattractive face. I didn't understand why people were so rude, when they'd become so rude. I thought about calling the store and leaving a complaint. Her name tag said Kara.

"Thank you, *Kara*," I said. I could teach her some manners. "I think next time I'll do my shopping at Walmart." At Walmart, they never asked if I wanted to become a member or commented on my purchases. I could even use one of those self-checkouts and talk to no one at all.

"And you ought to check on those ferrets," I said. "I'm pretty sure they've expired." I pushed my cart into a stack with a clatter.

As I was walking out, an older woman wearing a T-shirt

claiming she was a proud member of the basket of deplorables was on her way into the store. I pretended I didn't see her, and let the door close just as she was about to enter. Trump wouldn't want that woman in his basket. He would hate that old woman and she didn't even know enough to know that.

At home, I gave the dog the busy bone. She was thrilled. She tossed it into the air and chased it across the room and tossed it again. She tossed it a few more times before settling down as far away from me as she could get and still be in the room.

"I see you like your bone fine," I said. "Kara had her doubts. Kara was a real bitch who knows nothing about your likes and dislikes."

She looked at me with what could have been interpreted as suspicion, her paws handling the bone easily, turning it this way and that like human hands.

"I don't want your bone," I said. "I gave you that bone. You remember that." I considered taking it out of her mouth and giving it back to her to demonstrate my generosity, to show her who was providing for her. Instead, I called Maxine.

"Dad?" she said. "Hey. How are you?"

"Hey, Maxi. I wanted to thank you for the cheese."

"You got it?"

"I did. Thank you."

"You're welcome. I thought it'd be something different."

"It certainly is different," I said.

"But you liked it?"

"Are you kidding? I put it on some toast this morning and had it for breakfast. Two pieces!" I hoped she would say she had to go—she was in the middle of something—like she usually did.

She was feeding the baby or dressing the baby or fixing the baby's hair or helping the baby off the toilet. The baby was four or five years old but that's what she called it. "Well," I said. "How's that baby of yours?" She called the baby a baby so often I forgot its name, at least when I was called on to remember it.

"She's good, we're really good. How are *you*?" she asked. "How's everything? I haven't heard from you in a while."

"Everything's fine here, nothing to report."

"I was hoping to see you soon."

"That'd be nice. I don't know when I might get over there, though."

"How come? Are you busy?"

"No, it's not that. . . . I don't drive all that well anymore."

"Is it your eyesight?"

"My eyesight's alright."

"How come, then?"

"I get tired. I don't like to drive too far these days."

"What do you mean? Do you zone out?"

"Sometimes," I said. "Sometimes I do." Sometimes when I was driving—actually, frequently when I was driving—I felt like I shouldn't be on the road, was surprised to find myself at my destination alive and intact. A chunk of time missing. There was something wrong with my brain; my brain was a different brain from the brain I'd once known. I remembered how, as a young man, I'd had a nearly photographic memory, or someone had called it that once and so I had believed it to be true. For years I told my brain that it was photographic, the brain of a goddamn genius.

"Are you getting enough sleep?"

"Oh, I don't know," I said. "I sleep okay."

"Lucky called me the other day and I went by his office. Have you heard from him?"

"Not recently. That son of a bitch doesn't return my phone calls."

"You should call him," she said.

"I'll call him right now," I said. I thanked her again for the cheese and told her someone was at the door. It would buy me a few more days, at least.

I saw Maxine three or four times a year—about once a season—even though she lived less than twenty miles away. I could drive there right now and knock on her door, shake hands with her nice-enough husband and see my grandchild. The child was a girl, which I hadn't been thrilled about when she was born and still wasn't thrilled about. Maxine named her Laurel Maxine—that was the baby's name—a name that set the kid up for problems. What was a laurel—a tree, or a bush? And naming a child after yourself? What an ego! In my head, a lot of the time, I still thought of my daughter as Margaret. Margaret should have been her name, such a wholesome classic name, after my grandmother. Things would've been different if she was Margaret.

I imagined sitting on the floor with her, moving plastic eggs around a plastic skillet in a make-believe kitchen. Taking orders like we were running a diner.

The Maxine I'd known as a girl was gone. I could hardly remember the child that had liked to fish and sit for long hours in the woods. She'd been blond then, quiet but peaceful; she had loved me better than anybody in the world. She'd reach for my hand, take it and hold it until I couldn't bear it any longer and had to let go. But for all of the time we spent together, my memories are generic and unspecific. The only girl I remember in any detail was seventeen years old, when my thoughtful child turned reckless overnight. When I was convinced she'd kill us all. She left the doors wide open and the stove on, snuck out of her bedroom window at night. I put locks on the windows, painted them shut, and she'd walked right out the front door while we slept. She ran away. Came back. Ran away a second time and stayed gone five days. Her mother had a migraine the whole time and for weeks after.

She crashed two cars that summer.

The second accident occurred a month before she left for college. She broke both of her legs and cracked her pelvis and knocked her head pretty good, and I wasn't sure, from that point on, whether her brain was forever damaged. She spent a week in the hospital, her mother sleeping up there with her, and me alone at the house thinking of them and what I had done wrong and if there was any way to fix it. Trying to do the routine tasks that seemed to keep a household going—buying groceries, washing clothes—wondering if all of the hope and love that had existed in the beginning, and there really had been a lot of hope and love, of course there had to have been, was gone for good.

Our small family, a family of three. It would have been easier had there been more of us. Had Ellen and I had other children—additional chances, friends for Maxine. If we'd tried harder or loved each other more or been willing to sacrifice ourselves for the good of the whole. Those were the darkest days of my life.

Maxine looked different when she came home, something about the eyes and a slight limp she has to this day. We watched for signs that she was different, that she'd changed.

In the end, we decided she was the same and also somewhat improved by the injuries, possessing a caution she hadn't had before. She stayed inside, watching cartoons and eating bowl after bowl of cereal, like she'd regressed a dozen years, but she was pleasant. Agreeable. She didn't seem unhappy—on the contrary—she laughed more than she had in years, but it was a kind of frantic, nutty laughter. We had a small party to celebrate her eighteenth birthday, just the three of us and a boy she called her boyfriend that we never saw again, and then we sent her off to college. After that she was gone, really and truly, and there was no way for us to keep track of her. I had no idea what we'd been trying so hard for—all of the time spent worrying, the alarm system and the locks, the efforts we took to keep track of her comings and goings only to buy her new clothes and send her halfway across the country. She didn't visit once that year, not even at Christmas.

CHAPTER 4

I AWOKE FROM A dream in which Maxine had run away. This happened whenever I spoke to her; everything got stirred up. She was a grown woman now, in her mid-thirties and by all accounts a responsible wife and mother, but I couldn't forget the Maxine I'd lived with that final summer, the one who had cost us so much before vanishing altogether.

It was my fault that I couldn't get past it. Maxine had left that girl behind. Ellen had, as well, and the two of them were closer than ever. Why didn't I want to see my grandchild? they asked me. Why didn't I want to be a part of their lives? It was too late and I wanted to tell them to forget about me, to move on. Ellen wasn't coming back, and Maxine called and asked me to come by out of a sense of duty. When I was gone, she didn't want to have regrets. I was old enough to know you always had regrets, no matter what you did or didn't do.

I imagined running into Ellen at Rouses wearing a dress I hadn't seen before, with a haircut I hadn't seen before, and tried to imagine how I would feel. I liked the idea of fighting for her affections—bringing her flowers, showering her with gifts that this money would allow, finally, after all these years. I still loved her—that was the problem. Ellen still loved me, too, or so she claimed. *I've always loved you and I always will*, she said, signing the divorce papers. *But you never could accept my love. You were never happy and there was nothing I could do to change that.* She always knew the best way to hurt me. That's what a good relationship teaches you. I would provide for her once the money came through, though, would take care of her, regardless. And I would take care of Maxine. I had told them this and it wasn't just something I said because I hadn't seen the money yet. People are willing to make all kinds of promises before they see the money.

In the dream, I was standing in the doorway of an unfamiliar house calling out to my daughter, yelling her name as she moved about the yard. She wasn't hiding but changing locations, disappearing from one place and popping up in another. She couldn't respond, or wouldn't, as my voice grew louder and more frantic. It was horrible to call to someone without any response, especially when they could see you, when they knew you were there. But the dream wasn't so bad. It was nothing like the ones I used to have in which she would die; over and over again she'd die and I'd convince myself they were premonitions, that I'd have to bury my daughter and the dreams were my brain's attempt to prepare me for her death.

The dog had heard me moving about, her tail thumping against the nightstand. *Swish, swish* on the carpet and *thump* against the nightstand. *Swish, swish, thump, swish, swish, thump.* I wondered whether I should write Maxine and Ellen lump-sum checks—a one-time deal sort of thing, or send the money in installments. I didn't want to have to mail checks every month, though, or even every year. That was a lot of trouble and I might forget or find I wasn't the generous man I'd figured myself for after all. I leaned over to look at Layla and her tail wagged faster: *swish swish thump swish swish thump!* And then I was singing a little ditty that went *swish swish goes the tail! Swish swish thump goes the tail, the taily taily tail!*

I hoped to God it didn't happen when people were around. I might have to broach this subject with other pet owners or find this information on the worldwide web. Surely there was a forum for this kind of thing: do you break into song uncontrollably? Do you forget the song as soon as it's over?

I patted the spot next to me and called her up. She licked my cheeks, my lips, my forehead. She especially liked to get me on the mouth. I tried to block her but she really felt the need because she'd missed me so much in the hours we'd been apart. I was the bologna man, the foot man. Lived in the house where fajitas were spilled. But then I got the image of Bruno, the saddest dog in the world, in my head so I got up and started the coffee. After that, we went outside to get the paper and I walked slowly so she'd have time to do her business. The lovebugs were still out but they'd be gone soon. It was like that every year. There'd be millions of them clogging up everything, all over your car and messing up your paint job, flying into your eyeballs and up your nose and then not a single one anywhere.

While Layla licked the pavement, I looked at the sky, the moon faded and halved. I had a headache but it wasn't terrible. I'd grown accustomed to feeling bad all the time—or if not *bad*, exactly, certainly less than good. I knew I should feel ashamed but shame was mostly relegated to nighttime, to the darkness and the old mattress.

I poured myself a cup of coffee and went to the bathroom; the dog followed me in there to watch. I picked my nose. She didn't take her eyes off me. I wondered what the hell was going on in her head, but it seemed like it was only *I love you I'm happy what are we going to do next?* I put the words into her mouth without realizing I was doing it: talking in a voice that wasn't my regular voice and attempting to articulate the thoughts she couldn't speak for herself as accurately as possible. I would act as an interpreter, I thought, as if she were a foreigner or a mute.

I switched to my regular voice to tell her I had to go to the doctor. "I won't be gone long," I said. "You can relax here until I come back. Your bird friend'll keep you company." I explained where the doctor's office was because I was worried about the parking situation. "What kind of doctor's office is downtown?" I asked her. But when I got there the parking was fine. I found a spot easily and didn't have to walk too far. If I could be reimbursed for the hours spent worrying about nonevents, I'd be the richest goddamn man in the world.

The waiting room was nice and clean and there were plenty of magazines, ones I might even like to read if I weren't in a waiting room. I sat and did nothing. The room was full of blind people, people in wheelchairs, people with patches over their eyes and missing limbs. I got up to fill out some additional paperwork with a spring in my step. Pushed out my chest. The diabetes hadn't affected me too much. I was still able to fish and drive and cook my own food and cut the grass, though I'd recently hired a neighbor boy to do the yard work.

This was a new doctor, a doctor I'd been referred to because my old doctor moved to Pensacola. I'd liked my old doctor, who had generally seemed pleased with me, with my numbers, complimenting me whenever I lost a few pounds. And there had been regular types of people in the old doctor's waiting room, normal people with all their legs and arms. I thought of my brother in a hospital bed in Vietnam, though I hadn't seen him there, had only imagined it. He'd been wounded, his leg in one of those white casts suspended from the ceiling like a cartoon—*in traction*. He could've come home after that, to Pamela, the girl he said he loved, the girl whose picture he carried in his wallet, but he'd chosen to go back. It had been so close to the end, too. If he'd been injured even a few months later he would have come back to us.

Where was Pamela now? Did she think of him? I wished I had her picture so I could carry it for him.

I was reuniting with Pamela, lovely nineteen-year-old Pamela, when the nurse called my name twice before I managed to stand—a question, always a question, as if this were the kind of place folks up and walked out. She was pretty, short and shapely. I used the voice I used when I talked to pretty ladies. I knew I was using a different voice, much higher than my usual one, similar to my dog voice, but I couldn't stop myself. She weighed me, took my temperature and blood pressure—it was high, she said she'd try again in a few minutes, that I should relax and take some deep breaths—and asked me the usual questions. Then I waited some more in a different room, sat in a chair because I wasn't sick.

The doctor knocked as he opened the door. He was white, about my age, and had done a lot better for himself than I had. We had some people in common but they were people I didn't know very well, people Ellen had known.

He tried to scare me with numbers, said I needed to lose twenty to thirty pounds yesterday, and prescribed new medication, which he explained was more serious than the medicine I had been taking. I still hadn't picked up my other medicine, had run out—when had I run out? I told him my knees were bothering me, particularly the right one, and extended them a few times to demonstrate, but this just gave him the opportunity to talk about how fat I was again. We went back and forth until I indicated that I appreciated the gravity of the situation, and then the pretty nurse led me to a woman behind glass where I was to pay. There were signs everywhere: *If God brings you to it, He will bring you through it*; *If God is all you have, you have all you need*; *When life gets too hard to stand, kneel.* She slid open the door and gave me the total and I tried to make a joke about the kneeling one, how I guessed I'd have to continue standing because of my bad knees, but she didn't think it was funny. Or I hadn't explained it well enough.

I drove home thinking it was the last time I'd ever go to the doctor.

Layla was thrilled to see me on my return. This was a good incentive to go places without her. I petted and kissed her and the corn chip song came back to me just like that. I was afraid to stop singing it for fear I'd forget it again.

"I thought we might check out the dog park," I said. I had charged my iPad and Googled it and found one four miles from the house. There were a few reviews that said it was pleasant and the people friendly. One cited a lot of mud. Another said it was full of dog shit and this was why we couldn't have nice things.

I poured a beer into a go-cup, got the dog in the car, and we cruised with the windows down.

There were a few other cars in the lot, seven in total, two of them obscenely yellow hatchbacks parked right next to each other.

"We can do this," I said, observing the people gathered in clumps. It looked like a social club. But that was why we'd come, wasn't it? Otherwise I'd just walk her around the block or sit with her in my own yard. Layla was wary as well, so I explained to her that we were at a place called a dog park and it was where dogs ran free, etcetera, etcetera, and I'd be with her the whole time and it wouldn't hurt us to be friendly and we didn't have to stay long. We'd pop in and out and be done. That'd be that.

I opened the door for her and she hopped out. She immediately found a bone of some kind and chomped it up.

"Parking lot trash," I said. "Nice job." Her tail circled round and round. She was already having a grand time.

We stopped at the gate to read the rules, which were numerous, so many rules wherever you went and so many of them unnecessary, a test to see if you would follow them. Well, I wouldn't follow them. Or I would follow some of them but not others. I would pick up Layla's business, if she did her business, but I wasn't going to put her on a leash to walk the twenty feet to and from the gate. That was ridiculous. Nor was I going to hop up and down on one foot or touch the latch three times and do a spin before opening it.

There were two gates. We were inside the first one and standing there sort of trapped because a group of dogs had come over to check her out, including a Rottweiler with an aggressive bark.

"He's friendly," a girl yelled, and then she had a hand on the dog's collar and was pulling it back. She was saying that the dog just had a mean-sounding bark. I opened the gate and all the dogs sniffed Layla's ass and Layla sat; she walked, sat, walked, sat. The Rottweiler tried to mount her. The woman went on explaining that the dog's bark sounded the same whether he was happy or defensive and his body language was how you could tell the difference.

"I don't know your dog's body language," I said.

"Of course you don't," she said. "Of course not. Anyhow, he's fine. See?" He was slobbering all over the place. What a goddamn mess. "My dog's Bruno," she said. "Like Bruno Mars."

"I don't know him," I said, but the sad dog was named Bruno, or I had named him Bruno. How odd to meet another. I was still thinking about the two Brunos when she started singing the song she was sure I'd heard—terrible, awful sentimental shit. "It's on the radio all the time. What's your dog's name?"

"Layla."

"You love that song?" she asked.

"I do not."

She looked a little confused but held out her hand. "I'm Beth. I haven't seen you here before."

"Louis McDonald, Jr.," I said, thinking that I was this person, this Junior, which made more sense now that my father was dead. No—it made less sense. I was the only one. I felt like a new person, though, or new*ish*. Junior had a dog and a different diabetes doctor. He was single, a man-about-town. He could buy and sell this dog park if he wanted, if it didn't belong to the city. If his money ever came through from the original Louis McDonald, deceased.

A couple of loose children chased each other around a bench.

"Leave me alone!" they yelled. "Stop!" Why weren't they at a park for dogs *and* children? And then one of them let out a piercing scream and a woman walked over to them screaming her own head off.

I had to watch every step as I navigated the piles of shit, as Layla and I moved in and out of an open circle with a bunch of other people and their dogs and it became clear that I was uncomfortable with the people but okay with the dogs and Layla liked the people alright but was uncomfortable with the dogs. I should have been a dog and Layla a person. And the whole time I was smiling like a lunatic. They were friendly enough, though, like this Beth, a few years out of high school with her dog called Bruno. I watched her, how she let the dogs smell her hands. I put out my own hands for the dogs to sniff, petted a few of them. Wiry-haired, dirty.

"She looks like a Layla," Beth said. She got my dog's face in her hands and leaned in close.

"I've never met one before, so I don't know what one might look like."

"I knew a girl—she was a lady, actually. She had very soulful eyes just like these," she said. "She died of the flu. It's hard to believe that people actually die of the flu, but *thousands* die each year, apparently. Mostly old people, I'm sure, but still. . . . This Layla wasn't old."

"That's a terrible way to go," I said, though I didn't know if it was a terrible way to go. It didn't seem that bad, really—it probably didn't hurt much and was fairly quick. I thought of an old high-school friend who'd died in his chair one evening, fell asleep with the TV on and never woke up. That was either the best way to go or the worst. Best because you're gone, painless, no time to repent or grasp what's coming. Worst because of those things, too.

I wandered out of the circle and Layla followed. A bulldog followed us, too, trotting alongside trying to get our attention. The bulldog ran under her and she looked confused, but I found it delightful and clapped. I came upon a dirty rope and flung it. They ran after it and Layla picked it up. The bulldog tried to take it from her and there was a tussle but their hearts weren't in it.

"Bring it here!" I called. "Bring me the rope."

The bulldog ran back to its owner. I walked over and flung the rope again and Layla went after it, picked it up, and sat in the grass. We did this a few more times and then walked out of one gate and the other as I wondered whether it was bad manners not to say goodbye.

"Well," I said. "You can't fetch. I'll add that to the list of things you can't do. You *do* know how to chase something, though. You've mastered that first part." I didn't want her to get too down on herself.

On the way home, I made one turn and then another, and realized I was going to Harry Davidson's house. I just wanted to see if the balloons were there, if his dog giveaway was over. Layla sat up straighter in the back seat. I looked at her and then reached my arm around to pet her, veering off the road.

"Don't get worried, girl," I said. "I'm not taking you back. You're all mine. Harry Davidson, LPN, doesn't know what he's lost. Or maybe he does. I'm surprised he hasn't called me and tried to Indian-give you. That doesn't make sense but you know what I mean. He doesn't have my number, anyway. No way for him to get in touch. . . ."

I slowed and pulled up in front of a neighbor's house. The balloons were gone, as was the sign. There was a light blue car in the driveway that I didn't remember from before and a truck that I did. Layla began to whine, sat up straighter. I cracked the window so she could get a whiff.

"This is where you used to live," I said, "though I think you know that. You're smart. More like a person than a dog, really, just like the fat man said. You're also really shitty at being a dog, if I'm being honest about it, but you probably know that, too."

I nursed the warm beer and assessed the situation. I was getting hungry.

When the whining increased in volume, I told Layla to come on up as I yanked at her collar. She scrambled into the front seat and then she was sitting alongside me, exactly where she belonged. Why had I been putting her in the back? There was no reason for her to sit back there all by herself. I cracked the passenger side window a few inches and told her to calm down. I wasn't returning her. This was just a stakeout to see if we might get a peek at Harry Davidson's wife, if in fact he had a wife, which I had my doubts about.

I was thinking about Wendy's drive-thru in earnest by the time a woman walked down the driveway and stood at the mailbox, reached her arm all the way inside. She pulled her arm out and reached in again and then crouched to look. The woman was average-faced, neither fat nor thin. She was a lot younger than Harry Davidson and it was possible she was the daughter or stepdaughter instead of the wife. But she was too old to be the daughter, or didn't seem like daughter material. She wore her brown hair in a ponytail, blue jean shorts, and a white long-sleeve T-shirt that said PINK on it. I had seen shirts like it many times. What did PINK mean? Was it some kind of vaginal thing? I hoped like hell it wasn't. It probably just meant girls liked the color pink, though not Maxine or Ellen. Her dark-colored bra was visible through her shirt and I felt a tingle, a definite tingle, and readjusted.

There was nothing about the woman that was memorable except for a long scar running down one of her legs; it went from underneath her shorts all the way to her ankle. Reminded me of a lightning bolt. Would it be raised and bumpy if I ran my finger over it? It was like a colorful tattoo, a decoration. Her legs were rather thick, thicker than her upper half would suggest.

As I attempted to get a better look, my elbow hit the steering wheel and the horn sounded, just the briefest of friendly honks, more like a nudge or a wink. She turned to look at me, the mail in one arm as she shaded her eyes with the other. I drove off in a way that would, by all appearances, make me look guilty, as if I'd really been up to no good when I didn't know what I'd been up to. I hadn't been up to anything. I'd only wanted to see the woman and I had. But I also wanted to see her again, wanted to know her name. I thought about how I'd asked Harry Davidson her name out of the blue, without thinking about what I was doing, and how I'd known I would like her even then. And there was the sad dog named Bruno and the girl that had a dog named Bruno. There were all sorts of connections happening all the time if you paid attention.

How could a wife seem like such a curious thing simply because she wasn't mine? I knew what wives were like. I'd had one long enough. The longer you had one, the more unkempt they grew. They stopped shaving and painting their toenails, stopped wearing clothes that fit them properly, opting instead for T-shirts and boxer shorts from your own drawers as if they couldn't even be bothered to wash their clothes any longer, all while blaming you for the state of their lives.

As we were cruising along the beach, I talked it out with Layla. Why had I wanted to see Harry Davidson's wife? How had I known I would like her, without any way of actually knowing it? There had been something about her, many things: the scar on her leg and her long hair, limp as it was, that I wanted to take out of its ponytail and run my fingers through, her thick legs, the arm disappearing inside the mailbox and the sharpness of the elbow. I couldn't recall ever thinking about a woman's elbow before. And how she'd moved her hips back and forth as she walked even though there was no one around to see her. What was this woman doing with Harry Davidson? Life was a mystery. It was a goddamn mystery and I didn't like it one bit. It was also the only thing worth living for. I had a brief and bizarre image of Harry Davidson's wife working an elbow into my eye socket.

I drove through Wendy's and purchased three hamburgers—two for me and one for Layla—and then cruised along the beach as we ate. The beach was beautiful, white sand shipped in from far away and combed daily. The water was brown and murky but it was something you could overlook from a vehicle with the sun shining and the palm trees and sailboats, the stately old homes with their enormous oaks that had survived the storm. I liked to catch the flash of Mardi Gras beads in the trees, mixed in among the Spanish moss.

"It'll trick you," Maxine said once, "you'll be driving along the beach as the sun's setting and it's all so beautiful but it's all just a trick." Though she was born less than a mile from the beach, Maxine was like her mother, terrified of the water, but we insisted she learn how to swim; she'd hated every minute of those lessons—cried and pitched tantrums. I didn't know why she'd come back. There had been nothing here besides me and Ellen and she'd hardly been speaking to us at that point. Home was a funny thing. You returned and you didn't know why, you returned even when it was the last place you wanted to be, perhaps because it was the only place you could imagine. When Maxine left I'd hoped she would stay gone, not just because of how things had been, but because I'd wanted more for her.

I drove past the turn to our street with a feeling like we could keep driving, leave everything behind because we didn't really need any of that stuff, though I would miss my chair. I could get an identical one wherever we ended up, though. I'd have the money to buy ten chairs if I wanted. I didn't know how much my father had at the time of his death—he'd been a gambler—but even if he was dead broke there was the land; his father had left him over seven hundred acres in Pearl River County and I was the last one left to inherit it.

"Remind me to call that son-of-a-bitch lawyer again when we get home," I said, and then I asked her if exploring the world was something she might be interested in. I asked her why a lawyer was named Lucky, if she could tell me what kind of asshole went out into the world with that kind of name and how I'd ended up with him, though I knew how I'd ended up with him: my father's lawyer, Mr. Veach, died after a swallowed toothpick punctured his bowels.

I'd seen some pictures of a town—some place in Nevada—where every house was perfectly lived in and completely and forever deserted. Food still on the table and puzzles partially put together, coats hanging from the backs of chairs. I hoped that someone would find my house in ten years and wonder what had happened to me. Where I'd gone. Only I wouldn't have years. Frank would return within a week, perhaps sooner because we didn't get much of a visit in last time. He hadn't been able to ask me all of the questions he felt he must in order to give himself credit for having come. If I didn't answer the door, he'd return the following day and then he'd call Maxine. And Maxine would come over or call the police to do a welfare check.

The dog knew we were on a great adventure. She looked out the window and sniffed the air all the way to Alabama.

"Have you ever been to Alabama?" I asked. "I bet you haven't. We'll visit all fifty states, get a map and hang it on the wall and cross out one after another until we've seen every one. Would you like that?"

She licked my hand, faster and faster. I wasn't fond of my hands being licked. My face or my hands.

"I've always wanted to see the Grand Canyon myself. I believe that's a dream most men have. I'm a sixty-three-year-old American man who's never been to the Grand Canyon. Don't you believe that's a shame?"

She nodded or was just lowering her chin to look at the floor, which was her natural position. I would get her some confidence somehow. Getting her out into the world would do that for her.

"We're gonna get our confidence back," I said. "We're gonna steal Harry Davidson's wife and then I'll have his dog and his wife and the three of us are going to travel the world. What do you think about that?" She seemed to think it was a fine idea, fine, fine. I counted the states I'd been to, trying to visualize them on a map. I started in the West. I'd been to California and Oregon and Nevada and that was it out there. In California I'd gone through a roadblock and they'd asked if I had any fruit. In Oregon they wouldn't let me pump my own gas. In Nevada, I'd seen the Hoover Dam. About a hundred people died while building the dam, or was it a thousand? It hadn't been as awesome as I'd imagined, but it was still impressive; when there were so many people gathered in one place, herded from one area to another, things weren't as impressive. I feared the Grand Canyon would be the same way. I would have to ride a donkey down to the river in order to get the full effect and I wasn't going to do that. In the middle of the country, there were also great swaths I'd missed. Most of it, in fact, as there had never been any reason to go to Indiana or Ohio, Nebraska or the Dakotas. I didn't know anyone in those places. I thought I might like to know people in those places.

I pulled into a gas station and topped off the tank, then went inside to get a beer. On the way out, I stopped to check out the sunglasses. I tried on a pair, looked at myself in the tiny mirror.

"What do you think about these?" I asked the girl. "Do they look okay?" The tag was hanging down, obscuring my view.

"How do they feel?" she asked. "Are they too tight, too loose?"

"No, they fit fine. The lenses seem a bit . . . large, though."

She squinted and gave me a serious look. "Nope," she said. "Not too big and not too small." She smiled and it was a nice smile, like she was letting me know I wasn't bothering her, or that she didn't mind being bothered.

I thanked her and handed her a twenty-dollar bill, didn't look back. I would have to become more comfortable tipping people, with asking for things and accepting them. Though my grandfather had land and money and lived a rather lavish lifestyle, my father hadn't raised us that way. He said he wanted my brother and me to live as if we wouldn't inherit a dime.

I supposed we'd done it, though not in the way he meant.

The weather was excellent, sunny but a good assortment of clouds, low seventies. It was the best time of the year, early November, and the leaves were falling off the trees simply because it was time for them to fall.

I drove back the way we'd come, feeling better than I had in a long time, as long as I could remember. There was no reason to leave everything behind, no reason at all. The house would be paid off by Christmas. There was plenty of beer in the refrigerator and money for pizzas and hamburgers, everything we needed and nobody hounding us. It was a goddamn miracle.

CHAPTER 5

I T WAS AFTER five o'clock and the day was done. It had been a good day, and I felt like we'd accomplished a lot, though they weren't things you could check off a list. But we didn't need to check things off a list anymore—we were free birds, I reminded myself. I turned on the news, to my girl Christy who was stumbling over her words in a way that made me sorry for her. She did it again, and again. What the hell was going on? The more she stumbled the worse it was, like a snowball effect, until I couldn't take it any longer and had to change the channel.

Layla fell asleep soon after that and began to yelp. I didn't know if she was having a good dream or a bad one. What did dogs dream about? What were their nightmares like? I placed a hand on her until she woke up.

I had also been asleep, I realized, because it was after seven and I'd missed dinner but I wasn't too hungry—the hamburgers were still doing their work. I was thinking about getting myself a beer when I heard Frank's truck pull into the driveway. Dammit, Frank. I turned off the lamp, held my breath. He knocked as he called my name through the door. "Make sure that dog doesn't attack me again." It was weird for someone to talk to you through a door when there wasn't any evidence you were home. "Louis? You in there?"

I went to the bathroom, flushed the toilet. "I'm coming!" I said, breaking into a jog. "Frank? Is that you? I was taking a piss."

"I brought you some dinner." He peered in at Layla. She hadn't moved from her spot, but she was looking up at him with her white eyebrows raised. It was funny; you couldn't really see she had eyebrows most of the time. "She alright over there?"

"She's fine. She was napping."

"I tried something new, from someplace new—the blackened shrimp Alfredo," he said. "It's always a mistake." He handed me the box—oh, how I loved the box—but it was suspiciously light. I had the urge to open it right there and frown at the pitiful offering.

"That was nice of you."

"Well, I just wanted to give you that and tell you I'll be by tomorrow for a proper visit."

"That's alright. You don't have to do that."

"No, I want to."

Once his truck pulled out of the driveway, I ate the pasta with my hands, feeding noodles to Layla as her teeth scraped lightly against my fingers. There were only two shrimp left and I cursed Frank while Layla listened, her ears pricked. After that, we went and sat in the backyard. I had one chair back there, a cheap beach chair because Ellen had taken the good ones and I hadn't gotten around to replacing them yet. I knew I never would, same as the mattress, but I could pretend. The truth was I didn't care that much—so what if the chair was a bit low? It wasn't worth making a special trip to the store, wasn't worth the hassle of having someone come to the house to deliver stuff. Ellen had also taken the furniture from the office but I didn't need an office anymore. Other than her personal effects, she had only wanted things that held no memories at all: patio furniture, a desk and a desktop computer, a printer/fax/copier. Some white dishes she'd purchased at Tuesday Morning. I had liked those dishes. They were heavy and thick and when you dropped them they didn't break. She had also taken one of the TVs, a smart TV that I'd insisted she take since she'd been the one to make it do things, order it around. I refused to talk to a television set, couldn't even turn the damn thing on.

I watched Layla walk about the yard, sniffing and pissing in various spots, while I tried to conjure Ellen's face, but at the moment I was only able to recall her most unattractive features. One of her ears had been smaller than the other, folded in an odd way, and she'd struggled through periods of psoriasis that got so bad her scalp felt like a topographic map, flakes coming off in great chunks. Not to mention the fact that she had some of the thickest ankles I'd ever seen on a woman. While most people considered her an attractive person, when you thought about someone by their least attractive qualities, you could make anyone into a monster. Who would believe a deform-eared, thick-ankled, psoriasis-ridden woman could also have been a class beauty? That she'd received three marriage proposals before mine?

"You're happier than a pig in shit," I said. "Happier than a pig in mud." I was doing my best to get my spirits back up after poor Christy and the sad shrimp. "A pig in a poke," I went on. "A pig in slop. Pigs must be really happy 'cause there sure are a lot of sayings about how happy they are. Unfortunately, their lives are short and their deaths gruesome. They hang them upside down and slit their throats." I had no idea how pigs were killed, how long their lives were or how brutal their deaths, but it was fair to assume.

Layla sidled up to me and I petted her. If I could get her with two hands in the spot she liked best, she would grunt, quite like a pig. And then we went inside and she followed me to the bathroom and watched as I brushed my teeth. I'd read somewhere that you should brush for at least two minutes, though I was sure I'd never brushed for two minutes in my life and my teeth weren't so bad. I thought I might take up smoking again. I had loved to smoke. It had been a whole activity and I'd spent a lot of time on it, had been good at it. And if I died, *oh well*, but that was the sort of thinking you could only afford when you expected to live a lot longer.

I got into bed and tried to get comfortable, flopped about. I'd placed Layla's bed right next to mine so I could drape an arm over and pet her, though I worried I might step on her when I got up to use the bathroom in the middle of the night. I imagined the sign and the balloons going up at the hands of Harry Davidson's wife, the small pretty hands of his wife, who hadn't been able to stand the gagging or the shedding—the hair had already gathered under every one of my tables, retreated into every corner of my house. I fell asleep recounting the details of her: sharp elbows and the lightning bolt on her leg, her pretty hands and PINK shirt, short shorts, dark bra, mousy ponytail. Walking her up and down her driveway, back and forth. Mail, no mail. Ponytail, elbows, lightning bolt, PINK, ponytail.

- - -

FRANK CALLED at one o'clock the next day and reported to have a box of wings he had purchased all for me, not his leftovers but my own personal meal. That's what he said, "I got you your own personal meal."

"I'm in my truck," he said, "outside your house."

I knew that but I said, "Oh yeah?"

We were still on the phone, looking at each other, when he asked if I thought my dog would try anything.

"She was fine last night. Why don't you come inside and see?"

Layla and I watched him approach. "It's okay," I said, holding her collar. "She's fine, but you should let her smell your hand if it makes you feel better. That's what we do at the dog park."

He put out his hand and she turned away, uninterested, and went back to her bed, which I'd carried into the living room that morning. She needed two beds to be adequately comfortable, or else I'd have to tote this one back and forth forever.

"That is a strange animal," he said. "What'd I ever do to her?"

"She's not normal, it's true."

"I never imagined you with a dog."

"Ellen had a dog."

"That dog wasn't anybody but Ellen's," he said.

"You're right about that. Nipped at my heels when I walked. Barked its goddamn head off all day long." Frank didn't like it when I said "goddamn." He was a religious man who went to church on Sundays and visited shut-ins. But the dog had complicated my view of him.

Frank sat in his spot and I took the box of wings into the

kitchen: ten of them in all and the dressing untouched, celery sticks and everything. "What can I get you?" I called.

"Nothing," he said. "I'm all hydrated."

I opened a beer and left the box on the counter. He would leave soon and I didn't want a chill on them. I sat in my chair and turned the TV to Fox News even though I hated Fox News. I didn't like any of the news channels. They were all bought, all selling something. I muted it. I liked Shepard Smith alright, though, a Mississippi boy from Holly Springs, even though he was gay. He must've gone to school up north and lost his accent and become a homosexual.

Ellen and Frank had a cousin who was gay, but Frank pretended the other lady was her friend. Ellen thought gay people were born that way, except for the bisexuals—she had her doubts about them.

"I tell you, Frank, I don't know what it is. I guess this dog has inspired me to make some changes."

"You do seem, I don't know . . ." he said, "more content." He said it like he didn't think these changes were for the better but I also knew that people didn't like it when other people changed, for better *or* for worse. They took it personally. They liked to know exactly what to expect out of somebody and if you surprised them at all it made them question themselves. I recalled the time one of Ellen's friends lost a lot of weight. The more weight she lost, the shorter her skirts got, the more money she spent on her nails and makeup. Ellen had never been heavy and had no reason to be jealous, but they had a falling out, all their years of friendship out the window. I'd always liked the woman—had liked her the same skinny or fat and she hadn't seemed that different to me. She brought cookies over to the house on a weekly basis, saying she'd made too many, sugar cookies laced with Red Hots or peanut butter ones with Reese's Cups pressed into the center. That was her thing, putting candy into slice-and-bake cookies, and I appreciated it. When she was out of our lives, I asked Ellen to make the peanut butter ones but she'd refused. "You can do it yourself," she said. "You just shove a Reese's into a ball of premade dough and stick it in the oven. You don't even have to grease the sheet first."

Ellen claimed the cookies were meant to fatten her up, that they were cookies with bad intent.

"I have something I wanted to talk to you about, actually," Frank said. "Something Ellen asked me to bring up." Just then the bird banged into the window and Frank turned his neck toward the sound. The bird came in the mornings, and sometimes in the evenings, too. The middle of the afternoon was out of character.

"Does she want the house?" I asked. "She told me she didn't want the house."

"No," he said. "It's nothing like that."

"Well, what is it?"

"It's not about Ellen, exactly. It's more about Maxine. Well, I guess it's about the both of them."

"Spit it out, Frank. Jesus Christ."

Layla was looking at him now, too, had positioned herself a few feet away from him and sat, focused. He said the dog was making him nervous. I said he was making *us* nervous. The bird banged again. Layla thought nothing of the bird, acted like she didn't see it or hear it. Of course the bird had been banging into the window when I'd brought her home so she must've thought it was part of the deal.

"Listen," he said. "It really isn't my place. Why don't you give Ellen or Maxine a call and talk to them?"

"Talk to them about what? You're the one who came over here with some wings as a pretext to tell me something, so how about you just say it?"

"I think you should talk to Maxine," he said. "She should tell you directly. It's really not my place."

"Is she okay?"

"She's fine," he said. "Though she says you've been avoiding her."

"I just talked to her the other day, to thank her for the cheese. How'd you like the cheese, by the way?"

"Just call her."

"I'll call her," I said. "Tell me what it's about first."

"It's about the lawyer."

"Did that son of a bitch die?"

"No, he didn't die. What the heck is that bird doing?"

I threw my hands into the air and we sat in silence for a while, the dog still steadily watching him. "It likes to run into the window," I said. "Who knows why? This is an unusual time for it, though. Usually comes in the mornings, sometimes in the evenings, too. I've gotten used to it."

"You can do something about that, you know," Frank said. Then he said there was one other thing, one other matter of business—Claudia wanted to know if I'd come for Thanksgiving.

"That's a long ways off."

"Less than a month."

"I don't know. We may go out of town."

"We, who?" he asked.

"The dog and me, me and the dog. I think we might travel around, see the country."

"You don't travel."

"I didn't used to travel, but I'm retired now. A lot of people take up traveling when they retire."

"You gonna take a lot of pictures and make people look at them when you come back?"

"It's possible," I said, and I chuckled to try and lighten the mood. My father and his new wife—he'd been married to her for twenty-five years when she died but I'd always referred to her as "new"—had traveled after his retirement. They'd take hundreds of photographs wherever they went and then throw dinner parties where they'd project the pictures onto a wall before feeding their guests. They had done other things that had been odd, like they were always on the phone with you at the same time. You couldn't just talk to one of them. I tried not to think about my father, but it was harder now that he was dead.

"Well, if you're around we'd like you to come. Claudia wants to see you."

I seriously doubted that. Claudia didn't like to see anybody, so far as I could tell. There she was, curled up on the couch with her book. She probably read romance novels and talked about the characters like they were real people. "How *is* Claudia?"

"Same old Claud," he said. "She's started cooking a lot more, though. All sorts of things—soups and stews, mostly."

"But you're still eating out for every meal."

"I didn't say she was any good at it. She's been baking, too. But she's always substituting one thing for something else so nothing ever quite turns out."

"Will Ellen be there?"

"She'll be with her new friend."

"Her *boyfriend?*"

"Yeah, with Rick's family. Somewhere in the mountains in Tennessee."

"Well, I hope they're happy together," I said. I hadn't known his name, hadn't even been certain the man existed. Ellen must have told him to tell me, insisted he tell me. *Just let it slip out. Mention his name.*

"Where would you go? If you traveled?"

"I have some places in mind. We went to Alabama yesterday. Maybe we'll buy an RV or a little pop-up camper and go out West."

Right about then, Layla started doing her gagging thing, which was embarrassing. She looked at me like she would've held off for Frank to leave if she could've. "She just gags sometimes," I said, and found myself doing Harry Davidson's bit—a hand at my throat making palsied movements that struck me as birdlike, a birdlike fluttering. She made a beeline for the back door and I let her out so she could frantically eat leaves. The leaves made the gagging worse, but it endeared her to me, this attempt to cure herself even though the cure was all wrong. I got myself another beer and called her inside. She was still gagging, but she managed to bare her teeth at Frank.

"I don't know what it is, but this dog really hates you. She's so meek she won't look anybody else in the eye."

"I don't think I've ever been hated before," he said, and he smiled, and I smiled, and I walked him to the door.

As we watched him go, it occurred to me that Frank might

be an imposter. I thought of a friend I'd had as a young man named Jim Matheson, a boy I'd played ball with for years, and how he'd become convinced I was the shell of Louis taken over by a stranger. He approached me in the library one day after lunch, his voice becoming louder and more insistent, shoving me with one hand, and I'd been so confused I'd just stood there. I hadn't thought of him in years, supposed he was dead. His mother called me that afternoon to tell me Jim was sick, cried as she'd asked me to remember Jim as he'd been, as my friend, but the whole episode had terrified me. For a long time after, I wondered why he'd singled me out. *Who is Louis McDonald, Jr.?* I'd ask myself. It was a strange thing to think about—if you were acting like yourself, if a disturbed person could pick up on something you hadn't, know something you couldn't.

I opened the box of wings and dug in.

"Can you handle chicken bones?" I asked, dangling a small one. "Are they too soft for you? I heard somewhere that chicken bones are bad for dogs, they splinter or something." Layla jumped, rolled over, danced on two legs. "I think you can handle it, but sweet heavens to Jesus if you start gagging again today I'm gonna have to leave you outside for good."

Standing over the counter, I ate the meat off the bones before dropping them to the dog. And for a moment it seemed we'd all been sold a lie, that we didn't need anyone else. I was fine, just me and the dog and we had all we could ever want. No, we had more than we could ever want. We could spend our lives eating chicken wings and cruising the beach. Looking at pretty girls. I could embrace this feeling—I could be free and happy on my own. And then I wanted someone to witness it.

Once all of the wings had been eaten, I cracked open another afternoon beer and checked my account balance. It was a paltry sum now that everything was going out and nothing coming in. When I'd first spoken to the lawyer he'd told me these things took time, sometimes six months, perhaps even longer with estates like mine. But more than five months had gone by and I was growing increasingly anxious. I thought about the day I checked my balance and what it would feel like when there was a preposterous sum, a shockingly large sum. I wanted to look at myself in the mirror as a rich man. The money was mine—I was the rightful heir with my mother gone and my stepmother gone and my brother, there was no one else.

I called Lucky. His secretary said he was in court so I left my name and number, insisted on leaving my number. He was never just sitting in his office waiting for my call—I always had to leave a message and then wait for him to call me back days later only to tell me he was working on it, I'd have to be patient for a little while longer, sit tight, and then I'd get off the phone feeling bad about myself. Had these feelings of shame begun with Jim Matheson? Jim Matheson accusing me in the library, shoving me in front of my friends and teachers and Linda Rafferty while calling me a fake and a phony. Telling me he wanted Louis back. *What the fuck had I done with Louis?*

I poured the rest of my beer into a cup and put the dog in the car, shotgun. We drove the same route to Harry Davidson's house. Harry Davidson's wife—I loved Harry Davidson's wife, wanted to marry Harry Davidson's wife. I *would* marry her. I had never spoken to the woman and these thoughts surprised me. They just popped into my head. She could be missing half her teeth for all I knew. I could buy her new teeth, though, a whole new set of the good kind, implants, that would be like real ones. If I had to buy her, so to speak, it might be okay—an arrangement where everything was clear, so long as she liked me well enough and had warm feelings toward me, so long as she could put up with certain things without seeming like she was just putting up with them.

Layla was happiest in the car—so much to look at, the smells changing frequently. She never gagged in the car. I cracked our windows and then lowered them halfway knowing she wouldn't jump out.

"Trust," I told her, "is Tampax. There used to be a commercial like that, I think, or Maxine said that to me once when she was saying things to offend me. You don't have to worry about that, though. You're fixed. Wouldn't have to worry about it, anyhow." I looked over at her; she had no idea what Tampax was. I could literally say anything.

At a stoplight, there was a black Ford pickup with a license plate that said CONVICT. People loved their personalized license plates but I'd never seen one like this before. I imagined the man asking for this particular plate, the back-and-forth exchange, how he'd paid extra and waited for it to come in the mail. I wanted to take a picture so I got out my phone and clicked the image of the camera. I held it up and tried to stop my hand from shaking, tried to get it perfectly lined up and centered. Then I pressed the button again. Easy. Now I had three pictures: two of my freaky grandchild and one of a truck. I imagined calling the cops to report a crime and telling them the man in question had a license plate that said CONVICT.

We stopped a few houses down from Harry Davidson's, not as close as we'd been the previous day, and turned off the car. His truck was gone, but the blue car was there. I wondered if I might knock on the door and pretend to be selling something or handing out religious pamphlets, anything to get a foot in. What did the inside of the house look like, smell like? Was it messy or clean? Harry Davidson's wife did not look like a particularly neat or clean person but that was okay. We could hire a maid.

Layla wasn't as nervous this time but she had some questions.

"We're waiting to see if the wife comes out," I said. "You remember his wife? Short shorts, long hair? I hope she wears the exact same clothes again today. I'd like if she wore them every day, like a uniform. But not that white shirt, a different one."

"I'm sure it's his wife, yes. Not his daughter. She didn't look anything like him and she's too old to be his daughter unless he had her when he was fourteen or something. Wait—is that right? What am I saying?" And then someone leaned into my window and I jumped.

"Can I help you?" the man asked. He was freshly shaven, wearing a tie.

I tried to look sober and sane, becoming immediately self-conscious of my appearance: barbeque stains on my shirt, hair uncombed. The beer half-drunk in the cupholder, looking exactly like beer. I was a damn slob, a child molester with a dog in the passenger seat.

"Yes," I said. "I'm looking for an acquaintance's house, from church. Harry Davidson. He gave me his address and I wrote it down but I lost the paper and couldn't remember the number. I'm not sure . . ." Stop talking, I thought, that's enough. Don't say any more. Only liars elaborate.

"It's that one there," the man said, pointing. "You go to First United?"

"For a few weeks now," I said. "I'm just trying it out, going to visit a few to see which I like best."

"Oh, you'll like it there," he said. "It's a good place—I'm sure you met Pastor Mark? A fine man, fine, fine. We're fortunate to have him." He introduced himself as Kevin Hood and stuck his hand in the window. It was an awkward angle. We shook but it was terrible, my hand all clammy and my grip, it was not what it should have been.

"Louis McDonald, Jr.," I said. I was sweating profusely. I probably smelled bad, too. It had been a few days since I'd showered— how many?

"You related to Myrtle?" he asked.

I hope Myrtle keels over and dies right this second, I thought. I chuckled. "That's exactly what Harry asked when we met—no, no relation. I hear she makes a mean carrot cake, though."

"That's right—she sure does. It's Ellery's favorite. Ellery's her husband, of course." He seemed pleased about this, and about me, now that I had sufficiently checked out. Myrtle and her damned carrot cake. "All of her cakes are good, though," he went on. "I'm partial to her red velvet. Got one for Little Kevin's birthday a couple weeks ago. If you ever need a cake, she's started her own business—German chocolate, Italian cream, the whole lot."

We nodded at each other for a bit.

"I feel you might be more of a pie man," he said, as he peered in at Layla. I waited for her to growl or bare her teeth but she didn't; her contempt was reserved solely for Frank. "Doesn't look like Harry's home right now, but Sasha should be there. Harry works till six most days."

"I am a pie man," I said. "You've got me figured."

"I hope to see you on Sunday." He knocked on the hood twice as if to send me off and I told him I'd be there. And after the service I'd be sipping iced tea with one hand and balancing a too-full plate of casserole with the other, scanning the long tables for a place to sit, my plastic fork clattering to the floor. It didn't sound too bad. Not too bad at all. Cake and pie and cookies for dessert, a whole spread. A couple of nice fat church ladies making eyes at me as I made my selection.

For this to happen, I'd need a fresh pair of slacks, a starched button-down, and a good shave. I'd also need a haircut. Ellen had taken my clothes to the dry cleaners. She'd cut my hair because I hadn't liked for my head to be touched by strangers—a peculiarity I'd had since I was a boy. Ellen had also bought the special dandruff shampoo I liked, and I was out. I wasn't even sure where she'd gotten it. I'd looked for it at Rouses and Winn-Dixie but she must've ordered it online. It seemed Ellen had done more than I'd given her credit for, but anybody could drop off some shirts and order stuff online, push a few buttons. I'd take my clothes to the dry cleaners in the morning, locate an empty bottle of my special shampoo and look it up on my iPad. I didn't need Ellen to do those things for me.

"Sasha," I said. "What a beautiful name—a lot like Layla with that nice 'a' sound on the end."

We crawled by her house and looked at the windows, which were still dark. What was she doing in there closed up like that all the time? Was she in bed? Was she sad? Did she have migraines? Would she be willing to iron my shirts? Probably she was fine, happy enough, just watching TV or reading a magazine, painting her toenails, but I liked to imagine I could save her. Sasha in a closet, bound and gagged, Sasha tending to the bruises under her PINK shirt, furtively smoking cigarettes in the back-yard while plotting her escape.

CHAPTER 6

THAT EVENING WE planned a return trip to the dog park, hoping we might make inroads, become a part of something simply by showing up.

Layla enjoyed being outside and smelling new things, pissing on them, but I hoped she'd learn to like other animals. Seeing her watch the other dogs chase and play had bothered me, reminded me of the time when Maxine had come home from school crying saying she didn't have any friends. And then she'd pretended to be sick for a few days and we'd babied her even though we probably shouldn't have. But she *did* have friends, she'd always had a handful of close friends, and they'd just had a fight was all and the next week everything was fine again. I can still remember how hurt I'd been, imagining her eating lunch by herself, hiding in a bathroom stall. I knew what that felt like. Even if you were the type who was happy alone, even if you preferred it, there are very few people who would choose that kind of life for themselves.

Layla was still young and now that she had a good home she would adapt to her chicken-wing-and-dog-park lifestyle. She hadn't gagged in about six hours—and before that it might have been as many as twelve—but just as I was thinking we could put that awfulness behind us, I heard her swallow hard. Shift around nervously in her seat. Incredible! What a world!

"You don't do this in the car, remember? I thought we had an agreement. I thought this had been agreed upon." She looked at me with eyes that betrayed the humiliation of her bodily weakness.

- - -

WHEN I opened the door, she barreled out on my side, panicked and in search of leaves. There were more cars and people this time, lots of dogs—a whole pack at the double gate to greet us. No Beth. I had been hoping to see her, our ambassador. There were a number of large dogs with their large owners. I'd figured that dog-park people would be fit, but it was just a place where folks could go and sit, same as they'd do at home.

I was intimidated by the large group so we walked across the field to the least crowded bench where a regular-sized man and an enormous woman were hanging out with their Great Dane. The dog immediately took an interest in Layla.

"Oh wow," the woman said. "He really likes her."

"He doesn't usually do this?"

"No, never, he doesn't even know he's a dog."

"I know how that is—more like a person than a dog, complex emotions and all that." And the nervous gagging. The pitifully low level of self-confidence.

"Oh! He really likes her! What's her name?"

"Layla."

"She's mighty pretty," the woman said.

"Thank you."

Layla greeted the man and then the woman, allowing each of them to pet her, as we discussed shedding and drooling. Their dog had a problem with drooling in particular, and the man had a handkerchief for wiping its mouth every so often. The drool was getting all over Layla's nice white coat, and I was going to say something about it when I noticed a lizard on the woman's leg.

"Is that one of those dragons?" I asked.

"Yes, a bearded dragon."

"Does he like it out here?"

"Not really," the woman said, "but I like to have him with me. I take him to the grocery store and the bank, wherever I go."

"He's your—what do they call it?—a comfort animal."

"My emotional support reptile," she said, and she laughed, her whole body convulsing. Neither her husband nor I laughed but I smiled and nodded, which she noticed and seemed to appreciate.

We watched the Great Dane tower over Layla, slobber cascading from its mouth. The dog was mesmerizing in its size, like a horse. I wanted to say it very badly—*he's like a horse*—but figured they heard that a lot and the dog wasn't like a horse. It was nothing like a horse, really, it just wasn't much like a dog. It was more like a dog than a horse but more like a horse than any other dog, except perhaps other Great Danes but I didn't see Great Danes that often. I couldn't stop my mind from going round and round. I wondered what we looked like sitting on that bench: an enormous lady with a bearded dragon on her leg, a Great Dane drooling all over my pretty white Layla, and a couple of nondescript white men.

For some reason I decided to tell them about my oriole problem.

The woman suggested I print out pictures of birds and plaster them all over my windows. "It works like a scarecrow," she said. "And be sure to use colored pictures, not black and white."

"That's the stupidest thing I ever heard," the man said, wiping the dog's mouth again. "They make tape for that—shiny ribbons that rustle in the wind and scare them away—among other products. Though printing out pictures of birds could work, too," he said, as an apology to his wife. "What the hell do I know?"

"Yeah, what the hell do you know?" she said.

Layla wandered over to the fence and I followed her. The smells seemed to be strongest around the perimeter and she made her way slowly. I looked at the people in their loose circles and all of the dogs chasing balls and ropes and occasionally raring up into tussles. We weren't going to be a part of that. If I took her out there every day for a month, we'd still find ourselves walking the fence line.

"You think we should be vacuum salesmen, knife salesmen, or Jehovah's Witnesses?" I asked her. "I'm leaning toward Jehovah. I'll get one of those white short-sleeve button-ups and a tie and some black pants and get my old bike out of the attic. And I'll need to find some pamphlets. We'll have to go to their church, wherever that is, and get some. Or maybe we could just be regular ole Baptists or Methodists. Did you know that Dr. Livingstone only saved one person in his entire life and that man lapsed? I'm not sure where I heard that. Livingstone wasn't a Jehovah's Witness, but something else, I forget. Most people don't know this, but he was trying to find the source of the Nile—that was his true mission—and if he managed to save a soul or two along the way all the better. Except he was shit at it."

Layla did her business and I picked it up. She watched me tie it off in a grocery bag that had a hole in it. I bunched it up before anything fell out and walked it over to the can, still telling her about Livingstone, though I'd about reached the limitations of my knowledge. My favorite part was that his heart was buried under a tree in Africa while the rest of him went somewhere else.

As we started toward the gate, Layla navigated over to an old man to be petted. The man didn't pet her but bent down to look at her more closely. "Her ears are off balance," he said.

"One's black and one's white," I said. "It throws the eyes off."

"No," he said, "they're lopsided. This black one is much larger." He tugged on her black ear.

"Where's your dog? Go get your dog so I can insult her."

He kept walking. Maybe he didn't even have a dog but came around to rile people up. He was old, anyway, so I let it go.

On the way home, we stopped at the first church we passed and I went inside. There were dozens of pamphlets, most of them about tithing because Baptists were greedy sonsabitches: *Give cheerfully and gratefully and from the heart because you can't take it with you.* I liked one called *Baptism: Sprinkle? Pour? Immerse?* I might have to read that one. There was a donation box with a recommended two dollars per pamphlet, which was outrageous, but I put a twenty in and took enough to make me look legitimate. I put in five more dollars, which was the last of my cash, and cleaned them out. I needed a bag, looked around to see if there might be a bag. I could tell Sasha I was training to go to Africa like Dr. Livingstone and this was where I was beginning, door to door, getting my feet wet in my own backyard. Maybe she'd say something like she'd always wanted to go to Africa and then we'd go there and be missionaries together, what a strange thing that would be, but I'd be willing so long as we could take Layla with us. And surely I could save more people than the good doctor, beat his pitiful record. The more I thought about it the more I liked the idea. There was a lot missing in my life and perhaps what was missing was God, and Africa. I could build churches and orphanages, get my hands dirty. My hands dirty and my feet wet! I felt relief at the thought there might be an answer yet, and didn't care if pretending was involved. *If you pretend something long enough, it becomes real.* That had been one of my mother's favorite sayings, God rest her soul.

I was feeling like a convert already. I shoved the pamphlets into my pants and shirt and carried the rest out in my arms, waddled back to my car and emptied them onto the back seat. A few had shimmied down my legs. Layla watched calmly, unquestioningly. I wondered what I might do to surprise her.

I got back in the car and drove.

"What an adventure this is," I said. "All sorts of stuff happening now." I petted her and wished I had a bone to give her. I was excited—it seemed life held more than I'd ever imagined and all because of a dog. What might the two of us get into next? I decided we should eat again so I pulled into the Burger King drive-thru and bought a couple of Whoppers and a large fry. The dog could have her own burger and I'd share the fries with her, but I'd have to feed them to her one at a time. We drove and ate and it was getting dark so there was nothing to do but go home, which was disappointing. Once you started having fun it was hard to stop, to give up. It used to be that way when I drank liquor. I'd have one and then another and everything was going so well I thought I'd have just one more. But the turn was always right around the corner, closing in fast.

I opened a beer and resumed my seat in front of the TV. We'd missed the local news so I turned it to Fox to see what was happening in the world. Tomorrow I'd knock on Sasha's door, say I was in the neighborhood inviting people to worship with us on Sunday at whatever the name of that church was, or I could make one up, it might be better to make one up, and then hand her some pamphlets. All I had to do was ask if she'd been saved, simple as that: "Have you been saved, Sasha? Will we spend eternity together in the Kingdom of Heaven?" And God would take it from there.

CHAPTER 7

I N THE MORNING while I was having my coffee, the bird banging into the window at five-second intervals, Maxine called.
I thought about not answering but couldn't stop myself on the
fourth ring—I'd never been very good at ignoring the phone—
and what if something was wrong, if she needed me?

After the hellos and how are yous, I told her I'd gotten a dog.

"I heard. I didn't think you liked dogs."

"I like certain types," I said, and described some of Layla's
more attractive features: the black and white ears and feet, the
soft white coat, how docile and kind she is to strangers.

"You never let me have a dog. I must've asked a hundred times
and you always said maybe and I'd get my hopes up, but the
answer was always no."

"I'm sorry about that. I just hated to disappoint you. You'd
like her, I think. Her name's Layla."

"Like the song?"

"Yes," I said. "I named her after the song. It's a great song, a
classic."

"Well, you're full of surprises these days."

"She's good company, too. We take long drives and eat hamburgers. It's a lot like when you were little—we ride around and look at things, talk about the world, the places we might go."

"That's nice," she said. "We got a new cat while back. Now we have two—Penny and Ginger. Ginger is the new one. We're trying to fatten her up because she's so skinny."

"Is Craig a cat person?"

"Yeah, that's weird, huh? He doesn't seem like a cat person— he's so masculine—but he's made me into one, too. There's something really great about cats. And Laurel just loves them. She pulls their tails and carries them around the house and they're so sweet to her. Ginger's been waking us up at six o'clock in the morning to eat, though. I hope that ends soon."

"Since when is Craig manly?"

"I said masculine."

"What's the difference?"

"Stop, Dad."

"I'm pulling your leg, Maxi." She sighed a long one and I wanted to hang up but didn't.

"Are you going to hunt any this year?" she asked.

"Probably not." I didn't belong to a camp anymore. She knew that. It had been three or four years since the owner had sold the land and I'd been on the outs with them long before that, anyhow. Ellen said we were worse than a bunch of little girls with our gossiping and infighting, somebody always mad at somebody else. "That place hadn't been very good, at least not for deer hunting. I'd have to shoot a doe to have meat and I didn't like doing that." Once I'd shot a doe before seeing her two fawns nearby and I'd never forgiven myself for it and never would. I could cry just thinking about it. Goddammit.

"Dad? Are you still there?"

"I'm here."

"I have to come to Biloxi tomorrow and thought we'd stop by after I get my hair done."

"You and Laurel?"

"Yes. Laurel and I."

"That'd be fine, but let me know in advance so I'll be here."

"It'll be about three o'clock."

"We have some things to do tomorrow. Why don't you call first to make sure we're here?"

"Okay," she said, "but I'm telling you it'll be about three o'clock," and then I said okay and we said goodbye and hung up and I thought Maxine didn't want me to be happy—no one wanted me to be happy, not really, which was all the more reason to find a life in which I could be, but it also seemed like a reason to give up. Life was confusing that way. Ellen and Maxine and Frank, they wanted me to be the Louis they needed to check in on and visit and feel sorry for because it made them feel competent and responsible, like they were in perfect control of their own lives.

I picked up Layla and held her in my arms, legs splayed, stiff. She didn't try to get away even though she didn't like it. She wanted to be petted but not held. I'd heard most dogs were that way, that if you put your arms around them they felt trapped.

"I can change my damn phone number if I need to," I said, placing her back on her bed at my feet. She licked my ankle once and began to gag. The bird banged. I stomped over to the window and waved my arms around. The bird flew out of range as I examined the glass; it was hard to believe it hadn't cracked, though the window was very dirty, so dirty that if there were small chinks or beak holes in it I might not be able to tell. The bird returned—flapping its wings at me, seeming to look right at me—so I knocked on the window and Layla trotted over to the door. I was collecting the stupidest goddamn animals in the world—at some point I might open a museum, or a petting zoo.

"That was me," I said. "You saw me do it. Watch again."

She looked back and forth from me to the door like she didn't understand why I wasn't opening it, gagging all the while. "You're lucky I'm not the type to kick a dog because you would be a prime candidate for kicking if I were the type. Which I repeat I'm not. You don't have to worry." She looked worried, though, so I petted her until she quieted and then let her lick peanut butter off my fingers.

An hour later, we were in the car. I'd dressed myself in a pair of slacks and a shirt and tie, though everything seemed to have shrunk. I'd forgotten how uncomfortable the whole getup was, and wondered how I'd done it for so many years, but I had to look presentable for Sasha. Like someone she could open the door for and allow inside. I had the pamphlets in a black briefcase and, along with the clothes, felt like I was in disguise. I needed a mustache—no, a mustache would be too much. A hat might be nice.

Layla sat shotgun, sniffing out the window as we cruised along the beach on a mild and sunny morning.

A couple of bozos on the radio were talking about their Second Amendment rights, how we should all be stockpiling magazines. They were so angry I could practically see the veins popping out of their necks. I didn't think anyone was going to take away my guns—nobody was threatening to do that and never had—and yet they were getting me all fired up about it so I had to turn it off. I tried to bring myself down by imagining the nice cool living room of Sasha Davidson. Sasha in her black bra and panties, painting her toenails as I perched on the edge of a chair with a beer in hand. Fire-engine red, cherry. If only she would let me paint them. What I would give.

It was after 10:30 but I swung by McDonald's for a small coffee and a sack of Egg McMuffins to celebrate the all-day breakfast phenomenon that was still going strong, tossing pieces of Canadian bacon to the dog as we drove. Eventually, I'd have to learn how to cook a few more things, or at least buy some multivitamins. When was the last time I'd had a vegetable or a piece of fruit?

"Goddammit," I said, as a hunk of cheese and egg slid out of a muffin and onto my shirt, coming to a stop at my crotch. Layla made a pass at my pants and I jerked the wheel, the car crossing into the other lane. There was an extended honk and I righted the wheel just in time to miss a FedEx truck, the driver's leg hanging out of it. He craned his neck and honked a few more times for good measure but I didn't look because it was my fault and I never looked when it was my fault. You could only wave like you were sorry, or else give them the finger and act as though they'd been the one in the wrong, which might piss them off and escalate the situation further, and I wasn't in the mood for either.

I pulled up in front of Harry Davidson's house—small blue car, no truck—and it struck me that someone going door to door trying to convert a person wouldn't pull right up to their house, but then again they had to park somewhere. They were always on foot or bicycles and I was flubbing it from the get-go but it was too late to park down the street and walk.

"What do you think, Layla?" I asked, assessing the amount of sweat visible through my shirt. Add the sweating to the grease stains and the too-snug shirt and pants and it all seemed like a failure, like a great big failure that could only go badly and might possibly get me arrested. At the very least, I would be humiliated.

"Shit," I said. "Shit." I said it a few more times and then I took my briefcase out of the back seat and walked—no, I strided, I strode—up the sidewalk.

A big plop of bird crap fell beside me as I climbed the two steps to the door.

I knocked and waited, avoided peering into the wavy side windows like a creep. I nearly always felt like a creep or a delinquent when alone in public. Whenever I went into a liquor store, I acted as sober as possible, even though I generally *was* sober, or sober enough. It was like I thought they would assume I was drunk and I wanted to prove I was just a person who happened to have a reasonable amount to drink on occasion. Or I was having a party, a small get-together in which upstanding citizens might have a cocktail on a Saturday night.

- - -

I HEARD footsteps and then the door opened and Sasha was standing there. She wasn't wearing her blue-jean shorts but a blue-jean skirt—she loved her jeans. Her hair was still in the ponytail, though. It was strange to see her up close. Her eyes were a surprising bluish-gray color—like a thunderstorm, but also kind of greenish, like it was gonna be a bad one. I had to stop myself from saying her name.

"Hello," I said. "I'm—." I paused. Would Harry Davidson have told her my name? Surely not. "—Louis McDonald, Jr., and I'm a member of Grace Memorial Baptist Church. Do you have a minute to speak with me?"

"My husband and I already have a church home," she said.

"Have you been saved?"

"Yes, of course I've been saved."

I didn't know what to say after that. Jesus, it was hot out and I clearly hadn't thought far enough ahead. I would ask if she'd been saved—that was my opener—and she would say she had and then what? There was nothing to say after that because I was supposed to be converting people and saving their souls and hers didn't need saving so I should move on to the next one.

I mumbled something about praying together and went for the pamphlets, raising a knee to prop up my briefcase. I nearly spilled the pamphlets everywhere but recovered.

"I thought for sure you'd lose them," she said.

"You and me both. I'm new to this whole thing—not the Christian part but the saving-people part. I'm trying to become a deacon," I added, but then thought that was the wrong denomination. Deacons were Episcopalian or Catholic. Oh, boy, I was really flubbing it. She was going to call the police any minute and have me carried away in handcuffs. *There's a real pervert here with a bunch of stolen religious pamphlets claiming he wants to save me. . . . Parked right in front of my house. That's right, a Baptist deacon, that's what he said. . . .*

And just like that we were standing there smiling at each

other. I could tell only one side of my face was doing it so I tried to get the other side on board as quickly as possible and then I could feel my whole face doing it and I couldn't help but look back at Layla. She was frantic, pawing the window and panting with her mouth open like a goddamn lunatic. Oh shit.

"That's Katy," Sasha said, and then she was screaming "Katy! Katy!" as she ran to my car and opened the door and Layla hopped out and jumped all over her and barked and barked. My God, that dog could bark! And then she was crying and Layla was whimpering and they fell onto the grass holding each other. It was one of the most touching things I'd ever witnessed except that this was all going horribly wrong—horribly, horribly wrong. I was nearly bowled over by the depth, by the sheer impossible depth of my stupidity. If I hadn't done it myself I would've said people as stupid as I am should be killed off, should be barred from procreating at the very least.

When I walked over to them, Layla seemed torn. She licked my pants and then she went back to Sasha who was in the grass with her legs going every which way, her blue-jean skirt hiked all the way up. If I looked—I wasn't going to look—I probably could've seen her panties. And then I did. They were yellow.

"Who the hell are you and why do you have my dog?"

"Layla," I said.

"No, this is *Katy*."

The dog was Katy and Harry Davidson had stuck some balloons and a sign on his mailbox and given her away while Sasha was out of the house. But it didn't really make sense. There were neighbors who would've seen the sign, people passing by, but perhaps there'd just been me and it had all happened so quickly no one had been the wiser. It was an unlikely story and yet it was clear that he had given away his wife's dog without her knowledge.

"She ran away last week. Where'd you find her? She should've had a collar on with all her information and everything." Layla was still whimpering and Sasha's back was sort of heaving up and down as she tried to catch her breath. She looked up at me with a horrible face, one that reminded me of the girl at the pet store and my daughter caught sneaking out her bedroom window; so many women had looked at me this way and often I didn't deserve it, but this time was different. I considered grabbing the dog and running to my car, driving off before she could stop us. She didn't have my license plate and had never seen me before and there'd be no reason that she ever would again, but my feet wouldn't move.

"She didn't run away," I said, adding that I was just as confused as she was.

"You pull up to my house and knock on my door asking if I've been saved and you have my dog in your car? *My dog. In your car.* Who are you? Just who the hell are you?" She stood at this point and shoved me with one finger. The nail was long and pearly as a seashell, perfect. It didn't match the rest of her at all. Her nails should've been bitten and chipped, the polish garish. I wanted both of them—if I couldn't have them both I would never have anything.

"Listen," I said. "Is your husband coming home anytime soon?"

"You know my husband?"

"Yes, will Harry be home?"

"How do you know Harry?"

"I want to explain everything but I'm having trouble with my words," I said. Trouble with my words! What a thing to say. I was also having trouble catching my breath. It was my heart. I was having a heart attack. I had been expecting it for years and it was finally happening. My heart was failing me. I would keel over in her yard and she'd have to deal with it. I distracted myself from my impending death with the mascara running down her face in streaks. Ellen had never worn mascara. When she cried there was never black stuff on her face.

"Look," I said. "Here's what happened," and I started at the beginning, with seeing my ex-wife's car and the detour I'd taken along the beach, and to my surprise she let me talk. I told her I lived by myself and didn't know how lonely I'd been until Harry Davidson gave me this dog, this dog he called Layla, claiming he had fourteen or some such in total. I paused to see what she'd say. She blinked and wiped the black stuff with the palm of her hand but her tears kept coming and the black stuff came with it. She was not a beautiful woman—up close I could see that her eyes were too far apart and there were a lot of wrinkles on her forehead and around her mouth and the skin on her neck was loose. I wanted to know her age, how she came to be an old woman in the body of a young one. Her breasts were perky, her legs smooth and shapely and nicely tanned, marred only by that lovely scar. It looked like someone had taken a hot poker and dragged it down her side.

"Goddamn that son of a bitch, Harry. I knew he was lying, goddamn him."

"How'd you know?"

"He wouldn't help me put up flyers, for one. And he told me

Katy was dead and I asked how he knew and he said one of the neighbors said they'd seen a dog that looked like her on the side of the road so I'd asked him which road but he made some excuse, like he didn't want me to have to see that, acting like he gave a shit but of course there was no dead dog on the side of the road because he'd given her away." And then she started bawling, out-and-out bawling. I looked around to see if any of her neighbors were watching us.

"Why would he do that to you?" I asked.

"He hated her."

"How come?"

"Because I let her sleep in the bed with us at night and he didn't like that. And I'm sure you've noticed the shedding," she said, and she hugged the dog's neck, which looked very uncomfortable, but Layla licked and licked and continued to whine in excitement.

"And the gagging."

"Yes, that too. Harry couldn't handle the gagging."

I sat with them on the grass and Sasha let me pet the dog, too. She'd stopped crying but she still had the black streaks and I thought about all the times I'd seen women I loved cry. Each time it happened it could never break you like it had the first time, and it became less and less effective until, at some point it, it was as horrible and ugly as it looked. When Ellen and I were learning to hate each other, she'd cried a lot, once or twice a week. How to care after a certain point?

She stood and said, "Come inside."

My first impulse was to say no. I looked up and down the street for Kevin Hood, for old ladies peering from behind their curtains. I knew how old people were and this was the kind of neighborhood that was full of them. But it was also the kind of neighborhood where a man could put up some balloons and give away his wife's dog with no one the wiser.

The three of us went inside, Layla bounding up the steps and going straight for the L-shaped couch, where she curled up on one end waiting for Sasha to join her. I hung back in the kitchen. The house was cluttered, the counters full of dishes and appliances and stacks of newspapers, bottles and cans, bills, magazines, seven or eight boxes of cereal. There were vases and jars of flowers spread about and most of the flowers were in various stages of dying. I'd imagined it exactly, except for the flowers and cereal.

"Harry brings me all the flowers," she said. "He picks them from the side of the road half the time, I think, or from other people's yards. That fat bastard. When I ask where he gets them he says, 'the gettin' place.' Can I get you something to drink?"

"What do you have?"

She opened the refrigerator and stood there until it started beeping. "I have lemonade?"

I didn't care much for lemonade but agreed. She poured two glasses and directed me to the rocking chair, where I sat, and she sat next to the dog and they continued their reunion while Layla shot me side-eye glances like what we'd had had been very nice but it had been a casual sort of thing, of course it wasn't meant to last, I shouldn't be surprised, she was sorry if she'd led me on. I had been there for her, though, and she appreciated it despite how little I'd actually meant to her. I was reading too much into it, but she really did seem to be trying to convey these things to me: her indifference along with her appreciation and an apology. Already she was less and less like Layla, which had never been her name but a story that Harry Davidson had been dying to tell about George Harrison.

I'd never seen the dog so happy. She'd spent most of her time with me sleeping or licking my feet in what I now saw was a highly depressed manner. This was Sasha's dog, not mine, and I would leave without her. I told myself this a few more times to make sure it hurt.

"When Harry comes home, what do you think he'll do?"

"Oh, I tell you what he'll do—he'll pack his shit and get out," she said. Then she turned to the dog and called her mama's sweet little baby, asked if she wanted a turkey treat. Layla bounded off the couch and they went to the refrigerator where Sasha lowered each piece into her mouth one at a time. No wonder the dog couldn't catch. I thought about the discs of bologna I'd flung into the air. Which did she prefer? I wished I could ask her.

I drank my lemonade, which was too sour and made the insides of my cheeks pucker. "I've been feeding her bologna, for the most part," I said. "She really seems to like it."

"I've never given her bologna before. I guess 'cause I don't eat it. My dad used to make bologna sandwiches when he went fishing, though, and it brings back fond memories."

"Me too," I said. "I mean that's the only time I ever really eat them. Or it's the only time I like them." I wondered if her father and I might go fishing, if he was still alive.

"Are you hungry? It's the good deli turkey."

"I'm fine, thank you," I said, impressed with my politeness. "I saw something in the news the other day about these two Piggly Wiggly employees who refused to serve a cop some deli meat because he was in uniform. Did you see that? They just flat-out refused."

"No," she said, "I missed that, but everyone deserves deli meat. This is America."

"That's what I think." It was highly possible she was drunk or on drugs. I wasn't usually good at picking up on that kind of thing but she seemed loopy, beyond the normal loopiness. The way she'd sat in the grass with her skirt hiked up—that wasn't normal. And her shirt was too big and kept slipping off one shoulder, or maybe it was supposed to do that. That was the style. I'd noticed women had started to wear shirts with holes in them to show off portions of their shoulders and arms. Mostly fat women.

"Do you think you'd really leave him?"

"No, I told you, he's going to leave me," she said, settling herself back onto the couch. "I like this house. Katy and I are happy here and I've been working on an herb garden out back. I've got mint and rosemary so far."

I doubted this was true, though I didn't know why. Anyone could have a few herbs in a pot. But if there was one thing I knew for sure, it was that this was Harry Davidson's house and had always been Harry Davidson's house. Sasha probably hadn't lived in it more than six months. She buried her face in the dog's neck and the crying started again. I felt like some kind of pervert, a voyeur. I had always liked that word—*voyeur*. I said it to myself a few times, mouthing it to see what it felt like.

"I still don't understand," she said. "Harry gave you the dog and you like the dog, but you came back. Why'd you do that?"

There was a way to explain it, I was sure, that didn't make me sound crazy. "I guess, looking back on it, I knew something wasn't right. Harry told me he had fourteen dogs he had to get rid of and he only let me see this one. And he mentioned you, said 'his new wife' was allergic and that's why he couldn't keep them. And you weren't around so I wondered where you were, if he'd made you up. To be completely honest, I wanted to know what kind of woman would marry a man like that." I paused to see what her face was doing—both of her eyebrows were raised, her eyes wide—like she was telling me to keep going. "And then I drove by a few days later because I wanted to see if the balloons were still there, if he'd gotten rid of the rest of the dogs. I was trying to figure out what was going on, I guess, if he'd even *had* any other dogs, but I couldn't just knock on the door and ask so I decided to pretend I was a proselytizer." I paused again and said, "I guess I have a lot of time on my hands right now—too much time. I retired not long ago and my father died and my wife left me. Though not in that order."

"Oh," she said, taking her face out of Layla's belly. "That's a lot to deal with all at once."

I looked at my lemonade and tried to appear pitiful. It wasn't hard. I imagined Ellen and her new boyfriend hiking in the mountains of Tennessee, the two of them wearing coordinating outfits, boots and hats. She didn't have migraines anymore, had no use for them.

"Was he old?" she asked. "Your father?"

"Old enough. Eighty-four, eighty-five." I took another sip—the sugar-to-lemon ratio was all off. I wondered if everything she made was bad. I liked the idea, though of course it wasn't the kind of thing that would stay charming for long.

"Does it need more sugar, you think?"

"What? Oh, no, it's fine. It could use a shot of vodka but I suppose it's too early for that."

"Why not?" she said. "We deserve it."

She stood and straightened her skirt, which had twisted and lifted and done other inexplicable things, and then the dog got up and we followed her. I imagined a life in which we followed Sasha from room to room and place to place and worshipped her and it didn't seem like a bad life. I had nothing else to do. I took a seat at the bar and watched her pour vodka into shot glasses, dump two shots in each and top them off with lemonade. I wished she'd put more ice in mine or a spoonful of sugar. She passed the glass back to me without stirring it, spilling some on her hand.

"What's your name again?" she asked.

"Louis McDonald, Jr."

"To Louis McDonald, Jr.," she said, raising her glass. "My hero."

In my experience, women only said things like this to men they would never sleep with. The nicer a woman was to you right off the less likely she was to have sex with you, or this had been my experience in the past. But my signs had gotten all mixed up at some point, and the past felt like a long time ago.

CHAPTER 8

S EVERAL HOURS LATER, we were still going round and round on the same topics: what a rat bastard Harry Davidson was, what a great dog Layla was, the ways in which people disappoint you. We were a couple of drinks in and I was growing more and more anxious. Soon the afternoon would turn into evening and I'd be in my car alone, no dog, nothing. I was also drunk. I had given up hard liquor when Ellen left, or had stopped buying it out of some sense of self-preservation I hadn't even known I'd had.

When I wasn't looking at the scar on Sasha's leg or the shapeliness of her behind as she sashayed to and from the kitchen, I was studying the room, making mental notes: the brands of things, names of magazines and cereal boxes, the colors of the flowers since I didn't know anything about flowers, how the piles were stacked and ordered, if there was any order. I thought it would help me stay on my toes. I was searching for signs of Layla and Sasha and how they fit into the picture but they didn't fit into the picture at all. There wasn't a dog toy or a dog bed or anything pet-related, nothing feminine except the flowers. It could all be a setup. They might have found out I was coming into a substantial sum of money. It seemed unlikely but it was possible and you couldn't be too careful these days. You just couldn't be too careful.

I liked the idea of a setup, though, that I was in the middle of something that could go badly.

"Just to get this clear," I said, "there were never any other dogs."

"That's correct," she said. "Harry has had dogs in the past, but they were outdoor dogs, and they were before my time. Katy and I came together—a package deal."

"Why didn't he drive her out to the country like a normal person? Let her out and tell her to run free."

"He's not that cruel. He knew you'd take good care of her—anybody can look at you and see that. And let's face it: this dog wouldn't survive a day out in the wild. She's a real fraidy cat." She turned to Layla and used a funny voice, a lot like the one I used at home, and said, "Aren't you a big ole fraidy cat? You are! You *are* a fraidy cat!"

I hoped she'd break into song but she didn't. When the moment started to become awkward, I said, "She's special. As soon as I saw her I knew she was . . ." I stopped myself from saying "the one." There was no such thing as "the one," even when it pertained to a dog. I'd lived long enough to know that. The fact that I could love an overweight dog that gagged all the time and couldn't catch a slice of bologna proved to me that there were other animals, and perhaps even people, out there that I could love.

We looked at Layla, and every time the two of us focused on her, she was so happy her tail moved in circles, strong and fast enough to knock our drinks right off the table. Sasha went to the refrigerator and fed her turkey again, one piece and then another until it was gone. I imagined her putting her arms around me, telling me she'd been looking for me her whole life and now here I was, had just walked right up and knocked on her door, which is the thing people say opportunity will never do. I wished I were fifteen years younger.

"I don't know what to do now," I said.

"You mean right this minute or in general?"

"Both."

"Well," she said. "Right this minute you're going to drink your drink. And when you finish, you can have another if you like or I'll heat us up the lasagna I made last night for my darling husband because it's his favorite. And then you're going to take the rest home with you because fuck him. But let's not think that far ahead."

"Do you cook?" I asked, a bit too excitedly. I wasn't able to look at her straight on, much like Layla wasn't able to look at me. I imagined Sasha lifting my chin, forcing me to gaze into her eyes.

"I make four things," she said. "Lasagna, spaghetti, meatloaf, and pimento cheese sandwiches."

"You're being humble." I took a sip of my drink. It was going down easy now.

"No," she said. "That's it. I used to make tuna fish but Harry hates tuna now. I guess I can also scramble eggs but I won't do the other breakfast stuff—no bacon or grits or even biscuits. I *will* toast bread, however. But it doesn't matter 'cause we like to eat out a lot."

"I love meatloaf."

"I refuse to touch raw chicken," she added. "Never done it and don't plan to start."

"What are you going to do when Harry gets home?" I asked, wanting to see if her answer had changed.

"I've been thinking about that. My name isn't on the mortgage or anything—you probably guessed that much. Nothing in this place is mine except for my clothes and personal stuff. Literally nothing here is mine," she said, moving her arms about, "not even the groceries."

"I have plenty of room at my house."

"You're sweet," she said. "I don't know where we'll go. My mother has a place over in Long Beach and we could stay with her, though I don't really get along with her all that well. She doesn't approve of my *lifestyle*, as she calls it. Who says that anymore?"

"What's wrong with your lifestyle?"

"Well for starters, Harry is my fourth husband, which I realize is a lot of husbands to have at my age."

I made a noncommittal sound. What was her age? It might be anywhere from thirty to fifty-five.

"I always fall in love after about a minute and marry them right off and then find out later that I hate them, or they hate me or that we hate each other, and then there's a lot of ugliness and paperwork which really sucks because I hate signing my name— I don't know what it is about signing my name to official documents but I don't like it—and then I move back in with my mother until the next one comes along. It's a pattern and I can't seem to stop it. I try to stop it but then it happens again and it's like I've forgotten that it's happened a dozen times before, like I have amnesia or something until things go bad and only then can I remember. Like now. Like right now I don't ever want to date another man ever again but in six months some bozo'll come along and I'll let him take me out to dinner and buy me a few things and . . . The pattern, you see. It's all very strange. I don't know what to make of it."

I recalled a game Maxine had played as a child while watching *The Bozo Show*; she used to call a phone number and scream "Pow!" I couldn't remember anything about the game or its purpose. I would have to ask her about it. I'd scream "Pow!" in her face and see if it jogged any memories. "Yes," I said. "I've been thinking the same thing lately, about patterns." I wanted to tell her I wasn't a bozo, that I could make her life better and we could make each other happy, but I couldn't say those things. They would only confirm what she'd experienced in the past, where love seemed like the answer to every question and then you disappointed each other and were alone again, the same person with all of the same problems only more disappointed.

"My mother says I need a hobby."

I imagined her in the guest room at her mother's apartment, too many decorative pillows on the bed and a window that overlooked a parking lot or a brick wall. I tried to picture her in an office in business clothes but couldn't. She would always be in the grass, legs splayed and flashing her yellow panties, mascara running down her cheeks.

We were quiet for a while, the two of them on the couch and me in the chair. I felt like I should go, like it was past time for me to go, but I couldn't make myself stand and walk to the door.

"I feel bad," she said. "None of this is your fault."

"I know," I said. Of course it wasn't my fault. I was an idiot but I wasn't guilty of anything but that. My conscience was clear.

As if sensing that things were winding down, that her time

with me had come to an end, Layla hopped off the couch and walked across the room, head bowed in its usual position. She'd never learned to use the doggy door. I hadn't taught her to fetch or catch. If I had one regret, it was that I should have taught her something.

"I wish we could split custody . . ." Sasha said. "You know what? We can! There's no reason we can't. I can bring Katy to visit and the three of us can go on walks and meet up at the dog park or the beach. And you can take care of her when I go out of town. It'll be a win-win for everybody."

"I never took her to the beach," I said. "Every day I meant to take her there so she could scatter the seagulls. And I wanted to see what she thought of sand."

"You can still take her," she said. "You can watch her scatter all the birds—she loves that—and she digs and digs like a little kid, it's so cute." She made her hands into cups and started scooping. Then she crossed them over her heart and her chin scrunched up to show me how cute it was. "She loves to eat all kinds of dead things: fishes and crabs, whatever she can find. . . . Once she found a whole T-bone by the dumpster and snatched it up before I could yank her away so I just sat on the curb and let her finish."

"She really does love to eat trash," I said, and we sat there smiling and nodding at each other. "Does she swim?"

"Oh, yeah. Loves to swim."

I could see her out there, swimming like a goddamn champ. She was a contradiction, like so many of us, strong in some areas and weak in others. And sometimes weakness only looks like weakness but is really strength. Layla could swim for miles and live on trash, a champion of the land and sea, and I was smiling to myself and shaking my head as I heard the sound of Harry Davidson's truck pulling into the driveway.

"He's home early," she said, ushering me out the back door, and I made a run for it just as Harry Davidson was coming in the front. It was like a song on the radio. I heard his voice, no doubt asking who was parked in front of his house. No doubt recognizing my car as he saw that Layla was back. At the gate, I encountered a bike lock and felt sure I was done for, that the jig was up, but I pushed and it clattered open.

As I was putting the car into drive, he came bounding down the driveway at me full speed, which was not very fast, his whole body in motion. It was really something to see. Knowing I had a few moments to spare, I watched him with my foot hovering over the gas. It was grotesque and beautiful. I wanted to punch him in the face, knock him straight out. I felt the bones in his face crack at the strength of my fist, the referee calling the match. What a mistake it had been to come and yet it only felt like part of the story and the story wasn't finished.

I knew I'd done something good, something beyond my knowledge and capabilities. And I felt certain that Layla would come back to me, and Sasha would, too. When it was nearly too late, when I'd nearly been caught, I mashed my foot to the gas and left the scene, which was how I thought of it, as if a crime had taken place.

CHAPTER 9

To prove to myself I was okay, that everything was fine, I stopped at Rouses on the way home. Oddly, I felt sober, or sober enough. I got a cart instead of a basket, a full-sized one. I almost always got a basket that could not accommodate all of the things I needed to purchase so I'd end up leaving without essential items like laundry detergent or toilet paper and would have to go back the following day. I supposed it gave me something to do, though I hadn't thought of it that way before. I'd tell myself I was in a hurry, but I was just the type of person who felt like he was in a hurry because I didn't like to be in public, was afraid of people, afraid of running into a neighbor or one of Ellen's friends, a woman who would look at me and frown. But even at home I often felt hurried. I'd wash myself in the most efficient manner, make coffee and food in the most efficient manner. Only when I was in my chair or the bed did I feel like I could relax.

Harry Davidson. Harry Davidson, LPN. It was about time I had an enemy; it had been too long. I felt alive in a way I hadn't in years. I wanted to fight and fuck and break things. I decided to purchase a pack of cigarettes, ask the checkout lady to fetch me some, if that was how it was done nowadays.

I went up and down every aisle putting things into the cart, impulse items like olives and nuts and weird cheeses, a variety of crackers, and before I knew it I was making an appetizer platter. I also bought a lot of beer. I bought other things, too, because I had room—it was so nice to have room!—an eight-pack of paper towels, toilet paper to wipe an army, root beer, frozen pizzas, deli turkey and ham, bologna, two different kinds of bread, and stuff to make meatloaf and pimento cheese.

The checkout girl was one I'd had before, a black little person. She was friendly and smiled a lot and being a black little person didn't seem to bother her, which impressed me. She was very black, like a crayon—I wanted to hold a crayon up to her or a piece of cloth to compare. With the comparison I imagined she would look brown. She didn't have to stand on anything in order to reach what she needed to reach; she was short, but not so short that she was unable to perform the tasks of the job. I liked her, and appreciated her friendliness.

"How're you doing this evening?" she asked, and she actually looked at me when she said it.

"It's been a hard day," I said. "I lost my dog."

"Oh no! How'd you lose her?"

"I guess 'lose' is the wrong word." She looked at me encouragingly, sympathetically, so I went on. "It's a long story but basically a man gave me a dog that wasn't his to give and I had to return her to the rightful owner—his wife."

"Wait a second," she said, shaking a box of crackers at me. "You telling me this man gave away his *wife's dog*?"

"Yes, he did. That's exactly what he did."

"Awful, that's awful."

"I agree."

"If some man tried to give away my dog, I'd shoot him," she said.

I imagined her holding a gun. It would have to be a tiny gun. "It was just a bad situation I got myself involved in." And then a guy came over and started bagging my groceries. I recognized him, too. There was something not right about him—he was autistic, maybe. And one of his eyes was always looking at his nose. I thought of Layla and how much I missed her already.

"I know what that's like," she said. "I'm always getting myself mixed up in other people's business."

"Really?"

"Oh yeah," she said, and she stopped to give me a look like just because she was a little person didn't mean she couldn't get herself mixed up in stuff, too, or that she didn't have a life as complicated as everybody else's. It was hard to think of her going to parties, going much of anywhere except the grocery store and her mother's house which had been set up to accommodate her: the light switches low on the walls, step stools and children's play tables, water faucets that turn on with the wave of a hand. "I have a big family," she said, "a lot of sisters and a few of them are real *b's*, excuse my language."

"I never had a sister," I said.

"You can have mine," she said. "Take all of 'em!" And with that, the conversation was over. I knew so little about women. I'd had a mother and a wife, a couple of grandmothers, a daughter and a granddaughter—I still had a daughter and a granddaughter—

but I had no idea what they wanted or how to make them happy. She told me how much I'd saved and circled the amount and then she told me I could complete a survey to win a five-hundred-dollar gift card and circled that number as well, and I was sorry she had to do that for every single person who came through her line. I was sure there were ramifications for not doing those things, that her boss watched to make sure she was circling and smiling.

In the parking lot, I opened my door and it banged right into the car next to mine. Mine was white. This other vehicle was red. There was a little white mark on his red car and a dent, as well. I considered leaving my name and number but it was more of a ding, really, and it seemed like a lot of trouble for such a small thing. Plus, I was almost certainly legally drunk. Nobody had seen me. Were there cameras in the parking lot? I stood there with my door open, one foot in and one foot out, and then hopped in and drove off.

At home, after everything was put away, I sat in my chair and noted the things in the room that I wouldn't need anymore: the busy bone she hadn't much cared for after the first day—Kara had been right about that—the bed I'd moved from room to room, the Kong (should've gotten the wobbler), the enormous sack of dog food hardly touched. Ellen's hairbrush. I shoved my feet into the bed, watched the hair float around as the last of the sun streamed in through the blinds, and cried for a while, humiliated and lost in the crying even though there was no one in the world to see it. People said you felt better afterward, like it was a release, but I didn't feel better. I didn't feel worse, either. But that wasn't true because there was the shame of it, which brought back the shame of other things.

When I was boy of thirteen, all of my grandparents died in quick succession over the span of a year, as though the four of them had lived together in a house and passed around a disease that had taken them all out. My paternal grandfather—a ship captain, captain of the high seas, which was how I'd thought of him as a boy, though he'd only had one ship and hadn't been a captain at all but a landowner—was the first to go, and then my grandmother on my mother's side and then the ship captain's wife and then my mother's father. Spending so much time in funeral homes and graveyards, our house filling up with the relics—chairs and tables and glasses and bowls, pictures and books, my parents seemingly unable to get rid of anything—my sleep grew more and more disturbed. I imagined the dead people watching me from the foot of my bed as I masturbated, sat on the toilet. Commenting on my study habits and the way I spoke to my mother. They had been with me for years, disapproving of my behavior as I went about my day.

I got myself a beer and closed my eyes and fell asleep, woke up to someone knocking with the beer still upright and balanced on my stomach. As I was remembering what day and month it was and all that had happened, I opened the door to find Sasha with an overnight bag in one hand and my briefcase in the other. Layla licked my hands, my pants. I bent down and let her lick my face and she whined as if she hadn't seen me in weeks.

"You left your briefcase," Sasha said. "And along with all those pamphlets, you had a box of business cards in there. I didn't know people put their actual home addresses on business cards anymore."

"I'm sure they don't. I'm old."

"Old school," she said. "You're not so old." She touched my arm, lightly grabbed it, and let go. It made me feel like I'd missed out on so much. Here it was, all I'd been waiting for: a woman could show up at your door, grab your arm, and walk inside without an invitation. It seemed simple and yet nothing like it had ever happened to me before. I'd had some fun times in college—dates and parties, romps in bedrooms that weren't mine—though those fun times had been the exception rather than the rule.

"We left him," she said, tightening her ponytail, walking into my living room. I couldn't believe she was in my living room. "At least for the night. I felt weird going to my mom's house right now, though. I'm just not in the mood."

"Well, y'all are welcome to stay here. Of course you are."

"What a day! We just need somewhere to crash and then we'll figure things out in the morning." *Somewhere to crash.* It was such a violent way to describe sleep. "Do you mind if I take a bath? I usually take one before bed and I feel a mess."

"Of course," I said, wishing I'd had some warning, a chance to get myself and the house together. I took her bag and showed her to Maxine's old room, Layla trotting along behind us, a visitor now. I never went into this room, kept the door closed. I could feel Maxine in it, all of the hours she'd spent locked away to talk on the phone or stew or do whatever it was teenage girls did. How strange that a room could retain someone's energy after so many years. There was a queen-sized bed, a table on either side of it with a lamp on each. There was a bookshelf with some books on it, a random assortment of paperbacks and hardcovers that Ellen had purchased at library sales—the kinds of books people had when they only wanted to look like they read.

Maxine would be coming over tomorrow, I remembered, and the baby would be with her. I felt a jolt of anxiety. I would have to work on having some feelings for the baby, at least. I would hold her for a while, would smile and say things like, "Come to grandpa!" Perhaps I'd brush her hair or fix her a fruit cup. I didn't have any fruit.

Sasha sat on the bed, testing it out with a few bounces.

"It may need some dusting—I could dust it real quick—it's been pretty closed up in here. Or you could open a window."

"It'll work," she said. "It's fine, it's good."

"I'll light a candle." I went and got a candle from the cabinet where I kept the emergency supplies in case the electricity went out. It didn't have much of a smell but it would at least look nice. I turned on the fan, which blew the tiny flame all about. Sasha was still sitting on the bed next to her bag, the dog at her feet. From a certain angle, she looked like Maxine—different hair color and style of clothes but there was something unmistakably Maxine-like about her. I wondered if Maxine would be able to see it and knew that she wouldn't. Sasha was lower-class. If you dressed her up and put her in a ballroom you'd still be able to see it in her teeth, a coarseness of the skin. The way she moved. Even if they'd looked like twins—they didn't, but even if they had—Maxine wouldn't be able to acknowledge any resemblance; it would have challenged her view of herself in a way she couldn't handle. And then I thought about Sasha answering the door, how Maxine would think I'd relocated without telling her.

The idea of the two of them meeting was preposterous, and exciting. *This is my new life*, I would tell her, *you thought you had me all figured out but you don't know me at all.* Why would I want my daughter to feel like she didn't know me? This was the tragedy of families, summed up in its entirety: you wanted to be known and loved for yourself and you also wanted to be someone who might be capable of living another life altogether.

I showed Sasha the guest bathroom and turned on the faucets: hot, cold. I hadn't cleaned the tub after bathing Layla, though I'd given it a decent rinse. "The towels are in here and there's soap and toilet paper. I think I have an extra toothbrush somewhere."

"I brought my own toothbrush," she said.

I knelt, cursed my popping knees, and sorted through the drawers filled with Ellen's toiletries. There were more of them than I remembered: deodorant, makeup, various shampoos and body sprays and a lot of small tubes and bottles of things she'd gotten for free. The woman had loved free samples. I picked out what looked like a bottle of fancy shampoo for color-treated hair and a body wash that said Pure Grace.

"Is your hair color-treated?"

"It doesn't matter," she said.

"Do you like body wash or soap?"

"Both." She held out her hands and I gave her the bottles. "Now why don't you go sit down and relax? Have a beer. I can take care of myself."

"Do you need anything else?"

"Actually, I think I might like a beer, as well. A beer in the bathtub is always nice."

"Bud Light or Coors? I might have a Corona hiding in one of

the drawers." Ellen had liked a Corona every once in a while, with a slice of lime.

"Corona's great."

"Come on, girl," I said. "Let's leave your mama alone." I wanted to keep calling the dog Layla, though I supposed it wasn't fair to her. If we were both calling her different names she might very well become confused. It reminded me of a scene from *Annie*, a movie I hadn't watched since Maxine was a girl. Annie calling the dog so it wouldn't get taken to the pound and then bringing him home to the orphanage and hiding him in a basket of laundry. I'd liked that song about what to name him: *How about Rover? Why not think it over?* It was surprising sometimes, what the brain remembered.

After I delivered the beer, I sat in my chair. Layla got in her bed and licked my feet. "You may be her Katy but you're my Layla. How's that? That okay with you?"

She stopped licking my feet and sighed. I didn't know if it was a happy sigh or a depressed sigh. It sounded like a depressed sigh.

"You should be happier than a pig right now," I told her. "A pig in shit. You have both of us." I closed my eyes, listening to the water run and what sounded like humming. I thought about Sasha in the bathtub and whether she was the type to stay in there for a long time like Ellen. It seemed odd to go to a strange man's house and then stay in the bathtub for an hour and I wondered if that was the difference between men and women. Were women able to sit and relax and not feel any pressure to do anything but enjoy themselves even when a situation was odd or unusual? Men didn't soak in the tub for a long time and read and light candles and women did, though there were probably young men in this day and age who had decided to do it, too, that they weren't going to feel emasculated by soaking and having private time for their private thoughts. I turned on the TV, muted it. Then I turned it on low enough to hear both Sasha and the TV. She shut off the water and I could hear her sliding around, the bottle making contact with the porcelain. Beautiful sounds.

After a while, I knocked on the door. "You hungry? I could put a pizza in the oven, or we could order a pizza."

"Do you only eat pizza?" she said, and I heard her ass slide again, and what sounded like water slop over the edge of the tub. I hoped she wasn't making a mess, but reminded myself that I didn't care about such things—this was a new life, a new day. If there was a mess, I could clean it. Or it could just stay there.

"There's other things," I said. "I went to the store earlier."

"Like what?"

"Pimento cheese. Crackers and cheese. Lunch meat, bread, stuff for meatloaf . . ."

"Let's order a pizza. Pizza's good."

"What kind?" I asked.

"I like pepperoni and spicy sausage but I'm open to suggestions."

"Where do you want me to order from?" I could feel her getting put out with me. I knew I was asking too many questions but I didn't know how to make decisions for other people.

"Papa John's or Pizza Hut—wherever, it doesn't matter. Not Domino's, though. I don't like Domino's."

I stepped away from the door, which I'd been resting my hand against like a weirdo, and the dog and I went to search for a coupon. Most of them were for Domino's, which was my personal preference—what did she have against Domino's? I found one for Pizza Hut, but it was expired. I found another, also expired. I called the number and a computer voice asked if I wanted to hear the specials and I ended up ordering two large pizzas plus cheese sticks, which was a ridiculous amount of food for two people but everybody likes cheese sticks and I wanted a Hawaiian pizza, which was the ultimate in festive, if festive was the goal, which I hoped it was. Then Layla and I sat and waited. I petted her with my foot and the TV told me about all of the terrible things that were happening in the world but the terrible things didn't feel so important.

The water in the bathtub went on again and stayed on for a while and then it went off and Sasha was calling my name. It was a wonder to hear my name. *Louis. Louis.* I wondered if she would try to seduce me and I didn't know if I could handle that, if I'd be able to perform. What if she wanted to have sex and I couldn't get it up and she looked at me like I'd failed her, same as every other man had failed her. It would be better to disappoint her by rejecting her advances outright—if she planned on making advances—rather than the other.

"Yes?" I said.

"Could you get me another beer?"

"Okay, sure. Corona?"

"Si señor," she said, ass sliding. Was she doing that on purpose?

I got the beer and stood outside, knocked.

"It's open."

"I can just leave it here," I said, and she said she didn't want to get everything wet and then she said all of her naughty parts were covered up with washrags, and the word "washrags" seemed sad and awful and I wondered how many towels she was using, not that it mattered, but I was curious.

I opened the door. Layla hung back—she was the type of dog who didn't like to see you naked. She didn't mind me on the toilet but when I took off all my clothes she left the room. It made sense. If she showed up one day wearing pants and a sweater I wouldn't know what to make of it, either. Sasha had a small towel draped across her chest and a hand covering her other part, though I didn't look at it directly. I saw the blur of skin, imagining yellow. I turned my head toward the foggy mirror as I handed her the beer and took the empty away.

"Thank you," she said. "Today has been a nightmare, but it's also been kind of amazing. I got my dog back, met you, and now I'm taking a hot bath and drinking cold beer in a stranger's bathtub. It's tremendously exciting."

I thought she sounded like a TV character or someone in a movie. "Do you need anything else?"

"Did you order the pizza?"

"I did, should be here soon."

"You know that's the filthiest mirror I've ever seen," she said. "I can hardly even see myself in it."

"It's fogged up."

"I'm talking about before. It's okay, though. People have a hard time noticing their own filth. I won't hold it against you."

I let myself out and stood in the hall, stunned. Layla licked my hands and I wiped them on my pants. I went back to my chair and pretty soon the doorbell rang and Layla bounded over to it and barked.

"I see you're barking all the time now," I said. "Well, isn't everybody full of surprises? Now don't try to bite him." It was a woman, a hefty older lady, and I wanted the transaction to be over as quickly as possible—I felt as though I was doing something embarrassing or illicit even though nothing was embarrassing or illicit, we were two adults who hadn't committed any crimes— so I said I didn't need change and passed her the money and she passed me the pizzas and I said, "thank you," as I shut the door, tacking on "very much" so I didn't seem rude.

Sasha ate on the floor in front of the TV, feeding sausage and pepperoni to Layla, which would probably upset her stomach. Her wet hair was dripping down her back, soaking through her shirt, and she had on tiny stretchy shorts, the likes of which I'd never seen.

"If that dog has to go to the bathroom at two o'clock in the morning, you're in charge," I said.

"I'm in charge," she said. "Hand me the remote."

We watched a show on the Food Network in which two people competed and the winner got to cook against Bobby Flay; it was called *Beat Bobby Flay.* She stretched her legs out in front of her, flexing her toes, and told me she'd already seen it but couldn't remember who'd won. She talked to the Japanese man cooking steaks, the guy she was "rooting for," as she always rooted for somebody. I liked her, and I liked her in my house, but I was pretty certain she had some sort of mental deficiency, or a drug or alcohol addiction. I knew almost nothing about her except that I had stolen her dog, by accident, and that she was Harry Davidson's wife but might be anybody's.

I decided not to ask questions about who she was or what she did or whether or not she had any kids. Instead I asked how she decided who to root for.

"That's a good question," she said, "but I don't know. I just pick one without thinking. It's instinctual, organic."

"Interesting."

"If I had to guess, I'd say I usually like the foreign ones best."

"How come?" She did not seem like the kind of person who would like the foreigners best.

"It's all a mystery to me," she said. "But look how cute this little guy is. I mean, you're rooting for him, too, right? If you had to pick?"

"I'm neutral."

"You're Switzerland," she said, and I told her that was exactly right and spent the next few minutes wondering what other countries were neutral and whether it meant they'd stayed out of all the wars or just some of them. And did they have alliances or only depend on themselves? I was Switzerland. Untouchable, unbiased.

When we finished eating, she asked for a couch blanket, which I fetched for her, and then a pillow, which I took off my bed, and set herself up in a cocoon situation with Layla belly-up on her lap. We watched a movie called *Eddie the Eagle* about a ski jumper, which she kept calling a "feel-good movie." She would lean forward whenever Eddie was trying to land a jump as if she could help him. I wanted to point it out but I didn't want her to stop doing it because it was the best thing I'd seen in years.

When it was over, she looked at me and smiled. Her smile was crooked. I wondered if she was like me, if she also found one half of her face doing the thing it was supposed to do and had to remind the other.

"I loved that so much," she said. "I usually don't like movies like that."

"Sports movies?"

"No, happy movies. Movies with positive messages."

"How come?"

"That's not true, actually," she said, and thought for a moment. "I *do* like them. I just don't think of myself as the kind of person who likes them. I feel like I'm more of a realist." I wanted to hold her in my lap and put my face in her still-damp hair, breathe it in. Rock her to sleep.

She said goodnight and started back to her room, the dog following her.

"Wait," I said. "Take her bed with you."

She walked over and picked it up. "You bought it for her?"

"I did."

"That was nice of you."

"I'm a nice guy. Can I just ask you one thing?"

"Okay," she said. "But I won't necessarily answer you or tell you the truth or anything."

Who was this woman? I didn't know if I liked her or not, after all. She was mighty sassy. "Does your husband know where you are?"

"No," she said. "I told him I was leaving and would call him soon, and that he shouldn't try to get in touch with me before that or I'd call the police."

"The police?"

"I'm not really going to call the police, though a dog is considered property and if someone gives away your property without telling you it's illegal. It's always good to say you'll call the police, though. It gets the point across."

"Okay," I said. "Well, I'm glad you came here," which seemed like a risky thing to say but she could take it any way she wanted to take it. I didn't care. She tilted her head at me and smiled crookedly before she burst out laughing.

CHAPTER 10

"WOULD YOU COME sit with me for a second?" Sasha asked. "Just for a minute."

She was under the covers, her dark hair curled all over the pillow. I stood in the doorway, unable to move or speak. I missed my daughter. I wished I knew her and was sad to think I never would, that my not knowing her had been my fault. Of course it had been my fault.

I sat on the edge of her bed and she put her arms around my neck like she wanted me to piggyback her around the room. Her arms were freckled, hairier than I would have assumed. I could feel her breath on my neck, her heart beating against my back. It was such a strange place to feel a heartbeat.

"Do you like me?" she asked.

"Of course I like you." And then I stood, abruptly, and said, "Goodnight. Sleep well."

"I'm sorry," she said, and I wanted to apologize to her a thousand times for the wrongs I'd committed against others.

"I meant to tell you—there's a bird that comes in the morning and bangs into the window for a few hours. Usually starts pretty

early, around six o'clock. I could get you a box fan if you want. . . .
I know there's one around here somewhere."

"You know a lot of birds die flying into windows, like millions
of them each year. You should get one of those curtains or some
tape or something. You're going to kill it."

"I'm not doing anything to it."

"But you could do something to help."

I went and lay down on my bed, feeling like I'd never be able
to sleep. I hadn't thought about the bird dying, though I'd considered wringing its neck, scattering poisonous seeds about the
yard. I spent too much time thinking about that goddamn bird.
I wondered what all of it meant, and whether she would stay and
whether I'd want her to. I had money, or would soon enough, and
it could go a long way toward changing things for me. I had to
get in touch with that damned lawyer—why hadn't he called me
back? I would call and ask to speak to one of the partners, file a
formal complaint. And I was healthy enough, though I should
probably watch my diet and get more exercise. I wasn't too old yet.
I pictured Harry Davidson at my door with a baseball bat, ready
to bash my head in, only he wouldn't have a bat—we weren't in
sixth grade—he would have a gun and it would be small enough
to fit neatly in his waistband or the pocket of his jacket and when
he put it to my head and pulled the trigger there'd be no one to
stop him. There never was.

But it didn't seem like such a bad way to go, either, like dying
in one's chair. It would be quick. It would be painful but I had
never felt much pain and didn't know how to imagine it. More
than likely, I'd immediately black out. When I stubbed my toe
or slammed a finger in a door, the pain was so great I felt it in

my balls, got light-headed and sweaty. What would a bullet to the head feel like if I couldn't take a stubbed toe? I comforted myself with the idea of blacking out: a small, temporary death that would release me from pain until the pain was manageable or else I was dead.

I wanted to change my will first, though. I'd leave Sasha with enough money so she could buy her own house, a nice little spot on the water she could decorate any way she liked and that no one ever forced her out of ever again. This plan had the added bonus of pissing off Maxine. It didn't even matter if Sasha loved me, or even liked me. It would be my gift to her. My gift to women.

I awoke as it was starting to get light out, wondering if I'd dreamed it all. No—Sasha was in Maxine's room, and Layla, too. The previous day had been a blur. I'd started drinking early and more had happened in the past twenty-four hours than in the six months that had come before. Sasha eating pizza on the floor, wearing almost nothing. Wet hair dripping down her back. We'd watched a Japanese man beat Bobby Flay and a movie about a retarded man who'd overcome the odds to win some skiing awards. I'd been on Sasha's bed with her arms around my neck, her hairier-than-normal arms, though I couldn't say for sure that they were hairier than normal because I didn't go around looking at women's arms. I hardly even noticed a woman's arms, got close enough to notice them. These didn't seem like things that could have happened and yet they had.

I got up and peered out the window at the small blue Chevrolet parked in the driveway, an older model with hail damage I could see from this distance. I wanted to buy her something red or yellow, though I had never liked red or yellow cars. I liked the idea of buying her something extravagant, going to the car dealership with her and sitting in the passenger seat while she adjusted the mirrors. Smiling at me with her sunglasses on. They could leave before breakfast or stay forever, and we'd live together as friends or as man and wife. There was no way to know what was going to happen and I was just going to have to wait and see. It wasn't my decision, none of it was my decision, and it had been that way my whole life. Ellen would let me pick where we went to dinner, or what movie we watched at the theater, would make a great show out of letting me choose as if these small things might make up for all of the larger decisions in which I had no say whatsoever.

There was a lot of conflicting information on what it meant to be a man, what it meant to be a good man.

I started the coffee and went to let Layla out, opening the door just enough to see Sasha's body curled on its side and all the covers kicked off. She must have gotten hot in the night. I should have shown her where the thermostat was, told her to turn it up or down as she liked. She was wearing an eye mask, black with polka dots or stars.

I took the dog outside and she set off after a squirrel. She hadn't caught one yet but I liked to watch her chase them because it gave her such pleasure. One of my father's dogs, Jonesy, had caught them easily but always let them go, catch and release, until the day a squirrel bit him on the nose and he'd bled, bright red blood coming out of that black nose, and it was odd that something so bright should come out of it. I hadn't really believed he was full of blood same as I was until that moment—that we were both living beings who felt pain and joy and the only difference was that he never thought he wasn't deserving of joy or wasn't worthy of it. From that point on Jonesy killed the squirrels, had relished killing them, leaving their bodies scattered about the yard and my father proud.

I went to get a cup of coffee and rejoined Layla outside. I petted her for a while and then broke out into a song about how we were best friends and did she want to be best friends forever? When I stopped singing I felt slightly disoriented, like my body had been taken over by this other person, this stranger who sang ridiculous songs to dogs. And then, as had happened the time before and the time before that, all memory of it was lost. I recalled a cartoon frog grabbing a cane and a top hat—*hello my baby, hello my honey, hello my ragtime gal* . . . —and then the top hat and cane vanished and he returned to being a frog. But then he'd do it again. And again. I had a vague recollection of a Mexican man watching him. Were frogs always associated with Mexicans, or had this been embedded in the memory, the two of them forever intertwined?

Layla walked beside me as I went to get the paper. I looked down at her and she looked up at me and licked my hand. She wasn't ever going to carry the paper in her mouth but that was okay.

"Good morning, Louis!" Mrs. Sullivan called. She was walking her yippy Maltese back and forth in front of her house like she did every morning.

"Good morning, Judy." *Don't stop, don't stop*, I thought, but she was already asking her dog in an encouraging manner if it needed to take a poopy as the dog aimed its ass at my hedge. Mrs. Sullivan was something of a ringleader in the neighborhood, getting into everybody's business, though Ellen and I had mostly stayed out of all that. Once she'd gotten into a spat with Polly, the lesbian on the corner, and told her, "You ain't nothin' on this street anymore," which had been widely reported and commented on. Ellen had gotten such a kick out of it we'd started saying it to each other: *you ain't nothin' on this street anymore.*

"Have a good day," I said, and we got out of there before I had a chance to see whether she'd pick up the turds.

I tried to read but couldn't concentrate because the bird had returned to do its usual thing at the usual intervals and I was thinking about Sasha and how late she slept, how I could go in there and watch her if I wanted. I was also thinking about whether she had a job, how long it had been since she'd worked. And what time she might start drinking, or if yesterday had been a peculiarity, a difficult day and nothing more. It reminded me of one of Ellen's friends—Ellen had so many friends, presumably still did—a devoutly religious woman who was always waiting and seeing. It was all in God's hands and there was nothing to do but wait and see.

On top of everything, Maxine would be coming over. I should go to the store and have some of the drinks on hand that she liked—that sparkly water that tasted so awful, some juice or milk for the baby. I tried putting her out of my mind, which was impossible. She would knock on my door and I'd act surprised. *I forgot you were coming over today. . . .* And I'd hug her and say all the right things and we might both feel good about the visit, like we were finally moving in the right direction.

At 7:30, Layla and I set out for a walk. I decided we'd do something unusual, go somewhere we'd never gone before, so we walked down one street and up another and then out of the neighborhood altogether. I looked both ways and jogged across the road, dragging her along, as it was a pretty busy road, to the other side where there was a sidewalk. A jog! I felt damn near athletic and my knees weren't giving me any trouble at all. Then we walked along as the cars whooshed past and I paused to let her sniff the new smells, allowing her the opportunity to enjoy herself fully. I was never out in the world so early in the day anymore and had forgotten that it smelled different. Someone honked and I waved. Who was it? I didn't recognize the truck. I waved at the garbage men, a couple of guys working on a car in their driveway. Smiled at a young woman on a bike. Oh, she was lovely! Her hair flowing behind her. The garbage men and the workers and the young biking woman were tackling the day and I was one of them. We weren't wallowing in bed.

I came to a light and pressed the button to cross an intersection. I hadn't meant to go so far but it was still pleasant enough and the sun was shining, the birds chirping. I let Layla test the limitations of her leash to piss on a church rummage-sale sign.

On the other side of the street, an older black woman held the hand of a child—somewhere around the age of Laurel—only Maxine wouldn't let Laurel stand on her own two feet like that. She'd have the child in a stroller or would be carrying her. There was a grown man with them toting some bags from the dollar store. We were facing each other and I was trying not to look at them and then the walking-man sign lit up and we began to cross the street, which was quite a wide one, and Layla was acting weird so I was having to encourage her, drag her along. And then there were only twelve seconds left and then ten, eight, and the grandmother and child began to run and the man was running, too, his groceries bouncing everywhere. When we met in the middle, they were smiling and laughing and I returned their smiles. It was such a small thing, but their joy—and the way they had included me in it—made me feel like we were in it together. That we were all just doing our best to get safely across the road and it didn't have to be any more difficult than we made it.

CHAPTER 11

"**S**HOULD WE GO out for breakfast?" Sasha asked.

It was after eleven and she'd just emerged from Maxine's room. To my knowledge, she hadn't even gone to the bathroom yet. I'd pissed at least three times since I'd gotten out of bed. She sat on the couch with her knees to her chest as I poured her a cup of coffee, heated it up in the microwave.

"Might be too late for breakfast."

"McDonald's has all-day breakfast now," she said. "It's the best thing they ever did." Her hair was down and messy. I liked it. I wanted to tell her that she should wear it down more often but women didn't like it when you told them what you liked, or Ellen hadn't, and neither had Maxine. If I complimented one of them on their dress, they'd go and take it right off and put on something frumpy.

"You want McDonald's?"

"Not necessarily, I'm just saying we can still get breakfast somewhere. There's always Waffle House or IHOP—we could go to one of them."

"I haven't been to IHOP in forever."

"So let's go there," she said. "I can't remember what I used to order—I think it's called the Rootin' Tootin' Fruitin' or something like that."

"That doesn't sound right."

"I swear that's what it's called, or it's close."

"Then we'll both get it," I said, "whatever it is."

I handed her the mug. "Tell me if it's hot enough. I can heat it up some more or make a fresh pot."

She put her lips to it slowly, carefully, as I watched. I wouldn't say anything about her hair, ask to brush it, touch it. That would be weird. It was terrifying how easy it would be to mess it up. I felt like a pervert for having her in my home, at least fifteen years my junior, married. And she was wearing so little clothing, once again. One side of her shirt fell off her shoulder and she left it there, the top of a plump white breast exposed.

"I have an extra robe, if you want. It'll be too big for you but it's comfortable."

"Do you want me to cover up?" she asked.

"I thought you might be cold."

"You're sweet," she said. "I'm fine." The way she said she was fine—dead-eyed, stony—sent chills right through me.

"I'm going to hop in the shower and then we'll go," I said. "It'll take me five minutes." And I left the two of them on the couch where they were happiest. I hoped she wasn't the type to stay inside most of the day like Ellen, like me, though it was clear she was. I wanted to do things, get out into the world. We could rent kayaks and paddle out to Deer Island. I imagined us splashing each other, the sun shining on the water, helping Sasha pull her kayak onto the sand and exploring the island with her. I was sure there was a lot of trash out there; kids partied out there and left trash on the beaches. That ruined the fantasy a bit but we might find something good, even in the garbage. And we might rent a boat and go out to Cat Island. We'd pack a cooler full of beer and food and spend the day. I thought about the different scenarios, the ways in which Sasha and I and an island might configure, while I pleasured myself for the first time in a very long time.

At IHOP, there were a few tables of older couples eating lunch and three or four students scattered about, studying and drinking coffee, occupying entire booths by themselves. I remembered a time when Maxine was in high school and claimed that she was going to the IHOP by herself to "study." Ellen and I never believed her. I'm sure it wasn't easy being an only child, an only child with parents who didn't much like each other. We had failed to model a positive relationship and I hated that. I hoped she was happy with Craig, though he seemed more like the idea of a man than an actual man. Even his name bored me and I liked to call him Greg to fuck with him, or to fuck with her.

Our waitress was a friendly woman with one of the largest asses I'd ever seen on a white person. She had her hair piled into a brownish-gray puff on top of her head.

"What can I get you two?" she asked.

"Pepsi," I said. "And a water. Please."

"Same," Sasha said. This thrilled me and I was embarrassed that I'd let it show. But once we had our Pepsis, there was nothing to say. I wanted to ask if she loved him, if she'd loved him prior to the whole dog situation. It was a simple question and one people avoided asking or talking about. There was a time when Ellen insisted we go to couples counseling even though we were finished with each other by that point, but we felt we had to go in order to say we'd done everything—*we even went to couples counseling!*—and the counselor asked all sorts of questions and gave us all kinds of homework assignments like staring into each other's eyes for entire minutes without looking away, which I never could have done. The idea of it was a horror. Ellen hadn't been interested, either, never even broached the topic to me at home. But the counselor hadn't asked the most obvious questions, the ones that mattered: do you still love each other? Do you want to be together? Instead we talked about the bad things that had happened to us in our childhoods and young adulthoods and our past relationships as if they had any relevance on the present and the fact that we simply no longer loved each other and hadn't for years.

If the counselor had led with the questions that really mattered, she'd have been out of business within weeks.

"This Pepsi is flat," Sasha said.

"It tastes okay to me."

When the waitress returned, Sasha sent back her Pepsi and ordered the Rooty Tooty Fresh 'N Fruity and then I repeated it—she had been right, or nearly so—and we grinned at each other and raised our eyebrows. The breakfast came with everything—eggs and hash browns and pancakes, sausage and bacon, but I went ahead and ordered an extra side of bacon, anyway.

"You're mighty hungry."

"I thought I'd bring some home to Layla," I said.

She frowned in an exaggerated manner. "You mean Katy."

"She doesn't look like a Katy to me. How would you feel about changing it?" She kept frowning. "She seems to really like Layla."

"Whenever you call her Layla, she's probably thinking, 'I don't know who that bitch is.'"

"I doubt she's thinking that."

"You don't know what dogs think."

"That's true," I said. "But Katy seems like the name of a person, a human being."

"And Layla doesn't?"

"No." I wanted to tell her the story about Clapton but I couldn't remember it. He'd been dating a woman named Debbie or Pattie and George Harrison had stolen her out from under him. I had no idea where Layla came in, how Layla entered into the picture. Surely Harry Davidson had managed to tell her the story. He clearly loved that story and would have found a way to tell it.

"You don't change a dog's name after two years."

"You don't swap horses in the middle of a race."

"That's right," she said. And then, "I like that. I'm not sure it applies here but I like it."

Our food came out more quickly than I'd anticipated. We were just getting a good conversation going, a rapport. Her eyes were hazel, not like a storm at all—the green and brown swirling in such a nice pattern. I couldn't look at them for very long but hoped I was doing a decent job of maintaining eye contact. Not too little and not too much. I wasn't sure what was too little and what was too much. I didn't know anything about what it was to be with another person, even though I had been with someone for over thirty years. When Layla knew I was getting ready to leave the house but wasn't sure if I was going to take her, she would sit in front of me and stare off into the distance, like she was going to show me how good and quiet she could be, how unobtrusive.

I wouldn't even notice if she went along, she would be so well behaved.

At some point, Sasha said, "Let's slow down. We're eating too fast."

I was shoving an entire link of sausage into my mouth at that moment; what a horrible image this must have been for her. "I didn't know how hungry I was," I said, and smiled in a way that I hoped was self-deprecating and good-natured.

"Whenever I eat a lot at night I'm even hungrier the next morning. It's very strange," she said. "A very strange thing. You could get super fat that way."

"I know what you mean," I said, and I did, though I was always hungry in the morning, at least until I'd had my two cups of coffee and then the hunger subsided.

"Is something burning?" she asked.

Something was burning. There was yelling in the kitchen and the students began to look up from their textbooks and laptops. The yelling stopped and then it started again along with some clanking pots. Something shattered. We looked around at the other patrons and smiled and shrugged, resumed eating. I always liked breaks in the action like this, and it was the second time it had happened that day. I checked my watch: it wasn't even twelve o'clock. The world was magic.

"You have pancake on your face," Sasha said, and she stood in the booth and reached across the table. Instead of wiping it off, she touched it. "Or it might be egg. Yep, it's egg."

I wiped, covering a large area to be certain. "Did I get it?"

"You got it," she said.

Her phone dinged and she fished it out of her giant purse—

had it been so large earlier? Why did she need such a big purse? She typed something short, no more than two or three words, and dropped it back into her purse. A few minutes later the same thing happened again. I finished everything on my plate and the extra bacon, too.

On the way home, we swung by Home Depot at Sasha's insistence for some kind of bird deterrent. She wanted to wait in the car so I left the keys in the ignition, the radio and a/c on. The guy at the entrance asked if he could help and I declined and then proceeded to walk up and down what felt like dozens of aisles all the while thinking about Sasha in my car, running down the battery, growing impatient. I started to sweat as all of the other trips to Home Depot came back to me—every small part I'd had to return, the copied keys that hadn't fit. There were times I'd made three trips in a single day. After about twenty minutes I located a bin of Bird-B-Gone Flash Tape and grabbed four rolls to be on the safe side.

The car was still there, as was Sasha, eating from a movie-theater-size package of Twizzlers. I said nothing but studied her for longer than usual: her legs propped on the dash, the scar redder and angrier up close. It looked like it hurt. Had someone done this to her or had she been in an accident? Perhaps its origin was even less romantic, like a vein that had been removed.

"You have tape at home?" she asked, examining the rolls. Her head snapped back as she gnawed off a hunk of licorice.

"That's tape right there."

"This isn't sticky. You can use string, though."

"Why do they call the damn stuff 'tape' then? It says so right on the label."

She looked up the product on her phone and started reading the reviews. "Looks like woodpeckers and crows don't mind this stuff but you're not dealing with woodpeckers or crows so you should be okay. Oh, this is funny: someone asked if it can repel humans like his next-door neighbor and someone else responded, 'Haha! They could charge way more if it did.'"

Back at the house, Sasha set herself up on the couch, an enormous sweatshirt on top of her clothes with a blanket on top of that and two pillows she'd taken off her bed. Was she cold? Why was she so cold? She was still eating the Twizzlers, really working them over, while I inspected the tape. Now that I had a solution, or a potential one, I wasn't sure I wanted the bird to go away. I'd grown accustomed to the banging, its arrival every morning signaling a new day.

"You have a cheap cable package," she said, flipping around. "Bottom of the barrel."

"I only watch a few things." I considered mentioning *Naked and Afraid* but decided against it. I put the tape back in the bag.

"I bet you like Fox News," she said. "America's News Headquarters!"

It was edging closer to the time when Maxine would arrive and I was getting anxious. I could explain the situation—a daughter and a grandchild I didn't know all that well but was hoping to know better—and ask her to get out of the house for a while, go to a movie. She could buy herself another package of Twizzlers and a gigantic popcorn. I'd give her twenty or forty dollars, I didn't want to seem cheap, from the stash I kept in my sock drawer. I liked imagining her with her popcorn and soda in the dark, smiling at the screen.

I fed the dog some treats and Cloroxed the kitchen counters, rinsed a couple of pots and tried to appear busy because it was the middle of the day and I felt like I should be doing something. Perhaps, if Sasha weren't there, I'd be doing exactly what she was doing—no, I knew I would—and what a waste. Was this the extent of her days? It was so gratuitously self-indulgent it seemed impolite to look. I got out the vacuum cleaner and started pushing it around but it didn't seem to bother her at all other than the fact that she turned the sound up on the TV until it was blaring, until it could be heard clear over the damn thing. It was incredible. I almost admired her for it.

I turned the vacuum off, shoved it into a corner of the room. I couldn't recall ever having vacuumed before. It was a fact: the house had not been vacuumed since Ellen left. The kitchen floor had not been swept.

"Could you bring me a glass of water?" she asked.

"You want ice?"

"No thanks. I usually only like ice at Sonic—they have the good pebbly kind. More places should have ice like that, don't you think?"

"I never go there," I said.

"Oh, you're missing out. Although they usually burn the onion rings and they'll give 'em to you all burnt and dried out. Quality isn't at the top of their list but I like all the drink combinations. There are thousands, and I mean thousands, of options."

I handed her the glass and then squeezed myself onto the couch by her feet. It was an awkward thing for me to have done—there really wasn't room for me with her setup. She glared, but it was a fake-angry glare and then the dog jumped between us and jostled around.

"Good girl, Katy," I said. I looked at Sasha as I said it to show her I was coming around, would be able to change and adapt. It wasn't like I'd known either of them for long and if I had to call them something different, I could. But once you'd imagined something as one thing, even for a short while, it was hard to imagine it as something else.

"My feet are cold," she said, nudging them under my leg.

"I have some socks you can borrow," I said. "I mean you can have them, I don't need them back. Do you want me to get 'em for you?"

"No." She gave me a big toothy smile and shoved her feet beneath me more forcefully. There was a chip in one of her teeth that I hadn't noticed before, not a big chip, just a small one. Of course I had seen that her teeth weren't very good but I hadn't noticed this chip, which was fairly prominent, though not so prominent at all. It was both at the same time.

I went to the bathroom and took a piss, gathering my nerve to hand her a fistful of cash. I decided sixty dollars might seem better. I didn't want to give her too much, though, not enough to get a hotel room for the night, for example. I went back out and sat in my chair. She was watching a TV show in which a virus had broken out.

"I like this kind of stuff, end-of-the-world stuff," she said.

"I don't usually watch them."

"Once you start, you get really into them. You start wishing you could be challenged to see what you'd do in the situation."

"Oh, I *have* thought about that," I said. "Being challenged, different scenarios . . ."

"I want to see if I'm weak or strong, you know. Like, would I be brave enough to do incredible things? To save people's lives? Or would I give up because I was too scared? They're questions you can't answer when you're just sitting on your couch."

"That's true," I said. "Maybe you shouldn't sit on the couch so much."

She shot me a look that was certainly not fake-angry. *Watch out, mister,* it said. *You're going down a road you don't want to travel.*

"You could start training for something," I suggested. "A marathon or a triathlon, take up a martial art."

She was going to be angry for another minute so I waited. I wasn't going to press her on it. Then she said, "In *The Walking Dead*, Morgan practices Aikido. He's probably called a lot of attention to Aikido."

"I saw the first season but it wasn't for me."

"You were scared!"

It was true, I had been. I petted Layla with my foot and said, "My daughter's coming over with her baby in a little while and I need to spend some time with them."

"When?"

"About an hour." It was more like an hour and a half but it was clear she wasn't a fast mover.

She didn't say anything and I felt I'd made my point. We went back to the virus show. I'd missed some of it but it was easy enough to pick up on what was happening: they were trying to contain the virus to a section of Atlanta that had been cordoned off and no one was allowed in or out. But of course people had been divided by the walls and were desperately trying to get to one side or the other. The acting was terrible. I wondered again if this was how she spent her days, and why. I didn't do much with my days, either, but I was retired and my wife had left me. I realized I had been depressed, that until Layla had come into my life, I'd just been sitting in my chair. For months I'd been sitting in my chair waiting for something to happen and now it had and we were still sitting.

"Hey, Sasha," I said.

"Hey, Louis."

"Could you pause this for a second?"

"Sure." She turned the sound down and continued to look at the TV.

"No—could you actually *pause* your program?"

"My *program?*" she said. "I love that, my program. That's what my mom calls her soap opera. She doesn't talk to me when she's watching her program."

"You're welcome to stay here—I hope I've made that clear—but I want to ask you a few questions."

"He knows where I am," she said. "I told him."

"You gave him the address?"

"No, I told him we were staying with a friend for a few days and he asked if that friend was the 'goddamn dog thief' and I said it was."

"Wait, he's accused me of *stealing* Layla?"

"Something like that. Basically. That's the gist of it."

"Oh wow."

"The plot thickens," she said, moving her eyebrows all around. The dog was looking back and forth at us, following the exchange, eager to see what would happen next. Harry Davidson with his baseball bat, swinging it into the palm of his hand with nice little smacks. Pulling the gun from his britches. Searching his britches for his gun, the gun having gotten lost somewhere in the enormity of the fabric and folds. I took a few deep breaths and she asked if I would get her that pair of socks, after all. I went to fetch them, holding on to the dresser to steady myself. I was light-headed, fuzzy, and wished I could get back in bed and rest for an hour or two. I handed her the socks and she lifted a foot, pointing her toes at me, so I sat and got to work. Why was it so hard to put a sock on someone else's foot? She could've done it herself in two seconds. What an odd woman. I had feelings for her that I couldn't explain, that made little sense. I didn't particularly *like* her. I had always liked Ellen, or had for many years. We'd had fun together. I could talk to her about things.

I didn't know whether to leave the extra material bunched up at the toes or the heel. And then her program was back on, louder than it had been before: people running and yelling. I checked the clock. It was after two o'clock and Maxine would arrive soon. If I knew anything about grown-up Maxine, it was that she was damn punctual. And then there was a knock at the door and another and the door was opening and Maxine was saying, "Dad?"

It must've been a scene. Sasha's feet in my lap, all of the covers and pillows, and the dog standing in the middle of the room as if she'd also been caught.

"Oh! Is this a bad time?" Maxine said, her voice higher than usual. She was thinner than I'd ever seen her, wearing highwater pants and shoes that covered everything but her toes—peekaboos, Ellen called them. I called them silly, impractical. Toes just asking to be stomped on, begging for dropped knives and pots of boiling water.

I walked over to Laurel and picked her up. She was too big to be picked up, but I went with it and she didn't protest. She was a pretty child, with wide-set eyes and curly hair in a light reddish-brown color. She wasn't nearly as creepy in person.

"My, you've gotten big!" I said. How old was she—four, five? It was hard to tell.

"I like chicken nuggets," she said.

"Well, chicken nuggets are delicious. How old are you now?" I asked.

"Eight," she said.

"No," said Maxine, "you're five."

"I'm eight," she said, looking completely reasonable.

"Why does she think she's eight?" Sasha asked.

"Her cousin just turned eight," Maxine said to me. "Anson turned eight," she said to Laurel. "You're five."

"Me and Anson are both eight," she said. "And soon we'll be nine." She had her pointer finger out and shook it for emphasis. It was small and lovely. I grabbed ahold of it and it devolved into a game in which I kept holding on to it even though she wanted me to let it go.

"Well then," I said. "You're quite small for your age." I placed her back on the ground and she went and made herself a spot on the couch next to Sasha.

"Are you sick?" Laurel asked.

"No. I'm just tired."

"You look sick."

"I'm just tired," Sasha repeated.

"Whose dog is it?"

"Mine," Sasha said. "Her name's Katy. Isn't she pretty?"

"Where's your dog?" Maxine asked me. "I thought that was Layla."

"It's a whole long story, but this is Sasha's dog and they're staying here for a night or two. In your old room." I didn't know how to explain who she was or why she was staying with me or the whole dog situation so I repeated that it was a long story. I imagined how it sounded—she'd think I had lost my mind, perhaps start looking into old-age homes. Retirement communities, they called them. Luxury Independent Living.

"So that's not Layla?" Maxine asked.

"No, that's her, that's Layla. But she's also Katy and she was my dog for five or six days until I found out the person who'd given her away, Sasha's husband, had no right to do it. So the dog is Sasha's and her name is really Katy."

"That does sound complicated," Maxine said.

"The dog's name was never Layla," Sasha said. "To be clear."

Things were quiet after that, and tense, though Laurel happily moved to the floor with the dog and petted her belly.

"Does her belly smell like a corn chip?" I asked.

Laurel looked at me like she'd never heard of a corn chip so I turned to my daughter and told her that sometimes the dog's stomach smelled like one. Then I told her that her hair looked nice. Her hair was fluffy, much bigger than usual. I wanted to pat it with my hands, make it go down.

"You have great hair," Sasha said. And then she said, "I'm interrupting. I'll let y'all talk," and went back to her room, dragging the blanket behind her like a cape.

Maxine looked like she didn't want to sit in the spot where Sasha had been so she sat bunched in one corner looking as uncomfortable as possible. She had to work hard to look so uncomfortable and disapproving. "I wanted to talk to you about something but this is clearly a bad time."

"It's not a bad time. I'm sorry. I thought Sasha was going to leave so we could visit but you're early."

"I should have called first," she said. "You were right. Next time we'll call first." We looked at Laurel, who had her head buried in the dog's belly, Layla's legs peddling in the air. "Laurel, don't do that. Stop it."

"I bathed her recently," I said. "She's not dirty or anything."

"Well, she might snap."

"The dog doesn't snap," I said, but she was a dog and dogs were unpredictable. It was possible she could snap. You couldn't trust a dog any more than you could trust a person but I knew in my heart that Layla wouldn't hurt a child. She was good and she was kind, if goodness and kindness were ways to describe an animal. "Did Frank tell she took a disliking to him?"

"I don't know what you're talking about."

I was sure Frank had told her; it was the kind of thing he'd call her up to tell her. My image of him as a nice bland man, a dull and sober man, had really taken a hit.

Maxine wasn't going to let me off the hook. I'd known a number of people like her in my lifetime, the kind of formerly messed-up person who had gotten herself straightened out and led such a rigid and orderly existence that her only pleasure came from judging others. She genuinely seemed pleased by the situation because it confirmed her choices and place in the world. While the rest of us spun out of control, Maxine would do everything correctly, check off all the boxes. She was more of a grown-up than I'd ever been, would ever be, and I both hated and loved her for it.

"Laurel, honey, say goodbye to Grandpa. We need to pick up the ham and get home."

"I don't like ham," Laurel said.

"You like ham," Maxine said. "She's in her contrary phase, as you can see."

"I like chicken nuggets," Laurel said.

"Don't say that again," Maxine said.

"Do you know what contrary means?" I asked, kneeling down so I could look my granddaughter in the eye. She had a frenzied look about her, her eyes unfocused.

"Give your grandfather a kiss," Maxine said, and Laurel refused, and then Maxine and I shrugged and said goodbye.

Once the door closed behind them, I felt disoriented, flushed. I wanted to run screaming from all the women, go someplace where there were no women at all. I needed to check my blood sugar, which was something I was supposed to do every morning but I couldn't remember the last time I'd pricked myself and I still hadn't been by Walgreens to pick up my medication. What was wrong with me? Why couldn't I check my blood sugar every once in a while, take a few pills after my morning bacon and toast? There was nothing so hard about it, and yet I couldn't seem to do it, couldn't provide the most basic amount of care for myself.

Sasha came out of her room without the blanket and sat on the couch like a normal person. Crossed her legs, even. I felt like I was supposed to apologize but I was done apologizing. "I should have gotten you out of here for that," I said. "Maxine is difficult, always has been."

"She didn't seem difficult, she seemed nice. She's very pretty, and your granddaughter, too. They don't look anything like you, though."

"We're one of those families that don't look alike. Ellen and I come from the same kind. You should have seen my brother."

"What's he look like?"

"Handsome. Like a movie star, like a goddamn movie star."

"Where is he?"

"He died in the war. It was a long time ago."

"Which one?"

"Vietnam. He had the chin and everything. He had a little— what do they call it?—a cleft. A butt chin I used to tease him. Actually I never teased him, he would have beaten my ass, but I thought 'butt chin' whenever I looked at him. I would've killed for one."

"I'd like to see a picture."

"I have one somewhere," I said. There weren't any pictures on the walls or on the tables: no black-and-white photographs of my great grandparents, Laurel holding an Easter basket or on Santa's lap. And there certainly weren't any of my brother. I imagined hanging a picture of him in his uniform next to the window in the kitchen where I would be forced to look at him every day.

"Does Maxine have a limp?" Sasha asked. "It seemed like she was limping."

"She was in a car accident a long time ago. I hardly notice it anymore." This was an opening to ask about her scar—had she been in an accident as well?—but I didn't have the energy for it, or didn't care any longer. "I think I'll go lie down for a while," I said. "I put a key on the counter if you and Layla want to get out of the house, go for a walk."

She told me to take a nap, to take a nice long nap, said she'd fix me something good for dinner.

I went to my room and closed the door. I hoped she'd take the dog and leave, leave me there where I could be alone, where I knew what to expect. She was going to take Layla at some point and go back to Harry Davidson so it was better if we just got it all over with. I felt done, done with it all. And if I hadn't known before, it was clear what Maxine and Frank and Ellen had to tell me, why the lawyer wasn't calling me back. The lawyer was in no hurry to tell me what I hadn't inherited, what my father had not left me. Even on his deathbed he thought I should live as if I wouldn't inherit a dime, wanted me to pull myself up by my bootstraps, be a man. It was easy for people who had been given everything to expect others to make their own way.

CHAPTER 12

THAT EVENING WE sat down to a meal of meatloaf, mashed potatoes, and steamed broccoli. Sasha had her hair in a ponytail, was wearing her short shorts and a Rolling Stones T-shirt with that horrible enormous red tongue. She poured me a glass of wine and told me to dig in.

"I found the wine in your pantry. It was behind a bunch of stuff so I hope it wasn't special."

"It's not special. This looks great," I said. The wine was an anniversary gift from Maxine and must've cost at least fifty dollars, a bottle Ellen had been saving for a special occasion that hadn't come. I thought about the last time I'd prayed before sitting down to a meal and wanted to suggest it, but Sasha was already eating.

"Most of the time I serve green beans with this dish but I like broccoli better. Harry preferred beans."

"I like broccoli," I said. "It's a fine choice. And you were being modest—you didn't mention that you could make mashed potatoes and vegetables. You can do all sorts of things."

The food was surprisingly good and I was feeling better.

While we ate, it started to storm and Layla, who'd been under-
foot, slunk back to the windowless guest bathroom to hunker
down as though she knew it was the safest place in the house. It
was where Ellen and Maxine had taken refuge during hurricanes.
I'd settle them into the bathroom with pillows and snacks and a
hand-crank radio, a sink full of ice and a bathtub full of water,
and brave the storm alone in the rest of the house, feeling like a
king. Untouchable. Daring the wind to tear the house apart plank
by plank and brick by brick. There had been occasions when the
storm had taken me up on it, once sending a tree down on top of
the garage.

"Maybe I should go check on her," I said as I took another bite.
It really was good.

"She's fine," she said. "What a baby, such a baby."

"I had her out the other day and there was a loud crack of
thunder and she just turned around and walked me right back to
the house."

"That one was a real gully washer," she said.

"It was," I agreed.

After that, she told me about her trip to the grocery store,
which didn't seem remarkable in the least. In the soup aisle, two
old men talked about soup, recommending soups to each other.
She was still able to hear them from one aisle over! In the checkout lane, a lady cut in front of her and instead of getting angry
or saying something rude she'd just let the woman go ahead.
She reported that the dog had done all of her business. And then
she touched my leg and I was so surprised my knee knocked the
underside of the table.

"I'm sorry. I just wasn't expecting it."

She looked at me like she didn't know what I was talking about and then got up and started removing things from the table. I was still working on the potatoes but she took my plate, too.

"A man phoned while you were resting," she said. "Somebody called Lucky. I wrote down his number."

"What'd he say?"

"Just his name and number." She showed me her palm, the blurry numbers in blue ink stretched across it.

"I have his information," I said. "That's the lawyer who's dealing with my father's estate." *Estate* sounded so fancy. I liked saying it. *Estate*, I thought. *My father's estate.* I should enjoy it while I had the chance.

"Are you going to inherit a lot of money?" she asked, and turned the water off. I supposed I didn't look like the kind of man who would be coming into an inheritance, didn't live in the kind of house or drive the kind of car. My shirt had been washed but the barbeque stains hadn't come out.

"It's possible he's left it all to Maxine."

"Why would he do that?"

"I'm not sure."

"You must have some idea."

"Why do people do any of the things they do? Perhaps he wanted to leave me one last surprise. That would be enough reason for him."

"People like to surprise you," she said, "it's true."

We settled into the den to watch TV, back in our usual spots. She held Layla like a baby, her piggish stomach exposed, pink with brown splotches. Layla didn't protest, but she'd shoot me the occasional glance as though she would appreciate my help. The

movie we hadn't finished was back on, the one with the virus. I'd
lost track of what was happening and who was who because she'd
apparently watched some of it without me. They were still yelling
and running around. I closed my eyes, opened them. I liked all of
the running and yelling.

"We should go to the beach tomorrow," she said. "I'd like to
get some sun. And after that maybe we could go to the casino and
eat crab legs, play the slots."

"I could do those things," I said, though I didn't know how I'd
pay for them.

She talked at the TV, trying to assist the characters, telling
them which way to run and when to look out, advising them
that so-and-so was now working against them, for the other side.
She wondered where they were using the bathroom, the last time
they'd had anything to eat or drink. I wondered those things, too,
but told her the show was only so long and they had to cut that
stuff out, or it would only be important if, for instance, someone was starving to death or had to piss so badly they messed
themselves, but those things never happened, which was how it
differed from real life. I felt like I was teaching myself by way of
teaching her. And I appreciated her interactions with simulated
worlds, was reminded of how she'd propelled her entire body forward to help the retarded guy land his jumps.

When it was over, she promptly fell asleep, so I took Layla out
for a walk.

It was dark and clear and the stars were out. I let the dog stop
and sniff wherever she wanted to stop and sniff instead of jerking
her along. There weren't any cars around so I unhooked her leash
and then took her collar off because one of the neighbor ladies

said she'd gotten a ticket for having her dog off-leash. She said I'd get a ticket, too, if I wasn't careful. If anyone tried to give me a ticket I'd tell them she'd seen a squirrel and slipped her collar. I'd act frantic, ask for help. I felt downright clever and was feeling fine about everything but then I started to worry again. I knew exactly how much money I had in my accounts and it wasn't enough; it was nowhere near enough. I couldn't afford to pay a fine for such a goddamn stupid thing. I couldn't afford to take Sasha to play the slots and eat crab legs and I wondered if she'd have mentioned the gambling and the crabs if the lawyer hadn't called, if I hadn't told her about the thing I shouldn't have told her about.

The next morning, over coffee, the bird banging into one window and then flying around the house to bang into another, I called the lawyer. I was afraid of the lawyer as well as everyone associated with the lawyer and the law. They had done their jobs of convincing me of their importance. I took great big gulps of coffee to try and steel myself.

The secretary surprised me with her friendliness, asked how I was doing, said she hoped I was enjoying this beautiful weather before putting me through to Lucky. I imagined every morning she was given a sheet of paper with a list of names alongside a bunch of acronyms with meanings that only she could decipher: whether to take a message or put a client through, how friendly or cold she should be.

While the lawyer was going through his own set of pleasantries, I interrupted him to ask if the old man had left it all to Maxine.

"No, but I'd like to sit down with you and go through everything. Are you free this afternoon? Could you come in around one o'clock?"

"That should be fine," I said.

"Good, I look forward to it."

He was a good-natured son of a bitch, or that was the act he played. I supposed he had no other choice with a name like Lucky. When I first met him I'd asked about it and he'd said his mother couldn't get pregnant—all of the doctors had said so— and then he'd come along; he'd been called Lucky since he was in the womb. This disclosure, with its talk of wombs and pregnancies, had embarrassed me, and I'd disliked him for it.

I wanted to go to the beach. It was a nice day and I wanted nothing more than to take the dog to the beach before I died, and I wanted to do it as a potentially rich man, to continue living as though I might be a rich man while I looked out at the water with Layla, let her go for a swim—all I had to do was put on my shoes and get in the car—but I continued to sit and listen to the bird run headlong into the window, drink cup after cup of coffee. Sasha had yet to emerge and I could feel a dark force behind the door, a brooding energy, same as teenage Maxine.

- - -

I ATE a piece of toast and left a bed-headed Sasha and Layla bundled up on the couch, drove to the lawyer's office. The firm was one my father had been with for years, but since old Mr. Veach and his unfortunate toothpick accident, I'd been passed off to this young guy who wore funny glasses and had a shuffling, falsely humble way about him that made him seem even younger.

The secretary, who wasn't pretty, wasn't what I thought a secretary at a good law firm should look like, stood to greet me and asked if I cared for anything to drink.

"No thank you," I said, though I would have liked some water. My first response was to say no and I generally regretted it, but I'd already had too much coffee. I held out my hand to watch it shake.

"He's on a call but it shouldn't be long." She smiled and returned to her desk. I waited. These people always made you wait. I pictured Lucky in his office, eating salted peanuts and texting his girlfriend, shifting the power dynamic in his favor while I flipped through an issue of *Garden & Gun*. What a goddamn stupid name that was for a magazine. I read an article called "Good Dog," which was about a man who'd adopted a puppy after his son fell off a cliff in Italy, but then the puppy died in the third paragraph. This was what passed for literature these days, apparently.

"Actually, I *am* a bit thirsty," I said.

I watched the secretary type for a few seconds too long before looking at me in an irritated manner, which she immediately corrected, but only after she was sure I'd noticed, and then that same bland smile. She had a large mole on her face that was hard to look at but also the kind of thing you wanted to stare at all day. I berated myself for disliking her for something she had no control over—the mole, her thick legs. So many thick-legged women in the world. . . . She could have had the mole removed, though. It seemed like the sort of mole removal that insurance would cover. You'd tell the doctor it had grown in size, that it was suspiciously shaped. Any doctor could see it was suspicious. She could also lose thirty pounds, go to the gym a few times a week. Do it after work, or before work in the morning. I couldn't imagine her social calendar was full.

She brought me a bottle of water that was so cold it was dripping, as if it had been in an ice chest. It dripped all over my pants.

"Thank you," I said, getting a good look at the mole up close. I bet she constantly had to pluck hairs out of it. What was it about moles that made hair so eager to grow in them? I had a lot of questions and no answers. There never were any answers. The fact that I hadn't been named executor of the will should have been all I needed to know from the beginning. Ellen was the executor. Ellen, who had left me, who wasn't blood related and was no longer a part of my life, was the executor of my father's will. She had always been close to him, though, and nearly all interactions between the two of us had gone through her. She was the one he'd loved, not me. He would have married her if he could've. Of this I was certain. Instead, she became his daughter. He called her daughter and she called him dad. She'd kissed his cheeks, would sit with him for hours watching golf or the news, would cater to him in a way I couldn't have even if I'd wanted to.

It had been so easy between the two of them.

By the time Lucky came to get me my pants were dry. I sat across from him in his office full of leather furniture, a bookcase, pictures of things like tractors in fields and sunsets that were suspiciously like the ones Frank painted. I'd liked old Mr. Veach, who'd had taxidermy all over his office, not only on the walls but on the tables, too, animals I couldn't even name. They had shown how rich and successful he was—he could go to foreign places and kill foreign beasts. He wasn't afraid to make a statement, wasn't afraid to decorate his office with things that might offend people. Lucky was emblematic of young people today, who were scared to be anything but ordinary and safe. I'd heard some teenagers weren't even getting their driver's licenses but made their parents take them everywhere and they weren't even embarrassed about it.

"Give it to me straight," I said. "I can't take any more of this runaround."

"We'll get right down to it, then, Mr. McDonald," he said, presenting me with a document that must have been fifty pages long. "There's good news and there's bad news."

He didn't ask which I wanted to hear first. The good news was my father had left me everything other than $200,000 in cash, a hundred and ten of which had gone to Maxine and ninety to Ellen. The bad news, however, was that there were loans and liens and various other debts.

He licked his fingers and turned the pages: $8,000 to the funeral home, $165 to the *Sun Herald*, $150 to Reverend Grover Nail, twenty-two thousand to the lawyers, twenty-four to the nursing home. There were unpaid property taxes, debts to the bank and IRS—it went on and on and on. There were moving fees and cleaning fees and the rent for Ellen's beachfront condo. He continued turning pages, telling me who had been paid what. I interrupted to ask what was left, what the hell was goddamn left.

"Fourteen thousand dollars," he said.

"Fourteen thousand dollars," I repeated.

"Yes," he said.

"Fourteen thousand," I said again.

"That's right."

"And the land?"

"The bank owns the land," he said.

"The bank owns the land," I repeated. I couldn't wrap my head around it. My father owned upwards of seven hundred acres and it had all been left to me and somehow, someway, I had no land and fourteen thousand dollars. The inclination to kill myself had been right all along. Had I said this aloud? The idea that I might start a new life and have a second chance had been a dream. It was too late. It had always been too late and finally there was proof.

"I'm sorry," he said.

"This can't be right."

He directed me back to the papers again with all of their numbers. So many numbers. I stood, dazed, grabbed hold of his desk.

"I know it's not what you expected."

"I don't know what I expected," I said. "I guess this is exactly what I expected, which is the disappointing thing—I hoped I'd be surprised, that the bastard would surprise me for once."

"I'm sorry," he said, but he didn't seem sorry. He couldn't have possibly seemed sorry enough. "The check has already been sent via registered mail—you'll have to sign for it."

"I haven't signed for anything."

"Well," he said. "Keep an eye out." He went to do that move where he was going to put a hand on my back but had no intention of actually touching me. When had people stopped touching each other while pretending to touch each other from several inches away? I would have liked to stick a pen in his eye.

The secretary offered me cookies on the way out. She said she'd made too many for her son's bake sale and would I care for some? She didn't want to eat them all by herself and I'd be doing her a big favor.

"Are there raisins?"

"No raisins, but there's walnuts and chocolate chips. It's my grandmother's recipe," she said, "though I'm pretty sure it's just the recipe you'd find on any ole bag of chocolate chips." How many chocolate chips would it take to fill in her mole? If I melted it and spread it around, one. If they were solid, two or three. I thanked her and took a cookie.

"Take more," she said, "please," so I did. I piled one on top of another until I had a nice stack, and stumbled outside.

CHAPTER 13

IN THE PARKING lot, I ate one and tossed the rest. After that, I couldn't go home. Once again, my home wasn't mine. I had brought a woman into it and she'd taken over. I pictured her on the couch, watching TV with the dog, the air conditioner on full blast so she could curl up with all of my pillows and blankets. As much as I liked women, as much as I thought I wanted one, I didn't. Not when it came right down to it. Women had beaten me and they always would.

I drove to a bar called The Reef. It was one of those monstrous affairs on stilts overlooking the water, the kind of place where I wouldn't know anyone. I had been fairly successful in avoiding former friends and business associates since Ellen had left, which had been easy, especially because I'd nearly stopped leaving the house. But even out in the world it wasn't too hard. There were places that locals went and places that tourists went and they rarely overlapped. This was a tourist place. There was a whole line of them along the beach—Shaggy's and Snapper's and The Dock—and they all looked the same and the food was the same.

The waitress led me through the restaurant—it was bright,

so bright—and directed me to the outdoor bar, which somehow seemed less bright. I took a corner seat where I could see both the water and the people and set the *Petition to Close Estate and Final Accounting*, which was fifty-eight-and-one-quarter pages, down with a smack. The more I read, the angrier I became. There were two charges of $50 for Ellen's haircuts, gas for her car. Had my father told her he'd look out for her, provide for her? Lying on his deathbed, I saw him utter his last words: *I'll remember you in my will. I always loved you more.* I wondered how long they'd all known it would turn out this way, that I'd be left with nothing.

There was a good breeze and it was messing up my hair. I kept having to smooth the longer pieces that covered the top of my head back into place. I didn't know how I'd ended up with a combover, when I'd decided to have an old man's haircut; it hadn't seemed like something I had decided at all. It was my father's haircut and I would remedy that situation pronto, would do it myself when I got home: a close crop on the sides, the top smooth and bare as a baby's bottom. I wouldn't have to worry about the wind after that.

I picked up the menu—an enormous, colorful monstrosity—and tried to appear as gruff as possible to ensure that the few people around wouldn't try to talk to me, though there was no indication they would. Everyone was coupled, going about their coupled business. I flipped and flipped. I knew what I liked to drink and yet all of the choices made me question myself. I asked myself why I drank the same thing year after year when I might like something else better, when I might like a little variety. There was simply no way to know. Finally, I closed the menu and ordered a White Russian. I couldn't remember ever having had one before.

When the bartender delivered the drink, I asked for a pen and set the pen on the document, began some mental accounting. The wind kicked up and the papers ruffled. I smoothed my hair again and tried to angle myself so that it blew it in the right direction but then the wind shifted.

The drink was unexpectedly foamy, sweet and strong.

I wrote down my monthly expenses, estimating the ones that varied. I would have to apply for my Social Security benefits right away, and tried to remember how much I would receive—something like $1,400 a month if I took the money early. Maybe $1,500. The house was nearly paid off. The car wasn't. I'd bought a new one because Ellen had wanted to visit some cousins in Kentucky and said we ought to have a more reliable vehicle. The figures were bleak, even with a paid-for house. There would be no trip to the Grand Canyon. I might not even be able to keep myself in beer. The plan to end it and make a great big goddamn mess of things looked like the best option, and then leave the house to Maxine. Someone would have to come in and scrape my brains off the wall and then she'd sell everything for cheap because, so far as I knew, something like a suicide would have to be disclosed to the new owners and only the desperate would buy such a place. Or maybe a nice black family. Or a not-so-nice one. I wasn't going to make it too easy on her, though, wasn't going to do it in the yard. She should suffer at least a little bit.

I finished my drink and ordered another. My penmanship—when had my penmanship gotten so bad? Even the numbers were barely legible. It didn't matter, the only thing that mattered was there wasn't enough and I knew that as sure as I knew anything. I also knew I wouldn't call my boss and ask for my job back. Once you leave a place you've been for twenty-seven years, you don't call them up and ask to come back. You don't tell the people who bought you a cake and wished you good luck that you wanted to return. No, I would not do that. And a new job was out of the question. My skills were obsolete. I hadn't kept up with the technology. Every week there had been memos to alert me of changes and I was too old to keep up. Let the young men play that game. I was done.

On my third drink, a woman sat down, leaving one stool between us when there was a whole row of empties and no reason for her to sit so close. I recalled Ellen joining a gym about a year before she left, how she'd complained that all of the treadmills would be available and then someone would get on the one right next to hers. She said they were always runners, too, and their sweat would come flying off them and hit you right in the face. It made me feel sick just thinking about it. And the Asian ladies had worn so much perfume she'd gag. After she'd gone through all of the various horrors, she'd ask if I wanted to join her. Why did people do things like that? They would tell you how awful something was and describe it to you in nauseating detail and then ask if you wanted to share it with them.

I stared at the papers and sipped my drink, doing my best to go about my business, but I could feel the woman looking at me, at my papers. And then she leaned over so close I could smell her hair.

"Legal trouble?" she asked.

Instead of ignoring her or saying something ugly, I surprised myself by telling her that my father had left me hundreds of acres of land. She raised her glass of wine, said the next round was on me.

"But it's complicated. There were debts and liens . . ."

"Oh," she said, "that's too bad. But the land is still yours, right? You just have to pay some fees or whatever?"

I shook my head, trying to look like a good sport about it.

"How come?"

"Because the bank owns it now, or the government. I don't fully understand it. All I know is that it isn't mine, and never was. It was my father's but it doesn't seem like it was his, either. I didn't know all of that, or any of it, really—my father and I weren't close. I'm only finding out now, months after his death."

"I'm sorry," she said. "That's tough." She tilted her head and frowned, making all of the lines in her face rearrange themselves. Don't do that, I thought. Please don't do that again. The thing I hated most was for people to feel sorry for me, to pity me. It was what I'd struggled all my life to avoid, even if it meant separating myself from them entirely. I could've given her a good shove and watched her fall right off her stool, her granny panties on display. But perhaps she was wearing sexy panties and her sexy panties gave her confidence, the kind with the string that went up the butt. An image of Sasha flashed into my mind, her yellow panties and the green grass, how much I'd liked her before I knew her.

"Well, I suppose it's hard to miss something you never had." I'd never talked this way, and certainly not to a stranger. She was leaning toward me—close. She smiled and I could see too much of her at once, too many teeth, too much eyes and nose.

"That's very enlightened of you," she said, "very wise. I'm Diane, by the way." Once she'd backed up a bit she was attractive, though she had earned every one of her fifty-some-odd years.

She was age-appropriate, the kind of woman I should have been dating, but I didn't think of myself as sixty-three. My body was sixty-three but my mind hadn't kept up. If I could be blamed for anything in my life, it was that I had stopped developing at some point too early.

I took her hand and she gave mine a little squeeze before letting go. I felt something—fear or pleasure, some kind of fear-pleasure combination that I wanted more of. I also had a terrible urge to leave, to put twenty dollars on the bar and flee.

"That's nice, that little squeeze," I said, which just slipped right out of my mouth.

"It's what we do in prayer group, just before the prayer is over. A little something extra."

"It's very nice." I was jolted out of the conversation by the ringing of my phone, which was tremendously loud. Maxine was calling. I hit the red telephone button, hit it once more for good measure and asked what a lovely lady such as herself was doing at The Reef at two o'clock on a weekday.

"Is it two o'clock on a weekday?" she asked, and laughed like she'd said something funny. "I'm on a family vacation—my brother and his kids, my mother, my sister and her irritating lesbian partner and their adopted Chinese child—all of us in one house. It's not even on the water. I don't know why I agree to these things but I do, every time."

"Because it's family."

"Yes," she said. "But mostly it's because I forget how awful these vacations are as soon as they're over—I bury it completely. A lot like childbirth, from what I hear."

"This isn't much of a vacation spot unless you gamble, in

which case you should be staying at the Beau Rivage or the Hard Rock, one of the places with pools and spas, some kind of entertainment. You don't even swim in the water here unless you don't know any better."

"We should have called you," she said, and that laugh again. "We all got in the water today."

"Well," I said, "Northerners don't know any better."

"I'm not a Northerner!" she said. "I'm from Little Rock."

It had been a long time since a woman had tried to pick me up but I was pretty sure that was what was happening, even though I'd told her I was broke. The bartender set another drink in front of me, nodded and winked.

"You know what I wonder about?" she asked. "Seashells. Where are all the seashells? How come you find these amazing ones in stores but none on the actual beach? We couldn't even find any broken ugly ones. Or sand dollars. I really wanted to find a sand dollar, or a starfish."

"It's a good question and I don't have an answer for you." I thought about rocks. In some places you find diamonds and in other places there's only gravel. The ocean is vast. Just because it's a large body of water you shouldn't expect to find something beautiful. I was thinking these things but it felt silly to say them, and I wasn't sure what I meant, anyhow. Only that one beach isn't every beach, the same as one hill isn't every hill. People expected some sort of continuity out of their beaches, though, which was unfair.

"Here you mostly find trash," I said. "And fish carcasses. Chicken bones, candy wrappers . . ."

"I didn't see much trash."

"Well, that's very kind of you," I said, which was an awkward thing to say, but I felt responsible. When you lived someplace like Mississippi your whole life, you learned to apologize, and I was a little bit drunk. Had I eaten anything? I was starving. I wanted to smell her hair again. We looked out at the water for a while and said nothing and I tried to appreciate the beauty of it all, living on the beach, a place where other people went on vacation.

I finished my drink and signaled the bartender for the check, making an actual check sign in the air, which Maxine had scolded me about one night at dinner. She said it was enough to get their attention, to raise your finger slightly or nod, that you didn't have to draw an actual check sign in the air.

"You're leaving?" she asked, and that frown again, all of the wrinkles rearranging themselves. She was wearing too much makeup. If she hadn't been wearing so much makeup her wrinkles might not show so much. And then I noticed her neck and how it was a different color from her face. I wished you could tell people things like that—it would benefit them in the long run—and yet you couldn't.

"I have some things I need to take care of this afternoon," I said, picturing a six-pack of beer and a sack of burgers. I wished her the best of luck with the rest of her vacation, told her to be sure to visit the shop you entered through the shark's mouth, that the kids would love it. She held out her hand: flat out, palm down, like she was a dignitary. I guessed she wanted me to kiss it so I brought it to my mouth and pressed it to my lips.

"Give me your phone," she said, and I handed it over. She commented on how old and small it was, how it didn't even have internet access, as I watched her type her name and number.

"Now you have five numbers in here. I know you won't call but that's okay."

"Is that reverse psychology?"

"No, it's just a fact."

"Well," I said, and stopped myself from telling her that it was an opinion.

"Wait," she said. "Call me now so I'll have yours."

I pressed her name and her phone chirped crickets and then she hugged me awkwardly, shoving her chest into mine.

On the way home, I thought about Sasha. There was a pretty young woman waiting for me, if she hadn't already stolen my checkbook, taken my dog, and gotten the hell out of Dodge. Perhaps she'd packed up the suitcases I hadn't used in years, really loaded them up. I tried to imagine what she might take, what I had of value. I didn't have much, that was for sure. I hoped she'd take Frank's pictures off the walls in my study, thinking they were professional. What a day that would be! I wanted it to happen, wanted to see what I might do if my entire world imploded within twenty-four hours, how I would handle it. I relished the opportunity to lose my shit completely.

I knew I shouldn't have been driving—that bartender had a generous pour—but I took the beach, anyhow, so I could look at the water. The sun shining on the water, so pretty. I grasped the wheel tightly at ten and two, which I'd read was no longer the correct way to hold a steering wheel—something about the airbags shattering all of the bones in your arms. There was simply too much information available in the world and I missed living in a state of ignorance without having to apologize for it. Now there were people forcing information on you, telling you to educate yourself, that the information was only a few clicks away. I was so tired I closed my eyes. And then I stopped for beer and then, because it was right there, went into the liquor store for a fifth of Wild Turkey.

I took a quick swig before leaving the lot. And then one more.

The only thing that could make the day worse was if I got pulled over and then I was so nervous thinking about getting pulled over that I played it all out in my head: the handcuffs and Miranda rights, the cop putting his knee between my legs as I leaned against my car, the cold cell with all of the people in it and chatty wonk-eyed strangers asking me what I'd done. And what if there was no one to bail me out, what would happen then? At what point did they make you strip and give you prison-issue clothing, make you bend over to show them your asshole? I had spent my whole life with no one looking at my asshole and by God I was going to keep it that way.

In retrospect, the night I'd spent in jail after the fight with Ellen hadn't been so bad: the handcuffs had pinched, yes, but otherwise I'd been alone and drunk enough to not care too much. And no one wanted to examine my asshole for contraband; they hadn't seemed interested in me at all. I'd asked for a phone call and they'd taken me to the phone. I asked for water and they brought me a cup. But I knew it had been a fluke—I'd seen enough TV programs to know it had been a fluke. I got myself riled up into what could only be described as a full-fledged panic attack. I was sweating and my heart was beating fast. I kept checking the mirrors, convinced I could hear the sirens and see the blue lights. I understood why people tried to outrun the police, abandoned their vehicles to attempt it on foot.

By the time I made it home, car securely in the garage, I was a wreck. Once again I'd sweated straight through my shirt. I hadn't had much to eat and it was after five o'clock. The day had been wholly unlike my typical day, which consisted of TV and my chair and the occasional trip to the grocery store. Half the time I didn't even make it to the grocery store but shopped at the gas station. The closest gas station had become a humiliation, though, because the same young man was always there, and though he was pleasant enough, I felt he judged me for my purchases. I judged myself for my purchases so why shouldn't he? As much as I told myself he saw hundreds of people a day and didn't give a shit about some old man buying toilet paper and beer and ice cream sandwiches and male enhancement pills (to test them out), I didn't believe it. I was pretty sure he was a Muslim. He was Arab, anyhow.

Sasha greeted me at the door. She was like a different Sasha: curious and worried, wearing real clothes. The house was pleasantly warm and cheesy-smelling and I hoped to God there was an enormous pan of lasagna on the stove. She led me to the bathroom and told me to take a nice hot shower—she would have some delicious food for me and a cold beverage when I got out. She was wearing a dress—strappy, yellow as sunshine. I touched one of the straps, plucked it.

"Oh my," was what I said to her, and she petted my head. Smoothing the hairs in the right way.

I was dying to kiss her. I wanted her to touch my leg beneath the table and my leg would stay right where it was, still and calm. And then I would maul her. Jump on top of her and make her quiver, make her beg for more.

I finished cleaning myself and sat in my chair with a beer while she set the table.

"It's my birthday tomorrow," I announced.

"I know it is!" she said. "How exciting."

It didn't excite me much. A birthday would never be anything like it had when I was a child. It was like Christmas—you could try to recapture the glory of Christmases past, but the harder you tried, the more it felt like a sham. The best-case scenario was for someone to bake you a cake and you'd get to blow out some candles, but even this was a simulation.

I had experienced a lifetime's worth of emotions in a day, but my hair was nicely combed and my clothes were clean and I was feeling nearly cocky. I hoped she could sense it, and that it impressed her. I felt ready all of a sudden. It was the woman, Diane. She had done it. And then a terrible feeling was upon me again and I could see the document I had left in my car. No—it wasn't in my car, I had thrown it away, trashed it at the gas station. It had been one of those cans that tried to eat your fingers and I'd had to reach a good portion of my arm in to shove it inside.

CHAPTER 14

I WOKE UP EARLY and took an accounting of the previous day. I had passed out early, drunk, having driven my car home drunk. I did not feel well. I did not feel well at all. I'd met a woman and she had given me her phone number. Her name was Diane and I'd liked her, though I hadn't at first. She had grown on me. I had a headache and my mouth was dry. What the hell had I been drinking? White Russians. What an odd thing for me to drink, but they were delicious and I'd enjoyed them very much. And then there'd been Wild Turkey and beer and a plate of lasagna, Sasha in her yellow dress looking so pretty, asking if I liked her dinner and trying to talk to me about my day, but I'd hardly said anything to her before passing out in my chair. I must've gotten up and put myself to bed at some point but I didn't remember that part.

There was the usual shame, but it was manageable. I hadn't pissed myself. I was in one piece, my car in one piece. I wasn't in jail. I hadn't said or done anything terrible. I had just wolfed down a plate of lasagna and gone to sleep.

It was my birthday. I was sixty-four years old, which seemed like an impossible number of years to have lived, and I was alive. I didn't quite feel alive, though the hangover helped. Perhaps it was the reason, or one of the reasons—the main one being that I liked to be drunk—that I got hangovers as frequently as I did: proof of life. They also provided me with some immediate goals: drink a lot of fluids, sit in the sun and sweat, pop a handful of vitamins from the cache that Ellen had left, etcetera, etcetera. If the hangover was really bad, take a couple of ibuprofen and go back to bed.

In the kitchen, I drank a glass of water and then went to let Layla out of her room. As I reached to grab the knob, there was fear in my heart—they were gone, they'd left me—but Sasha was sound asleep and Layla was standing there with her tail wagging, eager to start the day. I petted her and her mouth hung open in what I'd come to think of as a smile.

We had a routine, the early risers, the two of us navigating the mornings alone. It was my favorite part of the day, hungover or not, and the bird was there to join us. I thought the usual thoughts about how I'd like to kill it, how it was driving me mad, had already driven me mad and yet I wasn't going to do anything about it because it was too much trouble and also I might miss it if it was gone.

I sat in my chair and petted Layla with my feet as I drank from a fresh bottle of Dr Pepper that had magically appeared in the refrigerator. It was a small, personal bottle, but I needed it more than Sasha did at the moment and I could replace it before she even woke up. After the Dr Pepper, I drank a cup of coffee and ate a piece of bread, which was awful and tasteless. There was no comparison between bread and toast, I thought, as I chewed. I chewed and swallowed and it seemed to go on a long time, much longer than necessary, as I pondered the good qualities of toast, how you could put the butter on before in nice thick pats and there'd be delicious buttery pockets or you could put it on after, which also had its merits, but would be difficult to spread and couldn't quite compete with those buttery holes. Then I took Layla out to get the paper but it hadn't come yet. I had beaten the paperboy. I wondered if the paperboy was actually a boy, or a man or a woman or a teenage girl. I hoped the paperboy was a boy about twelve years old on a bicycle but I knew he wasn't and then a car drove slowly by and two teenagers were chucking papers out of their windows. The driver tossed one at my feet and waved.

"Well," I said. "I'm going to take a dump and then we're going to the beach, goddammit."

Half an hour later we were parking in the lot. There was a sign that said dogs weren't allowed on the sand, but this seemed like the kind of rule that I could not, in good conscience, follow. First, though, I walked her over to the dumpster and let her sniff around, lick the pavement.

"Let's see if you can find a T-bone," I said. "Maybe you can find a bigger T-bone than the one you found before, or are they all about the same size? What bone is a T-bone, anyway?"

She was fast, efficient. She gobbled a whole bunch of shrimp shells while I watched a homeless man approach from a long ways off. I had a prejudice against the ones who were veterans, in particular, because they used it as an excuse—always holding up signs asking for handouts and I suspected half of them had gone to Canada while I'd lost my brother, my one and only sibling, leaving my parents heartbroken.

"I don't have any cash on me," I said. He looked like all of the other homeless men who hung around the beach, though a good bit younger than I'd initially thought. It was like they were all related.

"Oh, I don't want money," he said, as if it was ridiculous for me to think he wanted money. In my experience, unknown men did not approach you in parking lots for anything *except* money, that or they were going to rob you. He did not come over, for example, to compliment my dog, though he did that next, and before I knew it, he was giving me a story about driving over from Louisiana for an interview on an oil rig and getting separated from his friend and spending all his cash on a motel room and now he needed gas money to get back home. He was stuck. A request for gas money was a popular one these days. I decided to test his skills.

"Where's your car?" I asked, looking around. There were a few cars and trucks in the lot, four to be exact.

"It's at the motel."

"Which one?"

"One of the ones along the beach here," he said.

"You don't remember the name of it?"

"I don't know, man," he said. "I just got into town yesterday and my brother left me. . . . It's a motel. It looks like a motel. Why do you need to know where I'm staying?"

"I thought you said it was your friend."

"What? You aren't friends with your brother?"

I wasn't going to get into that with him. "Anyhow," I said, "that's tough luck, it really is, but I still don't have any cash on me. I only came here to let my dog eat trash."

He shook his head and thanked me anyway. His shoulders

were slumped, his head hanging down. The sight of it really socked me in the gut. And then I started thinking he probably just wanted a nice warm biscuit and a couple of cold beers, a pack of smokes, and who was I to judge? Who was I to deny a man a biscuit and a cold beer? I was no one. I wasn't anyone at all.

Ellen called and I hit Decline, goddamn Ellen with her fifty-dollar haircuts and beachfront condo.

"Sir!" I called. He turned, his whole face lifting. "Wait a minute." I went to my car and unlocked it. I kept a whole cup of change in the console, mostly quarters and dimes, and handed it to him. An entire cup! It must have been something like ten dollars. He didn't seem as thrilled as I would have liked, but he said he appreciated it and I knew this time when he was looking down it was into a cupful of silver. I had improved his situation slightly, but the main thing was that he was no longer bringing me down. My spirits, I thought, they are very tenuous, changing with the wind. It was my birthday and I still had a hangover but the dog had just scored a bone, though not a T-bone. All was right with the world, or at least okay. Then she took a gigantic dump and I didn't have any way to pick it up. I looked around, knowing I looked guilty for doing it but unable to stop myself, and dragged her over to the boardwalk. It was a long boardwalk, built after Katrina, and I had never walked it before even though it was a short distance from my house. It was a nice boardwalk. There were many nice things that I never took advantage of and I was going to have to start seizing the day.

We arrived at the end where a couple of guys were fishing. I thought about asking how the fishing was but they were weather-beaten and rough and I was afraid they wouldn't be responsive.

It was hard to tell, though. Some people who didn't look friendly were quite friendly once you engaged them. And I felt like I should also be fishing instead of just walking a dog up and down a boardwalk. So we turned around and walked back, got in the car right in time for Layla to start gagging.

On the radio, a young man was talking about depression so it had to be one of the God stations. He was going to tell me how his life had improved and how wonderful everything was because he had found God. He said he wasn't sad, that for him depression was an inability to imagine a future for himself. Something about that hit me: I had never been able to imagine my future, either. If someone asked where I saw myself in five or ten years, as they often had when I was younger, I answered in the abstract: health and happiness, enough financial security to pay my bills. But those things weren't a future. I wondered if I had been depressed my whole goddamn life. Since I was a child. Since I was in the womb. If that was just the way it was for some people and they didn't even know the difference.

When we got back to the house, Sasha's car wasn't in the driveway or on the street. I had a bad feeling, like the feeling I'd had that morning when I went to let Layla out of the room, but she'd probably just gone to the grocery store or run to the gas station for a new Dr Pepper. There was no reason to panic. I figured there was probably a note but there wasn't one in the kitchen or in the den. I opened the door to Maxine's room and her bag was gone. In the bathroom, which was a goddamn mess—lumps of toothpaste in the sink and hair all over the tub, scraps of toilet paper everywhere—her toothbrush was gone.

Layla walked the house with me, whimpering.

"Well," I said. "It looks like your mama has left us, which surprises me—not that she left me but I figured she'd take you with her. What a world we live in."

I truly felt Layla understood these words. Or she didn't understand the words but she got my meaning: Sasha was gone. I sat on the floor so I could look her in the eye. She wasn't feeling much like looking me in the eye, though, so I just let her stare at the floor while I petted her, flapping her ears slowly and covering her eyes and mouth. Blind, deaf, dumb.

"You never know with people," I said. "They're unpredictable. And it's possible your mother is on drugs, if I'm being perfectly honest, bad drugs. Something wasn't quite right with her, though this isn't to say that she doesn't have some good qualities. She does. I have tasted her meatloaf and enjoyed it very much, and her lasagna—I don't remember her lasagna because I was pickled but I bet there's some leftovers and I'm sure it's tasty. And there're plenty of other things, too, like her love of blankets and blue jean shorts. Showing off her shoulders."

It did not seem like a very good list, but it was thorough.

I drank another glass of water and then we went to the backyard and sat. There was a mouse running along the fence, a goddamned mouse. Whatever cool and breezy weather we'd had was gone. I felt unclean, the poison coming out of me. Somebody ought to shoot me on the spot, I thought, as I followed the mouse down the fence and around the patio. Once it was gone, I looked at nothing for a long time until a flock of birds passed overhead and then a plane. I wondered if Sasha would return for the dog and, if she did, whether I'd let the dog go with her. I couldn't imagine it. I would have to fight her on that one. She didn't have the money to sue me, anyhow, and had abandoned Layla by all accounts. It was possible she'd had something to do with getting rid of the dog in the first place, though I didn't see how that fell in line with the rest of the story. But the whole story was odd, the entire story was something I couldn't fathom, picturing myself walking up to her house with a briefcase of religious pamphlets, walking into that house with all its cereal boxes and dead flowers. I hoped I never saw her again.

I had her dog and that was that. And Layla was better off with me. I was a better dog owner, had proved that to myself. Since I couldn't remember if I'd fed her that morning, I fed her again.

My phone rang. Digging it out of my pocket, I managed to drop it. It was Diane.

"Is this Louis?"

"Yes, this is he."

"Are you okay?"

"I'm fine. I dropped my phone," I said.

She asked if I wanted to meet for lunch. I still felt like hell—sweaty and fuzzy-headed, not right at all—and I didn't want to leave the house again, but I also didn't want to tell her no. It was just bad timing, I felt, as if I had a million things on my plate, but most of the things on my plate were out of my control. I should call the Social Security office, though. Call Ellen back and bawl her out.

"I could really use some hair of the dog," she said. "And I'm on vacation after all, so I'm not going to judge myself for it."

"No reason to do that." The mention of a drink perked me right up. It sounded like exactly the thing I needed and I didn't know why I hadn't thought of it before, a nice cold beer or a Bloody Mary to take the edge off.

"And today's your birthday," she said. "We have to celebrate." She said we *had* to, no questions, no saying no. I walked back inside with Diane still on the line—she had started telling me what her family was up to, where they'd gone the previous night—and noticed the spare key was missing. Sasha had taken it. There was no use looking for it elsewhere in the house. I wasn't willing to risk leaving Layla alone so I'd have to take her along wherever I went until I had the locks changed. I wondered if this was something I might do myself, though I wasn't particularly handy. My brother had been handy, even at a young age, he'd been able to fix things. He hadn't just been the better version of me, it was like there was no relation at all.

"So, where should we meet?" she asked.

"Let me think," I said. I didn't know what to tell her. I didn't go to any of the places I used to go, couldn't imagine sitting in a booth that Ellen and I had eaten at dozens, if not hundreds, of times and yet here I was the local—and a man—and she expected me to give her a time and a place. I racked my brain for a festive restaurant that allowed dogs where I wouldn't see anyone I knew. All I could think of was the place next to the place that we'd been the day before, which was basically the same—colorful menus and fish tacos overlooking the water.

We agreed to meet in an hour at Shaggy's.

I showered and dressed, trying to think if I had any valuables to hide in case Sasha returned. This prompted me to take a quick look around the house for anything that might count as a valuable, and that might already be missing. The TV and DVD were still in the living room and there was also a smaller TV in my bedroom, untouched. But my iPad, which I'd last seen next to my bed, wasn't there. I checked my drawer for my wedding band and the good watch that needed a new battery, both gone. What else did I have that she might have taken? I walked through each room. In the kitchen, the blender was gone. A blender! I couldn't believe it. I had really liked that blender, too, a nice one Maxine had given Ellen and me one Christmas. It crushed ice like it was nothing, never gave me any trouble.

That seemed to be it: an iPad, a blender, a watch, and a wedding band. Good riddance to all but the blender. I hadn't worn the watch in over a year and hadn't missed it. The wedding band was worthless and I had only put it in the drawer because I didn't know what else to do with it.

Since she had taken off with my things, and because she couldn't tell if I was home since I parked my car in the garage, it was unlikely she'd return. She had known which items were worth taking and how few of them there were. And she wouldn't be back for the dog—she had had plenty of chances to rob me and take the dog, too. The dog was mine and I wished she'd challenge me on it. She'd regret it, I'd make sure of that. I was still going to change the locks and made a mental note to call the locksmith—I had used a guy before, what was his name?—and ask if he could come out as soon as possible.

I put the dog in the car and drove to the restaurant, imagining Sasha crossing over into Louisiana. She would go west and stop in New Orleans, stay there for a night, and keep moving. What had she swiped from Harry Davidson's house? I had an image of the two of us teaming up to go after her—guns in both of our britches, a whole thing.

The restaurant was crowded. It was Thursday, I believed, though it didn't feel like a Thursday. Since I'd stopped working, the days rarely felt like the right ones. There was always something a little off about them because there wasn't any reason to feel more hopeful or depressed on one day as opposed to another.

Diane was seated at the bar, which was almost exactly like the one next door but this one had a Jamaican vibe. She was drinking a Red Stripe, which she raised at me as I sat down.

"You brought your dog," she said. "That's cute." She didn't look like she thought it was cute. I signaled the bartender and ordered a Red Stripe as well, though I didn't know if I'd like it. He opened the beer and fixed me a big cup of iced water with a lemon wedge.

"Thank you," I said. "This is exactly what I need right now."

He nodded and told me it was no problem, which was a thing young people said today, and I thought about tipping him generously but I was nearly broke, so very close to broke, at least until the fourteen thousand dollars came through and I signed up for my Social Security benefits. I needed to do that ASAP, pronto. I heard the lawyer saying I should have already received the check, that it had been mailed last week. Or it had gone out last week, or had he said it was on its way? *Keep an eye out*. It was possible the check had already come and Sasha had signed for it. With registered mail, someone had to sign for it and they didn't care who it was in my experience, so long as it was the correct address. If Sasha signed for the slim envelope, she would have opened it. And of course she must have found my checkbook in the dresser where

I kept my watch and ring, though I hadn't noticed it missing. I hadn't noticed it there, either. I felt my blood pressure skyrocket as I pictured her writing checks up and down the Coast, in multiple states. I thought about Harry Davidson again, his situation.

"Louis?" she said. "You there? Earth to Louis . . ."

"Oh, yes! Sorry. The dog is kind of a long story," I said, which was a phrase I'd used frequently as of late. I liked it—it made me sound like I had a lot going on. And I did, boy did I. "If I left her at home I was afraid she might be dog-nabbed."

"I think it's napped," she said, "like kidnapped."

"Oh, of course it is, that makes sense," I said, though I wasn't certain. Perhaps it was one of those words where either was acceptable. "You'll have to excuse me today. My head's not quite right."

"Oh, I have a terrible hangover, too!" she said, reaching down to pet Layla. "Well, isn't this all very intriguing. Who's trying to dognap you, girl?"

"I ask her questions all the time but she doesn't answer," I said, and smiled my half smile and she smiled and we were off to a winning start. Layla took to Diane right away—she loved to be petted by strangers, black and white, rich and poor, fat and thin—all but Frank. I wondered where the hell Frank had been keeping himself. I ought to give him a call, I thought, surprising myself. He hadn't returned for that "proper visit" he'd threatened, which was unlike him.

"Soooo . . ." she said. "I've got nothing but time and I want all the details."

"You wouldn't believe it if I told you." I shook my head, hoping I appeared to have some swagger or charm or mystery about me.

"I would, I most certainly *would* believe it. And after I get another beer, you're going to tell me the whole story. Oh, and happy birthday! I wish I'd had the chance to bake you a cake."

"Someone once told me I look more like a pie man."

"What's a pie man look like?" she asked, signaling the bartender for another round. I decided the question was rhetorical and shrugged, braced myself to look at her straight on in the noonday sun. Just as I was deciding how pleased I was with her, wondering why a nice, classy lady might be interested in me, I noticed a small patch of chin hairs, three or four in a cluster like mushrooms popped up overnight, one of which had grown quite long. When was it appropriate, if ever, to tell a woman she'd missed a chin hair? To reach over and yank it out?

Before I could start in on the tale of Layla, she started telling me about her cat, aged nine, and how she had no feelings for this cat whatsoever and never had; she wanted to get rid of him but who wanted a nine-year-old cat? She'd only gotten him because she needed him to catch the mice in her apartment.

"You have mice?"

"No, I *had* mice. It's not uncommon in the city."

"In Little Rock?"

"Yes," she said, "in Little Rock. And it's a really nice building—one of the nicest in town."

"But if you got rid of him they could come back," I said. This cat had done its job and done it so well that it was being held against him. It was just like people. "Your cat should go on a strike and then, once the mice return, you'll be happy to have him again."

"Let's don't talk about mice anymore today," she said, getting huffy.

I drank my beer and thought terrible thoughts, imagining

unwanted cats and mice, hot checks written all over town as I drank once more with a vacationing woman in the middle of the day. I stole a glance at the chin hairs and she caught me, touched herself like she might have food on her face. There was this thing I used to do in work meetings when I was bored—I'd sniff and run a finger under my nose or do a quick pick as I looked at someone across the table. I liked to see who took it as a signal and mimicked my gesture. That person would lose. But sometimes I'd be called out: *Are you sick, Louis? Is everything okay with you, Louis?*

"This dog could be in the movies!" Diane said. "She's got so much personality. And these ears—the way they flop and the one black eye. She's got real star quality. She's got that 'it' factor. She reminds me of the dog in the RadioShack commercial, or maybe it's a different one, some dog food commercial."

"She's quite special."

The excellent bartender brought the dog a bowl of water, and asked if it was okay if he gave her a Milk-Bone. I said she'd love a Milk-Bone. They were classic. All dogs liked them. They were like McDonald's but for dogs and not full meals but snacks. I was saying these things aloud. I finished my beer and ordered a White Russian.

"Hardly anyone orders these anymore," he said.

"I've just recently been turned on to them. They're very good."

"Too sweet for me," he said, and smiled, and I smiled, wondering if I should call my bank and cancel my account. I needed to go home and see if my checkbook was there, but even if it was, I had no idea what check I'd recently written, what number I was on. There was a time when I'd kept up with it meticulously, balanced my account every month. I asked Diane if she could watch Layla while I made a quick phone call and she seemed a little put out but said she would keep this dog forever. It was a bad day for a date, for a woman to want to date me, though any day might be a bad day for it.

I checked my wallet: my debit card was missing. In the parking lot, I called the bank and told them to cancel everything because I'd been robbed. It was funny to allege such a thing, which made me think of an unknown assailant wielding a knife on a street corner instead of an attractive woman I had invited into my home. I didn't have to go into all of that, though. They didn't need to know the details. It was easy enough but I would have to go into the bank to sign a few papers for new accounts and fill out a report. A new card would be sent to me within five business days.

"What am I supposed to do until then?" I asked. "I don't have any money."

"You can go into any branch and withdraw cash," she said, as if I were stupid. What a mess. And I was embarrassed that the woman knew how meager my funds were. Why even bother with such pitiful sums?

I went back to Diane and she said Layla had been whining and looking around for me.

"Really? What was she doing?"

"Whimpering and turning her neck all about. It was really cute. This dog loves you a lot."

"You think so?"

"Oh, yes."

"I hate to tell you this but I have bad news," I said. "It's related to the dognapping story but it's another piece of it—my debit card was stolen and I had to cancel all my accounts."

"That's too bad," she said.

"It *is* too bad," I said. "I don't have any cash on me and I need to get to the bank real quick to withdraw some money and fill out the paperwork."

She looked at me like she had known plenty of men like me in her time, bums, bums who didn't want to work and just wanted to live off women, going from one to another if they had to. I wasn't a bum and had never lived off a woman—a woman had never paid a bill for me in my life—and yet I knew how it looked. I had heard enough songs and seen enough movies to know how it looked.

"There's no reason to go right this minute," she said. "I can buy you a couple of drinks."

"Are you sure?"

"I have vacation money," she said. "It's different from real money." She touched my shoulder. I was very aware of my shoulder being touched.

"Same as the day drinking," I said. "I'll pay you back, or take you out for a good dinner?"

She smiled and said that would be fine, of course I would, and her tone rubbed me the wrong way but I would prove it to her, show her a grand time.

"How long are you here again?" I asked.

"Till Saturday. It's been a long week, but I shouldn't complain. I really shouldn't. It's nice that a single lady like me has a family at all."

"Family is good. I don't have much family anymore, other

than my daughter and granddaughter and I don't see them too often. They came over the other day and it was a mess, as it usually is."

"How come?"

"I don't know, but I keep trying."

"Do you?"

I thought about it for a minute, since she seemed to want me to think about it. "Yes," I said, "but perhaps not as hard as I think I do." I told her she was very smart, a very smart lady.

Layla was breathing heavily. The weather had turned warm again and seemed to be staying that way. Though I'd never liked the idea of the cold, digging oneself out of snow to go to work, the bulky coats and scarves, I would have liked to wear a light jacket at times and not sweat through my shirt in November. It was hard to believe it was November. Soon Thanksgiving and then Christmas, my first Thanksgiving and Christmas without Ellen or my father, though I had the dog now. When she laid on my chest I could feel her heart beating, how it skipped, and it was different from a human heart but it was a beating heart just the same. I would take care of her, fight for her if I had to. I needed to take her to the vet, say I'd found her on the mean streets, get her a proper name tag that said LAYLA in big letters with my phone number on the back.

"You're having a hard go of it lately," Diane said.

"There've been a few setbacks but I think they're over now. I think I've got things covered."

"Sometimes these things are blessings in disguise," she said.

Instead of being pissed off, I decided to make a game of it. "When it rains it pours."

She took a sip of her drink and gave me a sly grin. "Good things come to those who wait."

"When one door opens, another closes."

"Oh," she said. "I like that one. It's just . . . so true."

Layla drank messily from the bowl, slopping water onto my leg. I finished my drink and told Diane I had to get to the bank, take care of some things. "Can I take you out tomorrow night?" I asked.

"I'd like that."

"And don't worry," I said. "If I've forgotten my wallet or don't have any money, I expect you to get up and walk out. Calling me a bum and some other choice words on your way."

"I will," she said. "In fact, I'll ask to see the cash up front."

"Okay then," I said.

"I'm kidding, of course."

"Well, it's a date. Let me think about someplace nice and I'll call you." I knew where I wanted to take her, but I also knew the number of former business associates and acquaintances I'd run into at a place like Mary Mahoney's. I wasn't ready for all that. Or I could drive her over to Bay St. Louis or Pascagoula, somewhere we could be anonymous, though it was nearly as likely I'd run into folks there, too; the Coast was one long beach connecting people to each other despite the boundaries of towns or counties.

"Do you text?" she asked.

"I think so," I said.

"You think so?"

"I've received texts before."

She grabbed my phone and gave me a tutorial, commenting again on how old and small it was. How featureless. It reminded me of the times Ellen had helped me attach documents to emails, sighing as she told me how easy it was.

As we said our goodbyes, she touched my leg. My leg didn't do that thing where it rebelled, but stayed in place, which made me proud of it, as if it were separate from the rest of my body.

The bartender handed me the check and I passed it to Diane.

"The lady is treating today," I said, feeling as if I could never show my face there again, which was fine. It was simply one more place to add to the list.

CHAPTER 15

I DROVE TO THE bank and went inside, sat in a chair waiting to talk to someone about the new accounts. It was all handled quickly, efficiently, so I went over to the window to take out some cash. The lady—one I'd seen dozens of times who was still a complete stranger to me—looked at my driver's license and told me it was my birthday. I agreed that it was.

"I've got some good candy suckered away in here," she said, grinning as she rooted around in her drawer. "None of those green lollipops for you today!" She seemed so pleased with herself as she passed me a bite-sized Kit Kat through the slot along with the slim envelope.

"Thank you."

"You're very welcome. I hope you have a wonderful day, Mr. McDonald."

"You know they have white chocolate ones now," I said. It was time for the next customer; she was done with me. She was cool as a cucumber in her button-up sweater, just like a bank lady. You never saw them sweat. "You should try the white ones sometime. I prefer them, actually. You don't have any white ones in your secret drawer, do you?"

She looked at me like I'd slapped her. Somehow it had gone wrong, I'd said the wrong thing. I hadn't meant to offend her, had only wanted to get a rapport going. Was I being racist, liking the white ones better, or simply ungrateful? My phone rang. I jumped, pulled it out of my pocket: Maxine. I punched some buttons, trying to make the ringing stop as the bank lady looked around like she might need to notify security. I chuckled to myself but nothing was funny, and then tried to determine why I'd said it, what I'd been thinking prior to saying the thing that turned a pleasant interaction into an unpleasant one.

I hit the button on my key chain to unlock the car and Layla moved her head all around looking for me. It was one of my favorite things. A few times I'd hidden behind other cars so she couldn't see me to extend the game. She was panting heavily and I should have taken her home beforehand but hadn't wanted to make the detour. "I'm sorry about that, girl," I said. "I'm a real shit. A real bastard. I don't know how you put up with me, how anyone does."

"Don't be so hard on yourself, Papa," I responded in my dog voice.

I turned the a/c on full blast and rolled the windows down. The phone dinged: Maxine had left a voicemail. I drove to the locksmith's. I couldn't call the guy because I knew the location but not the name of the place. It was just one guy, a friendly black man who'd spent his life putting locks on things, getting people in and out of situations. It sounded like an easy job, and full of interesting stories. I liked stories; the problem was I didn't like people. How it was possible to like stories that had happened to people but not the people themselves, I did not know.

I apologized to Layla again—and let her forgive me and tell

me how excellent I was, encourage me to believe in myself—as I parked at the strip mall. Everywhere it was strip malls. He was squeezed between a Little Caesars and a UPS store.

The guy, Marvin was his name, said he could come out in the morning and I told him I'd have to sleep with one eye open, which was sort of a joke but also not a joke. In my mind, Sasha had become a menacing figure: one part prostitute serial killer like the woman Charlize Theron played in that movie where she'd gotten fat and one part homeless meth addict with a dash of *Thelma & Louise* thrown in. And yet she seemed like such a simple creature, I hated to give her so much credit. She was just a woman who liked to watch bad TV and sit on the couch with her blankets. I couldn't even imagine her driving more than a couple of hours by herself because she seemed very much like the type of person who needed other people. But she didn't. And that was the thing that made me afraid of her. She didn't need any of us, not even the dog.

"You want me to come out there today?" he asked. "I could probably come by around six, if it would help you to sleep better."

"It would—it would help me sleep better," I said, "but I wouldn't want to put you out too much."

"It'll be okay. I can postpone that *Top Chef* marathon with my wife."

"You like those cooking shows?"

"I like *Top Chef* best," he said. "They're all living together in one house so things get complicated, though not right off."

"I'll have to watch an episode." Whether it was cooking or surviving in the wilderness, the main attraction was how people got along, or didn't, with others. And it was most interesting when things went badly. I shook his hand and thanked him. After that, I drove through Burger King and bought a sack of junior bacon cheeseburgers and fries and Layla and I ate our first burgers parked in the lot. I still didn't want to go home so I took a detour by Harry Davidson's house, just out of curiosity. Perhaps it was Harry Davidson I was obsessed with and not his wife, after all. The idea horrified me. It also excited me. Harry Davidson, that fat bastard.

I slowed as I approached, but his truck wasn't there. He was at work, as usual, just a normal day. A regular day even though your wife has left you and run off with another man and then burgled him and run off from him, too. I trolled, waited. I didn't know what I wanted to happen but I wanted something to happen even if it was Harry Davidson with his fat fingers around my neck.

Layla whimpered so I tossed her another burger.

"I wish I was a dog, things would be a lot simpler if I'd been born a dog. Of course your lifespan is shit but maybe that's all anyone really needs on this earth—fourteen, fifteen years. Seems like plenty." I picked up her paw and kissed it and the corn chip smell overwhelmed me—it had relocated from her belly to her feet, or it had spread—and the corn chip song came back to me. I felt a world of possibility open up and then someone was grabbing my shirt. It was Kevin Hood: overly involved neighbor, God-fearing churchgoer, the kind of guy who wants a Little Kevin so he can be the big one. Just like my father.

Big Kevin did not look pleased to see me. He had his phone out and was punching the buttons very aggressively like it was a prop.

"I'm calling Harry right now," he said. "I'm getting Harry on the phone."

"What are you, Harry's little bitch?"

"I'm the HOA president."

"Well isn't that something," I said. "HOA president. You're doing really great things with your life, Big Kev. Amazing things." I took a sip of my drink to show him how unbothered I was by the whole affair, and then stepped on the gas but the car was in park so the engine revved. I put it into drive and noted that my heart was barely even beating fast. I was training myself, putting myself into challenging situations to see how I would handle them. It had been a long time—I had been a young man—since I'd really pushed myself. I called out the window for him to go fuck himself.

I drove by the gas station on the way home and picked up a twelve-pack of beer and a couple of Pepsis. Then I stopped at Walgreens because it was right there and ran in to get my medicine. There were five different bottles and I wasn't sure which ones I was supposed to take since the new doctor had switched things up so I paid for them all. As I was pulling up to the house, the UPS man arrived with my check and I signed for it. I ripped open the envelope with the blind hope that there would somehow be more, a mistake had been made, but there was no mistake. At least Sasha hadn't gotten her dirty hands on it.

In the kitchen, I found a notepad and made a list of the things that were missing. I didn't want to call the police but I should call my homeowner's insurance to see what they would cover. And my checkbook was, indeed, gone. I thought I might have to call the police since I'd reported it to the bank, but I didn't want to call them—you called the police and they shot your dog or there was some confusion as you reached for your license because they

thought you had a gun and *bang!* It was over. They were shoot-
ing white people now, too, or so I'd heard, and all sorts of dogs,
though not small ones like Ellen's; no one would shoot a dog that
weighed ten pounds. I would like to see a cop shoot a Chihuahua
or a weenie dog, some tiny thing that had bared its teeth, see how
that played in the media.

I watched *Naked and Afraid* as we waited for the lockman to
arrive, petting Layla with my foot. I hadn't heard her gag in a while.
I tried to put it out of my mind so as not to jinx it, felt sure she'd
start back up any minute. Any second now she'd swallow hard and
then she'd start gagging and freaking out and the gagging would
resume right on schedule—four, five, six times a day until I broke. I
thought about calling the Social Security office and then I thought
about some other things and they led to other things until I was
thinking about something I hadn't thought about in a very long
time: how my uncle had given my brother and me a baby alligator
when we were young. It was a small thing but it grew very fast. It
grew so fast we started keeping it in the bathtub and even though
we'd raised it from infancy we had to be careful because it would
try to bite us at every opportunity. Our mother had a girl of about
seventeen who helped her cook and clean and we would torture
her with it and then she quit and we pretended like we were glad
she was gone, but I missed her and my brother did, too. What was
most surprising in this memory was the fact that our parents had
let us keep it at all, let it live in our bathtub for so many years. Perhaps the alligator in my memory was a lot bigger than it had actually been, and perhaps it had only been months, or weeks even, that
we'd had it. I wished I could call my brother up and ask him. That
was the worst thing about everyone being dead.

I woke up, startled by a knock at the door. The dog had also been snoozing. She barked once, sharp and high-pitched, on alert. I let Marvin in and Layla licked his hand: he was one more person who had won her over simply by not being Frank. I'd been dreaming of Sasha. Sasha and I had been somewhere together, doing something. I could see her on a boat, at the top of a building, waving down to me. I wasn't going to be able to piece the dream back together with him in the house.

"Can I get you something to drink?" I asked, impressed with myself for thinking of it. "I've got beer, Pepsi, water, milk." I did not have milk—I had half and half, but I'd been on a roll.

"Well, I'll be off work in ten minutes," he said. "No harm in having a beer."

I agreed and opened myself one, too.

While the man worked, I told him about my troubles, figuring it was what folks did when he was in their living rooms, giving him a story. I started with the women in my life and the ways in which they'd wronged me. And I told him about my father, the inheritance. He was black and we didn't know any of the same people so I could tell him anything. He was also half listening as he worked, or not even half listening, less than half. If he were around more often I might get used to talking about myself, learn how to do it without offending or alienating people.

He went out to his truck and I sat in silence for a while, not watching TV or doing anything, awaiting his return.

"I've been married twenty-nine years," he said, as he continued with the job.

"Do you still like her?"

"She's too good for me but she loves me for some reason—tells me I'm her best friend and she has a lot of friends so that must mean something."

"That's nice," I said, though it didn't answer my question. As he handed me the keys, however, he told me things. They were the kind of things I'd heard before and yet they felt remarkable: listen more than you talk, be thankful for every day, compliment the other person often, and if you have something negative to say, keep your damn mouth shut. Perhaps the remarkable thing was that someone actually followed this advice. I pictured Diane's chin hairs. If you really liked—no, if you really loved—someone, would you let them go around with a bunch of hairs hanging off their face? Surely not. Surely you would err on the side of hurting their feelings in order to protect them from the people who would judge them even more harshly.

He waggled his empty bottle and said he guessed it was time to go.

"You sure you won't have one more? You're officially off work now."

"Well, okay then. Twist my arm."

I got him another, got myself another. He sat on the couch and petted Layla and I introduced him to my program—a naked man and woman in the Louisiana swamps. I was surprised he'd stayed, but didn't want to appear as though I was surprised. And he didn't seem eager to get home to his wife, despite what he'd said about her. I could hear his phone vibrating in his pocket, see it lighting up. Dinner on the table, his wife there alone. . . . I supposed it was nice that he said kind things about her in public, regardless; it was better than saying shitty things about her and broadcasting their troubles all over town.

When Ellen and I were together, even when we'd stopped talking and lived as sullen roommates, I didn't say anything bad about her to my colleagues or fishing buddies. We didn't talk like that, about things like that. You asked how someone's wife was doing and the other person said they were fine and that was the extent of it unless she'd been sick, in which case he would say she was feeling better, regardless of whether or not it was true.

"Oh, these two'll never make it," I said, gesturing at the TV. "I've gotten to where I can look at them and tell. And the primitive survival ratings are bullshit, pardon my French. I don't know how they come up with them but they don't make any goddamn sense. Pardon my French."

He didn't seem to mind my French. He commented on the man's back hair and quietly drank his beer, one ankle resting on a knee.

I went to the kitchen and stood on my tiptoes to procure the fifth of Wild Turkey from above the refrigerator, but I couldn't reach it so I had to climb onto the counter. As I was cursing my knees, I heard Frank's truck pull into the driveway. I opened the door with the bottle in my hand before he had time to knock. "Come on in and have a seat—I've been expecting you. This is Marvin. Marvin came by to change the locks and stayed for a beer." I was pleased to see that Marvin hadn't moved. He was enjoying his beer and looking at Layla, the way her lips had curled up and away from her teeth at our new guest. I noticed that some of her teeth were broken and a number of them appeared to be missing altogether. Such was life for a dog like her. Who knew where she'd been, what she'd been subjected to, before she found me.

"Oh, Layla hates Frank here," I explained. "Attacked him once—got him by the ankle and latched on, wouldn't let go."

"I went to Chili's," Frank said.

"Well, it must've been a special occasion. Thank you for the birthday present."

"Oh, Louis, I forgot it was today."

"That's okay—I don't remember when yours is, either. Sometime in April?"

"March," he said. "Close enough."

"Come on in and have a drink to celebrate."

He couldn't say no at that point. I took the box into the kitchen—the dog hot on my trail—and snuck a peek: chicken fajitas. I'd been hoping for a burger and fries. Or something else, I didn't know what, but not chicken. I had a flashback of all the rotisserie chickens Ellen had tried to feed me over the years and call it dinner. She'd serve it with a can of beans or peas and some white bread stacked on a plate. What a lazy woman she'd been. I'd known it even at the beginning, which is what galled me most. I could track her laziness, her selfishness, all the way back to our very first date when she wouldn't give me a bite of the dinner I was paying for. I fed the dog a few hardened bits and went back into the living room, still carrying the bottle of liquor like I was just going to carry it around forever.

I wanted to confront Frank about the will, how he'd known all along I'd been screwed and hadn't said anything. Instead I offered him a shot of Wild Turkey, which he declined. He was sitting on the other side of the couch, Layla keeping a close eye on him though she'd stopped baring her teeth.

"I thought you'd given up liquor," Frank said.

"I did, I have. But it's a special occasion. You want a beer?"

"I'm fine. I can't stay long."

We continued watching the program and the man and woman weren't getting along at all. She called him shiftless and good-for-nothing but he claimed to be saving his energy for more important things. He spent his time dozing under a tree, drinking swamp water without purifying it with the mirror the woman had brought along as her special item. Meanwhile, she sat in the sun for hours at a time, shining it into a pot she'd miraculously found on the first day. We discussed whether or not someone in the crew had planted the pot, how likely it was to find a pot in a swamp. Since I was the expert, I did most of the talking.

I went back to the kitchen and returned with three glasses of ice. Frank sighed but took one, as did Marvin.

"Did you poison it?" Frank asked, after I'd splashed the whiskey in.

"Yes, Frank, I poisoned it. The whole bottle. I always like to poison my guests."

He set his glass down and picked it back up, eyeing me as he took a sip. He took another sip and another, and after a few minutes, a friendly mood came over the room, which was unexpected. The three of us drinking our drinks and commenting on the program—the man had been bitten by a snake—and it seemed we were all supposed to have convened like this, in these spots, like I had seen it before it happened. I couldn't remember what that was called but there was a word for it. I wanted to get out my iPad and look it up but remembered I didn't have my iPad anymore.

"You know they make tape for that bird banging on your window there—you hang it in the branches and they avoid the whole area," Marvin said, moving his arm slowly across the room like someone describing a beautiful sunset. "Works two ways, they don't like the rustle or the shine."

"I got some," I said. "I got a whole bag over there on the counter. I barely even hear the damn thing anymore, though. It hardly even registers."

Marvin said he'd hang it for me at no charge because he'd had the same thing happen a while back. Maybe it was because his wife kept the windows so clean. It was a relief to hear him say he'd dealt with the same issue. I wasn't being singled out by this bird. This bird wasn't a bad omen or bad luck, hadn't chosen my house in particular to torment. It was just a bird and you could hang some shiny stuff and make it go away. I thanked him but said I'd do it first thing in the morning.

"It's something I need to do myself," I said, as if it was really something special to walk into your own backyard and hang shit from a branch.

"You going to vote on Tuesday?" Frank asked.

"Of course I'm going to vote on Tuesday," I said.

"What about you?" Frank asked Marvin.

"Oh, yeah," he said. "I always vote."

"Me too," Frank said.

Stop it right there, Frank, I thought, don't say another word. That's a damn can of worms you don't want to open. We went back to the program—the man was killing snakes left and right and the couple was eating pretty decently. Turned out I'd been wrong about them. When it was over, Frank stood and said he'd better be getting home to Claudia, which prompted Marvin to stand, as well. It always happened like that: one person left and then everyone went with them.

I was sorry to see them go. I picked up Layla and held her like a baby, like Sasha had done, and she didn't try to escape so I said all of the nicest things I could think to say to her, that she was pretty and smart and kind, that she was a good dog, the best dog. My truest companion, my one and only now and forever.

CHAPTER 16

I N THE DREAM, Sasha had broken into the house. Hovering over my face so close I could feel her breath. I was frozen in place, unable to move anything except for my eyes and facial muscles, which contorted into horrible shapes as she smiled down at me. She held up a key, but in the dream the key didn't look like a key but a piece of fruit. I told her I'd changed the locks and she laughed. *You don't even lock your windows*, she said. This wasn't true. I never opened any of the windows except the one in the kitchen and only when I burned something—so far as I knew, the rest of the windows had been locked since Maxine left the house. Sasha laughed again and her key was just an ordinary key, though the teeth appeared larger and sharper than usual. *Wake up*, she said, and I did.

I heard Layla's tail thumping and called her onto the bed with me, rubbed her belly. The dream was nothing—Sasha hadn't broken into the house; she hadn't threatened me, pointed a gun at my head. She was just a woman, and a small one at that, and I felt silly for being afraid of her. For dreaming of her. The image of the fruit—a pomegranate—was stuck in my head. I saw it balanced

on her palm, bright red with seeds bursting out of it. I wondered
if pomegranates were in season.

"What do you think a pomegranate means?" I asked Layla.
"Did your mother have a thing for those? What if she told me
about it and I can't remember? Or what if she didn't tell me about
it and I knew anyway because we have some sort of special mental
connection? Do you think that's possible?"

She jumped down and we went from room to room checking the windows. I found the one in the office unlocked as well
as one in Maxine's room. What a wily, deceitful woman! She
could've stolen Layla right out from under my nose! I locked the
windows and then went around the house double-checking just
to be sure. After that, I sat on Maxine's bed and stewed for a
good ten minutes. I considered stripping the sheets, but instead
found myself under the covers inhaling deeply: the smell of dust,
decaying flowers. I had the terrible idea that Sasha had crept in
the window and slept there, vacating the room mere moments
before I opened the door. I picked a couple of hairs off the pillow and held them, not sure whether to flush them down the
toilet or swallow them or drop them to the carpet. I dropped
them. Considering how often I vacuumed, they might stay there
forever.

The bed belonged to both of them now—Maxine and Sasha,
their ghost selves, back-to-back with their arms crossed, dis-
pleased. I had only ever tried to please them but they'd out-
smarted me at every turn.

Layla licked my hand—she still had to use the bathroom—
and I got up to let her out. Then I started the coffee and called
the Social Security office. After an extended recording instruct-

ing me to do everything online, a woman answered. I told her I wanted to sign up for my benefits and she transferred me to someone who wasn't there. I had no intention of leaving a voice-mail so I called back and the same woman answered and transferred me to someone else who put me on hold. Seven minutes later, I hung up.

Layla sat watching me, ready for her walk. "You know what would be great?" I asked. "If you could pour me a cup of coffee. If I could teach you how to pour a cup of coffee I'd . . ." I couldn't think of what I would do. "Be very pleased." I petted her aggressively with one foot to try and stay calm.

On my third attempt, the same lady answered and I explained what had happened the previous two times and asked if she could help me make an appointment but she said she only transferred people.

"Are you telling me your whole job is to transfer people?"

"That's right," she said.

"That's your entire position?"

"Hmm hm."

"Do you take messages or anything like that?"

"No," she said. "I greet people and I transfer them."

"Do you know if the person you're going to transfer me to is actually at their desk?"

"Sometimes," she said. "If I stand up I can see just about everybody in the office."

"How often do you stand?"

"It depends on whether I feel like standing," she said. It sounded like she could do this with me all day, answering my questions honestly and without any sort of guilt or fear because she was a government employee and would never be fired. If she did a particularly bad job, she might be promoted. Up and out.

"How often do you figure you feel like it?" I asked.

"Ohhh," she said, like she was really enjoying this now, "I suppose not very often, especially if it's after lunch. I get pretty tired after lunch."

"Hmm," I said. I couldn't think of anything else to say except that I also got tired after lunch.

"Well, would you like me to transfer you now?" she asked.

"Will you stand up and transfer me to someone who's there?"

"For you I'd do anything," she said, and she sent me to a man named Jimmy who picked up on the first ring. I could tell he was obese by the sound of his voice; it was strange that you could tell something like that. Was it the cheeks—did they muffle sound? He encouraged me to fill out the information online but I told him I didn't want to do that, that I wanted to meet with a real live person and get everything taken care of in person.

"I don't make appointments," he said, blowing my mind, but then he said he had a cancellation for that very afternoon and could squeeze me in if I could make it work. He acted like he was doing me a big favor so I thanked him and told him I'd be there and he gave me a list of documents to bring along. After that I was exhausted. I looked at the day ahead, which consisted of a visit to the Social Security office as well as a date with Diane and I missed the days when I woke up and had nothing on my plate. I'd felt good when there was nothing on my plate even though I'd spent most of the time lonely and bored, wishing I had something to do.

I decided to make some breakfast. I was hungover but not too bad considering the beer and the Wild Turkey, and then, after Marvin and Frank left, a few more beers to celebrate the remaining hours of my birthday. I remembered Ellen calling at some point so I checked my phone but she hadn't, or she had, but not the previous night. I scrambled a couple of eggs and got the water boiling for grits while debating between deer sausage or regular sausage, deciding on deer sausage because Arnie's did a good job, better than anyone I'd used in the past. I drank another cup of coffee as I stirred and flipped and then the dog and I enjoyed our breakfast without turning on the TV. Of course the bird had returned to keep us company. Since I was on a roll, I gathered my whites—all of my underwear and T-shirts were dirty other than the V-necks Ellen had bought years ago in an attempt to make me fashionable—and put them in the wash. I dumped some detergent in and set it on a regular cycle even though the machine always made me feel like I should do something special. Then I sat in my chair and fell asleep. I did my best sleep in my chair and never had nightmares, didn't even remember my chair dreams.

When I awoke, I reheated a cup of coffee and drank it while sitting outside with Layla. The weather had turned cool again, the sky bright and cloudless. It was a perfect day, a clear bluebird day.

Layla watched a cat walk the fence line. She whined, stood on her hind legs, and looked at me as if I might get it for her.

"You want to kill that cat? Is that right, girl? You want to kill the cat?" I repeated "cat" a few more times so she could associate the word with the thing. I told her cats were our enemies, feral, godforsaken. I'd never had one and never would. Best-case scenario, the cat pissed on the dirty clothes you'd left on the floor, things you were planning on washing, anyway; worst case, it pissed on the baseboards and in the vents, on blankets that were dry-clean only. Hissed, scratched your arms all up. I picked up an acorn and chucked it at the animal. It missed. Then I went inside and searched through all of my important documents to find the ones Jimmy had requested—birth certificate, marriage license, divorce decree—and cried for a while.

At the Social Security office, I waited with all of the people who didn't have appointments until Jimmy came to the door and called my name. He had a file in his hand to make him seem important. He was even fatter than I'd imagined.

We shook hands and I followed him to his desk, which was separated by a partition from a coworker's. I sat where he pointed and he kept standing, continuing the conversation he'd been having before he'd come to get me. I coughed. Coughed again. Finally he explained that Gina was about to go to the dentist for a root canal, which I could plainly hear.

"I never had a single cavity until I was twenty-seven years old," she said from behind the partition. "For a long time it was my most impressive achievement. Now what do I have?"

"You have a nice head of hair," Jimmy said, taking a seat.

"No, it's frizzy and gets tangled easily. It's all knotted up right now—that's why I stuck it in a bun."

"Well," he said. "You *have* hair. That's something."

She sighed. I was desperate to get a look at her at that point, so I stood and stretched, smiled down at her. She returned my smile, showing me all of her teeth. Gina was a well-dressed woman in her early thirties, pretty, much too good to work in an office like this, in a town like this. You would think people like her would have graduated high school and promptly moved away, no reason to come back, and yet many of them did come back. Like Maxine. They went out into the world and experienced life in the big city and probably did drugs and had lots of sex and then moved home and reconnected with their high school boyfriend or some such. I looked at her fingers—nothing but a ring on her left pinkie—and tried to come up with alternative scenarios. Perhaps a teen pregnancy that led to the GED and junior college, her mother's house.

"Your teeth are still nice and white," I said. "And straight, too."

"Thank you. That's kind of you to say."

Jimmy seemed annoyed by our exchange and asked if I was ready to get started. A short time later, however, their conversation resumed and circled back to the beginning, only he managed to ask me questions and type them into the computer at the same time.

Gina stood and opened her mouth to indicate where the problem was.

"Don't show this man your nasty mouth," Jimmy said.

She looked at me and apologized, said she was very nervous. "I hope you don't mind."

"Not at all," I said. "I'm glad I didn't fill out the forms online—I would've missed all this."

"Well, good," she said, "but don't tell anyone that," and she sat back down where I couldn't see her. Did they always talk like this when clients were around? Though I didn't mind, found it refreshing even, it also seemed highly inappropriate. Made me wonder what kind of operation this was and how much work got done. Perhaps they acted differently with other, more important people, while I was just another middle-class white man who insisted on bothering them instead of filling out the forms online. I could hear Gina eating and wanted to see her, see what she had in her mouth, wished she'd been the one taking my claim. I'd have a reason to call her up and ask questions.

Because Ellen and I were married over ten years, she'd be treated the same as my wife, Jimmy explained.

"So she'll get part of my retirement each month?"

"No, it won't ever affect your money. But if you die before she does, she'll be paid as if the two of you are still together, like she's your widow. She could receive up to a hundred percent of your benefit, depending on her age."

"Divorced women all across the country must be praying for their ex-husbands to drop dead," I said, and Gina laughed and Jimmy said he was sure that was true but Social Security probably wasn't the reason.

I watched Gina stand and button her sweater. Put her sunglasses on top of her head. "Ugh. I guess I'll get this over with. Maybe they'll knock me out. I sure hope they do."

Jimmy wished her luck and I wished her luck and she was gone. I wanted to ask about her but showed some restraint, sitting quietly and signing the forms where Jimmy put the Xs. Then he walked me out and I looked around for her, waited. She could still be sitting in her car, stalling or putting on makeup—or she might've made a detour to the bathroom to brush her teeth first since she'd been eating—but I didn't see her. She was gone.

I didn't want to waste another second of the day, so I went home and put the dog in the car, drove to the beach.

As I pulled into the lot, I saw Harry Davidson getting out of his truck. I let my foot off the brake and sank down in my seat, reclining it like a gangster as I cruised past. Someone told me hoodlums leaned back like that so the bullets would miss them, and not because they thought it looked cool—or not just because they thought it looked cool—which had surprised and delighted me. As I got right up on him, however, I could see that the man hardly looked like him—roughly the same build and head shape, but this guy was shorter and clearly Hispanic. The color of the truck wasn't even right. I recalled a breakup with the only woman I'd loved prior to Ellen and how she'd dumped me without warning, or any warning that I'd seen coming. For months after, I saw her face in so many faces; it was like she was everywhere and nowhere all of the time.

Layla scrambled out of the car, trotted over to him.

"Leave the man alone," I said.

"It's okay," he said, petting her. "That's a nice dog you got there."

"Thank you," I said, feeling a surge of pride. "She's a good girl." Everyone was always telling me how good she was, how pretty, and it made me feel like I'd done something right. "Okay, well, goodbye," I said, and I hooked the leash to her collar and walked her over to the dumpster so she could take a sniff around. While Layla busied herself digging, I called Maxine.

"Good job!"

"Thanks, Dad."

"Hey, Maxi. Layla just found a bone—I was congratulating her—it's a really big one."

"You mean Katy?" she said.

"She's Layla again. Anyhow, I was just calling you to apologize about the other day. I know it was awkward and I'm sorry for it."

"Who was that person?"

"No one," I said. "No one important."

She pressed me on it so I told her that Sasha was somebody I'd tried to help because I cared about her dog but she was gone and the dog was back to being mine and mine alone. The more I said, the more questions she had as Layla dragged me around the lot to search out the next spot. "Look," I interrupted. "It's over, and we can all move on."

"Okay, then. . . . I don't know if you remember me telling you this—you were pretty distracted—but Laurel's birthday is Sunday."

I had not remembered. I did, however, remember going to visit the baby in the hospital, holding the baby in my arms while she screamed her goddamn head off. "That's right—just a few days after mine. She was my birthday gift that year."

"We're having a get-together at the house, around five-thirty. Her big party with all her friends'll be next Saturday—there was a conflict at the bouncy place, we called too late, I don't know why we left it to the last minute—so it's just a small gathering, pizza and cake. Do you think you can make it?"

"Of course I can make it, I wouldn't miss it. You'll have to give me some gift suggestions, though. I don't know what she likes."

"Mom will be there. Is that okay?"

"Your mother and I are on fine terms—we're on good terms."

"Really?"

"Well, we're not on bad terms. She called me the other day to let me know she'd sold her burial plot."

"That's a morbid thing to call you about," she said.

"It's just a practical matter. Something we all have to think about at some point."

"She wanted to tell you she'd sold it so she wouldn't have to be buried next to you for all eternity?"

"Exactly. That's exactly what she said."

"She is really something, that lady."

We discussed gift ideas, and she told me some of the things Laurel liked, which primarily seemed to consist of robotic animals. I tried to remember the names of them: Hatchimals and Little Live Pets, some kind of mice that may or may not have been different from the Hatchimals and Little Live Pets. So many animals in my life all of a sudden.

"I need to write all this down," I said. "Hold on, let me see if there's a pen in the car."

"I can text you, but you know what would be easier?" she said. "I just thought of this—Laurel saw a commercial the other day for an Easy-Bake Oven, like I had when I was a kid." I had forgotten about Maxine and her Easy-Bake Oven. She'd used it for years, unlike most of her toys and dolls that she had quickly abandoned. Those cake mixes had been outrageously expensive and she'd have me running out to buy more so she could bake something shitty for me. I could still taste the icing—thin and grainy—and the cakes were so dry I'd have to drink an entire glass of milk to choke 'em down. I had eaten every one she'd ever made me, though, and complimented her on her skills.

"Those cakes were so bad I wouldn't eat them myself," she said. "But you seemed to like them."

"I was just thinking about that."

"And I burned them half the time—how did I manage to do that? Weren't there fail-safes in place?"

We chatted for a few more minutes, and it was all quite pleasant. She didn't mention Lucky or ask if I'd spoken with him and that whole business seemed done, which was a relief. I was tired of worrying about it. And I was glad she had the money, what little of it there was, and was sorry I wasn't going to be able to leave her more. I would've liked my child and grandchild to never have to worry about finances again, for Laurel to go to any college she wanted and stay single if she didn't want to marry and be some kind of weird artist if that's what she turned out to be, which was pretty much a given so far as I could tell.

Maybe we would never talk about the inheritance that didn't come. And I was going to be fine. The house would be paid for. There was a retirement account I hadn't touched; it was small but coupled with my monthly Social Security check, I'd be fine. Perhaps I'd use that fourteen grand to update some things around the house—paint the outside and fix the gutters, put in a hot tub on the patio like a real bachelor pad. And buy some patio furniture, some nice stuff, so that Layla and I would be comfortable. She could chase squirrels and sun herself while I had a soak. A cooler of beer perched on the side, or built in. Surely they had something to accommodate their heavy-drinking clientele. Hell, I might even buy a new mattress.

I got off the phone thinking about those cakes and little girls everywhere baking them for their fathers. And then I recalled how Ellen had helped me get rid of them when I couldn't eat any more, burying them beneath the trash and feeding them into the garbage disposal. Had Ellen told her flat out she didn't like them, or had they only been offered to me? When Laurel opened the oven, Maxine and I could reminisce some more, and she might help me reconstruct other things, as well. Our lives before it all changed, how happy we'd once been.

Layla began to gag so I walked her over to a bench and sat down. She continued gagging and I continued to sit and look out at the water. The water was calm, the sun hitting it so it blinded you if you stared too long. I was thirsty and a bit dizzy, my blood sugar too high. Or too low. I ignored the gagging, pretended as if I couldn't see it or hear it even though she was doing that thing where her eyes were worriedly searching out mine so I could tell her it was okay, that it would soon pass. My new tactic would be to pretend there was nothing wrong. My new tactic did not seem to work any better than the old one.

After that, we attempted a jog, working up a good sweat within a few short minutes, and then we got back in the car and drove directly to Sonic, inspired by Sasha, that bitch.

It was high-tech now—you could slip your card right into the machine. I ordered two cheeseburgers along with onion rings and mozzarella sticks and a vanilla milkshake, really going all out so I'd feel like the best version of myself for my date with Diane. As I crammed the onion rings into my mouth, I noted that they'd been fried perfectly, weren't burned or dried out at all.

CHAPTER 17

THE CLOSER IT got to evening the more I wanted to cancel.
Why bother going out with a woman I'd never see again? I
couldn't remember ever meeting a person from Arkansas and tried
to picture a map in my head—it was close, but was it touching
Mississippi? I wanted to look it up but Sasha was on somebody
else's couch with my iPad, reading advice columns or celebrity
news or trying to purchase items with stolen credit cards.

I needed to contact my homeowner's insurance but I was
done with errands for the day. I was going to have a few pre-date
beers while I watched my program and Layla napped peacefully
at my feet.

By four-thirty, I still hadn't gotten in touch with Diane to
tell her where and when this date was going to happen, and this
seemed an easy way out—we'd only had casual plans, a loose
agreement, no set time or place, and I could simply not call her.
The relief was so immediate and intense I fell asleep. I hadn't
turned my phone off, though, because I never turned my phone
off—too few people ever called for it to even occur to me—when
it rang once, twice. Three times. It was hard to let it ring, but I

was growing more accustomed to it. There was a time in my life when I'd pick it up even when I knew it was a courtesy call—the cable company offering a new and better package, someone wanting money for disabled veterans or policemen who'd fallen in the line of duty. It rang a fourth time and went quiet. It was so quiet. I sat still, unmoving, as if Diane, or someone else, might see me. I imagined her sitting on a hotel bed in her beach dress, a damp swimsuit on underneath because she'd spent the day reading magazines by the pool, nursing mimosas and thinking about me. Maybe she'd even painted her toenails, shaved all her lady parts.

I went to the refrigerator and got another beer, talked it over with Layla. She seemed to think I should keep my word, but she was never going to say it and this was both the blessing and curse of an animal. What did they understand about human life? I took out a few pieces of bologna, tore them in half and tossed them underhanded, perfect easy tosses, nothing challenging. She missed tosses one and two but caught the third; she missed four, caught five. I regarded this as an immense improvement. If I practiced with her every day she would continue to improve, same as anybody.

But then she started gagging again.

"Goddammit, dog. You are really testing me now. You're really pushing me to my limits." I opened the door and forced her outside. "If you want to come in," I shouted, "you're going to have to use your door!"

The gagging continued so I went into the living room and sat in my chair, turned the sound up on the TV. On *Naked and Afraid*, the man refused to cuddle with the woman at night because he was afraid his wife would get upset. The woman was very put out by his reluctance to share his body heat because they were naked, of course, and it was cold, and she didn't have as much fat to keep herself warm. The woman was nice-looking and I imagined the man might have been more inclined to cuddle if she weren't so attractive. His wife would see him lying naked with this woman and all hell would break loose long after the show was over. The cuddling discussion went on and the man could not be persuaded and the woman wanted to leave him, saying she would be better off on her own, which wasn't true—they were never better off on their own. The ones who tried it failed. I wondered if she had seen any of the previous episodes but then I thought in a situation like that you weren't thinking about previous episodes; you were not a TV character when it was happening to you.

The man and woman silently, angrily, went about their business. I drank my beer, periodically checking my phone. It was five-thirty, five-thirty-seven, five-forty-one—I could still call Diane and explain things. We could meet and have a nice dinner and I could make her trip to the Coast something she would remember for years to come, or one of the things she would remember, if I wanted to. I could charm her, show her a good time. I was capable of it. I picked up my phone and called her, hung up before it started ringing.

She called right back and I answered before I could stop myself.

"Louis? Is that you?"

"It rang?"

"Yes," she said. "It rang."

"That's interesting," I said. "I didn't hear it on my end."

"Why would you call me and hang up?"

"I didn't mean to—my daughter was on the other line and I've been trying to get in touch with her for a few days. I thought it might be important."

"Is your daughter on the other line now?"

"No."

There was an extended pause and then she said, "You know, Louis, if you didn't want to go out tonight you could've just said so. I don't know why men do things like this—all you have to do is be honest. Why is that so hard?" She sounded like she was about to cry. It was awful, just awful.

"I'm sorry. I don't know what's wrong with me." I apologized again and she told me it was fine, she was used to this sort of thing, which made me feel like a piece of shit. I felt like such a piece of shit I thought it would be best to hang up and never speak to her again, but she said she still wanted to see me. This led me to speculate about how often men had stood her up, had hurt her, and it made me want to hurt her, too.

"Why don't you come over to my house?" I offered. "We could order in food and have a few drinks."

"I'm not sure I feel comfortable with that, going to a man's house on a first date." I poured myself a shot of Wild Turkey and tipped it down my throat. She explained that it wasn't proper. I poured another and wished her a safe trip back to Arkansas, got off the phone before she could berate me and tell me what an asshole I was. I didn't owe her anything, I didn't even know her. She was just a forward woman who had gotten up in my business.

I opened the door to let Layla in, but she wasn't there.

"Dog!" I called. "Layla! Come here, girl." I walked around to the side of the house but she wasn't there, either. The gate was closed and locked; there was no way out of that gate.

I stared at it for a while longer and then reached out, ridiculously, and shook it. It was iron, solid. There was no indication that anything had been tampered with. I wished I hadn't drunk that Wild Turkey. The Wild Turkey was affecting me. I couldn't think clearly. When Maxine was young I'd done my best to stay sober because what if she needed me in the middle of the night? What kind of man would I be if I was too drunk to drive my sick child to the hospital? But then sometimes I reasoned that Ellen would stay sober, and she had. Ellen hadn't even started drinking until Maxine left the house.

The dog wasn't in the backyard, which meant she was somewhere else—I couldn't think beyond that. I imagined her trotting down the street and onto the main road, looking for the house where we had recently seen all of the squirrels, a group of them taunting her from the base of a tree. Would she remember such a thing, try to find her way back there? What was a group of squirrels called? I got in my car and drove slowly to the main road, yelling her name out the window. The cars were flying past and I knew then and there that she was dead. I wondered what I'd do if she really *was* dead, how I'd handle it. I thought for sure it would be the end of me. I scolded myself for being so dramatic at a time like this. She was nearby, couldn't have gone far. She knew her way home. She was just out exploring.

I drove to the next street over, parked at the house that backed up against mine. Even though we shared a wooden fence, I didn't know them. The fence predated them. I had known the family that lived there before, the Hansens, but they'd moved to New

Orleans and a new family moved in. This new family consisted
of figures moving behind the slats. The man walking from the
house to the grill with plates of meat while the woman sat in a
chair and coughed great hacking coughs. There was one small
boy—a quiet and solitary child, like Maxine had been—but lone-
lier, as boys often are.

There was a sign on the door asking you not to smoke because
someone with an oxygen tank lived there. I knocked, thinking of all
the times I'd heard the woman hacking, how painful it had sounded.
I knocked again and peered into the windows, but it was dark. I had
a bad feeling about the house. It did not look like a friendly place.
It was maintained fine, the yard was trimmed and there were various flowers and a big oak tree, a welcome mat at the door—in other
words, there was nothing to give its unhappiness away.

I waited a while longer but no one came so I got back in my
car and continued driving, visions of Layla dead on the side of the
road. I thought about how I had yelled at her and slammed the
door in her face over something she couldn't control. It was indis-
putable. I was a bad person, a real garbage person. I didn't deserve
her, didn't deserve to be loved by her or Sasha or Diane or Ellen or
my daughter or anyone.

I realized at some point I was aggressively picking my nose.
I must have looked like a lunatic, head hanging out the window
shouting the dog's name, frantic, half-drunk. I hoped somebody I
used to know would see me and ponder the sad direction my life
had taken since Ellen left. *I saw Louis McDonald earlier today. . . .*
He was driving erratically and screaming out the window. You know his
wife left him, walked out and no one's seen him since. Poor guy . . . I hope
he's okay. . . .

Once I'd given up, I drove home. I was a wreck, my heart beating so fast I couldn't catch my breath. I only wanted to imagine the dog dead in case she actually *was* dead, to soften the blow, but I hoped to God she wasn't. I honestly didn't know what I'd do without her, couldn't imagine going back to the life I had when she wasn't a part of it. When there was no one to talk to and nothing to do but drink beer and feel sorry for myself, and my life was mostly that way still but it was also different. I hadn't even minded being robbed. It had been exciting—it had been *something.* If I had friends, it would've even made an interesting story—*and then the bitch robbed me! Took off with my blender and my favorite watch, too. . . .*

I circled the backyard again, checking the slats in the fence when I saw her muzzle, black nose and white hair trying to push its way through. She was in the yard of the oxygen woman—there must've been something over there she'd wanted to see, a squirrel or a cat, or she'd smelled a bone. She was an explorer at heart, compelled to climb the mountain because it was there. Though she'd managed to get through the fence, she couldn't get back to me so I had to lift the board and hold it while she pushed and struggled—her muzzle turned greenish yellow from the old wood—and the damn thing cracked. And then Layla was mine again and I was hers. We were back together. We fell to the ground hugging and kissing each other, just as she had with Sasha. I let her lick my face, my ears and eyelids and cheeks and nose. A flash of Sasha's yellow panties as her skirt hiked up. I slapped her a couple of good ones on the back end to make it clear I was mad, and then hugged her again, hoping she'd understand. She seemed to. It was hard to say, though. It was hard to say what the punishment meant to her when it was mixed with so much joy.

I licked my fingers and wiped her face, considered giving her a bath, but it wasn't going to teach her a lesson and I didn't feel like it. Dogs did the things they did without foresight, without thinking about the ramifications. At least untrained ones like mine. Somewhere there was a dog leading a blind man down a street, a dog that would not take off after a squirrel, dragging the man to the ground in its efforts to catch and kill it. There were dogs that sniffed out bombs and saved the lives of soldiers, moved quietly and calmly through airports. But Layla wasn't like those dogs and I didn't want her to be. I liked her the way she was. I liked everything about her except, of course, the gagging. I did not like that and could live the rest of my life without hearing it ever again but I would go easy on her about it. I'd just have to go easy.

I tried to check her for splinters but she seemed fine—a yellowed face and an adventure that I hoped hadn't been too fun, especially now that she knew she could get out. I would double-check every piece of wood. Get out my toolbox, hammer and nails. Before I tackled the fence, however, I needed to calm down. There was a reason people claimed their hearts were beating out of their chests. I could see it. No, I couldn't see it, but if I concentrated hard enough I'd have probably been able to. I sat in front of the TV with the bottle of whiskey and the drawer of deli meats on my lap, lowering the slices into her mouth one at a time. I adjusted the sound and was surprised to find the same couple huddled together in the dark—how had so little time passed when so much had occurred?—the man spooning the woman like a lover. Their primitive survival ratings must've gone through the roof.

CHAPTER 18

FOR SOMETHING LIKE the one-hundred-and-fifty-eighth night
in a row, I slept poorly. I woke up at two in the morning and
couldn't get back to sleep, thinking about the date I didn't go on
with Diane and the dog I was sure I'd lost and how I'd preemp-
tively buried her. Sometime around sunup I dreamed I'd found
Layla dead, saw myself curled up next to her on the side of the
road. And there was a whole Diane/Ellen/Sasha mash-up on hotel
beds, their bodies slumped in a way that accentuated their fat
rolls. As a child, my dreams had been nonsensical—at least as I
recalled them—but at some point they'd become terribly obvious.

I was depressed as hell but had to get Laurel a present and
Layla was there, licking my hand. She had slept like a goddamn
champ. She woke up every morning refreshed and glad to be alive,
eager to start the day. At least before her first gagging session.

I made a pot of coffee, drank a cup. It turned my stomach
but I poured myself another and forced it down. Then I showered and walked the dog around the block. She found a dead
mouse, blood dripping out of its mouth and onto the sidewalk,
its tail stiff. She carried it for a while and I didn't bother trying

to take it away from her. I was pleased with my resignation. It didn't seem so much like resignation as it did acceptance and I chose to see it that way. Dogs would escape and bank accounts would dwindle and women would leave, fuck you every which way, and you would get new ones, or you wouldn't. It didn't matter in the least.

I took Layla off her leash and let her run and sniff at dogs behind fences, chase squirrels; she came back to me, right by my side, every time I called. When we got home, I drank some water and rested in my chair for a while, noting that the bird wasn't around. Perhaps it was dead. I went to the window and looked out, thinking a cat might've gotten ahold of it.

After a short nap, it was time to go shopping. I would have to find a present for my granddaughter that would be good enough to compensate for all of the time and love I had failed to give her. I knew such a present did not exist. I'd get a card, too, and say something nice in it. I'd stick some money in there, as well, even though the money would immediately go into Maxine's pocket. I got out an old phone book to look up the number for Toys"R"Us, make sure they were open this early, but when I called it was disconnected.

I said goodbye to Layla and drove over there, anyhow. I hardly ever went to the outlets because the things that appealed to other people—so big, so many choices, all of the alleged "sales"—were the same things I hated. And it was a weekend, which meant it would be crowded. I walked and walked and finally stopped at a map. *You are here.* There was something so appealing about that. Here I am, I thought, touching the arrow as I saw myself as if from above, coming into focus. I looked at the numbers in the boxes and tried to find the corresponding ones to see what shops were nearby, but I couldn't seem to make sense of it. The stores were also listed by category. In the children's section, there wasn't a Toys"R"Us but there was a Disney Store and something called The Children's Place, a Gymboree, and an OshKosh B'gosh. I tried to match their numbers to the squares and rectangles and finally gave up and wandered once more.

I stopped to get a cup of Dippin' Dots, amused that I had once been charmed by the cold little pellets. I ate a few bites and tossed it into the trash within eyeshot of the guy who'd sold it to me. I was sorry I'd done it so I went back and ordered another one in a different flavor: birthday cake. He looked at me as though he'd never seen me before, which I appreciated. Then I sat on a bench and ate, enjoying the feel of them in my mouth, how I could track them all the way down my throat and into my stomach in a way I couldn't with regular ice cream.

After that, I went into Gymboree. A woman approached as I held a dress to my body in front of a full-length mirror. The dress had helicopters all over it in red and blue and yellow.

"May I help you?" she asked.

"I'm looking for something for my granddaughter—ideally an Easy-Bake Oven but I don't think I'm going to find that here."

"No," she said, no humor whatsoever, "you're not going to find one of those here, but you might find her a pretty new dress. How old is she?"

"Five, though she claims to be eight."

"Isn't that cute," the woman said, even more humorless than before. How did I manage to find all of the unpleasant women in the world, or were they all unpleasant now? It seemed possible they were, that they walked around with scowls on their faces blaming every man for the faults of the particular ones in their lives. Well, I wasn't going to be held accountable for all of them. It was true I could have done a better job but this woman didn't know that.

She asked me a few questions about Laurel but I didn't know if she was tall or short or big-boned for her age. "You mean fat—you're asking if she's fat?"

"No, that's not what I'm asking. I'm trying to get an idea of her size."

"She's a normal size, I guess, a normal-sized little girl. Her mother is quite health-conscious." I handed the dress to the woman, sorry to see it go. I wished I could wear something new and colorful myself. I'd been wearing the same pair of khakis for weeks, and one of two shirts. I had a closet full of clothes but it didn't matter because choices overwhelmed me. I vowed to clean out my closet, donate the whole lot to poor people.

I was still standing there like an idiot, but instead of giving me her usual sour face, the woman tilted her head and smiled. "You'll find the right gift," she said. "Don't worry."

"Do you know where I might find an Easy-Bake Oven?"

"You could try Walmart," she said. "Or Target."

"Aren't there any toy stores anymore?"

"The Toys"R"Us closed about a year ago, but Walmart and Target have all that stuff now. That's where I get my kids' presents or I order them online, but that only works if you've planned ahead."

"The party's tomorrow. I have not planned ahead."

"I didn't think so," she said, and she smiled again and gave me a little wink. The wink was spectacular. It sent a chill throughout my entire body and I would have paid her a lot of money to position herself in different areas of the store and wink at me all day long. I hoped she would do it one more time, wanted to ask her to do it, but I was afraid of women. I had been afraid of them my whole life. If I'd been a bully, if I'd mistreated or ignored them, judged them by their looks or weight, it had always and only been because of this.

"Thank you," I said. "I really appreciate your help."

"My pleasure." She continued smiling at me. I wanted to ask her out on a date but figured that would be inappropriate. She was also young, how young I didn't know. She was Mexican, too, though I had nothing against Mexicans.

"I appreciate you saying 'my pleasure.' So many young people nowadays say 'no problem.'"

"I've noticed that, as well," she said, scrunching up her nose.

"Back to the dress. . . . Do you think it would fit an average five-year-old, one that isn't too short or too tall or too big-boned?"

"No," she said, "but I'll grab one in the right size."

They wouldn't wrap it because nobody wrapped gifts anymore, she told me, so I would have to figure that out on my own. After that I felt inspired. I could make decisions, would have no difficulty completing this task.

I passed a bookstore, stopped and went inside. I navigated back to the children's section and asked another woman for help and we had an excellent time looking at books, talking about books. She asked about the books I'd loved as a child, and I thought about them and the nice feelings I'd had while reading

them for the first time in a long time. I took all of her recom-
mendations, spending over eighty-five dollars. I'd had no idea
they were so expensive but handed her a wad of cash as if I spent
money like this every day. And they really were beautiful—full
of bright colors and dumb jokes, funny-looking animals and people. I wanted to buy Laurel everything, wanted to give her such
perfect gifts that they would inspire her to live a great life, or
at least set her on the right path. I wished I were rich for the
sole purpose of having young women help me buy things for my
granddaughter all day. I thought about Layla, how she'd let me
hold her even though she didn't like it, how her arms and legs
would go stiff and she'd look tortured but one day she'd be so
comfortable with me and love me so much she'd fall asleep in
my arms, just like a baby, just like Maxine had. Just like Laurel
might one day.

I considered getting her a puppy but they were cat people.
I didn't want her to be a cat person, though, particularly not so
early on—it could ruin her life. I would get her a puppy. I couldn't
get her a puppy. I went back and forth as I drove to the pet store
but all they had were cats.

"Where are the dogs?" I asked the woman.

"We don't sell those anymore."

"How come?"

"There's a whole puppy-mill debate raging," she said. "It's
complicated."

"What's that mean?"

She shrugged and told me she just worked there, didn't know
the ins and outs of puppy mills. "Well, this whole cat situation—
and the proliferation of cat people—is getting out of hand," I said,

and the woman laughed so I told her about my granddaughter and how I needed to get a dog into the mix ASAP so she wouldn't be doomed. The woman laughed some more and we chatted for a bit about dogs and cats. She was an older overweight lady but I acted as though she was very beautiful, or at least like I hadn't noticed that she was old and overweight. Whatever I'd done it had worked and I decided to employ this tactic more often. She was a human being and I was a human being and we were all damaged and ugly and hurting, no matter what face we presented to the world. But if I made eye contact and smiled, said nice things, nearly anyone could be charmed.

I drove to another pet store and they didn't have dogs, either, but said the humane society would be there the following weekend.

"Where can I get a dog today?" I asked.

She told me about a few places I might try, wrote down the names and addresses on a piece of paper.

After that I swung by the house to get Layla so she could ride along, figuring the weather was cool enough if I had to leave her in the car for a few minutes. She hung her head out the window, the wind whipping her face into a smile, while I told her what a good life she had and how lucky she was and then I stopped to get us some burgers to prove the point. We ate them while cruising along the beach and I didn't feel like looking at dogs any longer. I'd gotten lucky with Layla but how often did that happen? The worst-case scenario would be to pick out a dog only for it to grow into an antisocial, food-aggressive animal. What if the damn thing bit Laurel? I'd heard plenty of stories and I didn't want to be responsible for something like that. And then, just as quickly as

I'd talked myself into it I had talked myself out of it. I was apparently going through some sort of midlife crisis but it was very late for that. It was a three-quarter-life crisis. They should write a book about that. All over the country, white men retired and then sat quietly in their houses until they shot themselves in the head or died of boredom. It was a goddamn epidemic.

I picked up a six-pack and cracked open a Miller Lite, considered cruising over to Alabama again, or perhaps the other way, into Louisiana, to show the dog New Orleans, but I was afraid to drive in New Orleans. There were all these one-way streets and too many cars on the road, but mostly there were a lot of black people, which was something we didn't have much of on the Coast. We had white trash and white trash were predictable. They loved the rebel flag and big trucks and shirts apparently made their skin hurt; they chain-smoked cigarettes and loved Trump because he hated everyone who wasn't like them, too. White trash were easy enough to avoid. I told the dog about New Orleans, about pralines and po'boys as we cruised the beach, driving back and forth but staying safely within Mississippi. There were times when I didn't feel as though I could cross state lines, either, much like the people of Arkansas. We were all moving around but we weren't going anywhere, or we weren't going far enough.

■ ■ ■

THAT EVENING, Frank stopped by. He passed me the white box as he entered and I was glad I'd taken a nap because I'd had a nice buzz a few hours earlier. As much as I liked to be drunk, my preference was to do it in private.

"Your good buddy Marv around?"

"That's funny."

"What? Y'all seemed like good buddies."

"I'll just have my locks changed again, give him a reason to come by. See, you bring me food—that's your purpose. If you came here without food I wouldn't know what to do with you." I opened the box: half of a sandwich and most of a loaded baked potato. "You didn't eat much."

"I've been trying to eat half my meal in order to drop a few pounds. I cut it in half right when they bring it out."

"I've never heard of any such thing."

"I'm practicing restraint," he said. "You wouldn't know anything about that."

"Frank! Throwing zingers tonight." I hoped it was over. I decided to sit and eat the sandwich right there. Then I picked up the potato with my hands. Ellen had liked to eat with her hands, as well—she'd liked quesadillas and corn dogs, in particular—and I'd joked that it was one of her defining features. I supposed it was one of mine, too. Something we had in common.

As I bit into the potato I looked at him and waggled my eyebrows. He laughed and shook his head, said there was something wrong with me. "You're probably starving over there. You're not even fat, Frank."

"You haven't seen me without my clothes on," he said, which was a very gay thing to say and which I didn't appreciate. I pictured him standing in front of a mirror examining the various naked parts of himself.

I licked my finger and hit a few buttons, turned it to Fox News so we'd have something to talk about if we were going to talk. Once the food was gone I was good and sober, perfectly sober. I placed the box on the floor so Layla could eat the scraps, lick the sour cream. She ate a pickle and I pointed this out to Frank but then she rejected it.

"The dog seems to have gotten used to you," I said.

"She won't come anywhere near me, and she's giving me the sketchy eyeball right now. Look at her eyeballing me."

"Well, at least she's not growling," I said. And then, "How come Claudia never stops by? I'd like to see her sometime."

"Oh, you know how Claudia is—she prefers her books. Real people she doesn't find all that interesting."

"I should start reading if people in books are so interesting."

"I think they're the same in books, mostly, at least the ones she reads—frustrated, angry—but in a book she can close it when they start to bother her. It's probably why she never wanted kids."

I wasn't sure what to say to that. Frank had never said that much to me about his wife or their life together. I mumbled something about women, the difficulties of them, because I felt like I needed to say something. He looked tired and I wondered how his sleep situation was going. I felt sorry for him but he had his job and his painting and Chili's, which was more than I had. He probably knew all the waitresses and bartenders by name. Hell, maybe he was sleeping with one of them, had put her up in a condo somewhere. Of course he wasn't doing anything of the sort but I liked to imagine his secret life now that he seemed to have one. Dogs feared him. He and Claudia were clearly having some kind of problem. He had decided to cut his food in half for no reason whatsoever.

When Tucker Carlson came on, I fell asleep, or pretended to—I hated Tucker Carlson, his stupid tie, his stupid face—and Frank let himself out.

CHAPTER 19

THE FOLLOWING AFTERNOON, I went to Target and browsed the toy aisles. There were only a few of them and it made me sad for all the children who didn't know what a whole entire store devoted to them felt like, a trip undertaken solely for them as opposed to an afterthought while their mothers purchased sheets or some such.

I had a spring in my step, as I was wearing a clean pair of khakis and a shirt I hadn't worn since I'd been employed. I'd shaved and used soap in the shower, too, lathering the different parts of my body instead of just standing under the water. I felt sober and decent, like an upstanding citizen once more. I would go to my granddaughter's party with a shit-ton of presents and behave myself, return home to walk the dog and eat a nutritious dinner—a piece of fish, assorted green vegetables—and get into bed without consuming a six-pack of beer. I could do these things, I told myself. It was nothing. It was easy.

I stood in front of the display of Hatchimals and selected one: *New Hatchimals from the Glittering Garden with twinkling wings and shimmering fur; rainbow eyes let you know your Hatchimal is ready to hatch.* . . . I grabbed several in various sizes because I didn't know what the hell they were and didn't care. Maxine could return them if she wanted, or trade them in for others. After that I looked at gift bags, choosing the biggest one along with some tissue paper in rainbow colors, which would go nicely with the rainbow eyes, and then went to find an Easy-Bake Oven. It appeared basically unchanged, though it had a fancier name—The Ultimate Oven, Baking Star Edition. I hesitated because it seemed like too much, all of the cakes and icings, the ongoing expense of it, and an oven wasn't a present for a young girl, anyhow. What was it telling her? That she should learn how to bake so she could stay home and make things for men? Maxine hadn't baked the cakes for Ellen but for me, as if she'd known her job in life would be pleasing a man. I didn't want my granddaughter to think that way, to think I thought of her that way. She was too young to understand but one day she would.

"Can I help you, sir?" a woman asked. Her eyes were kind. She had blue streaks in her hair the color of cotton candy. I wanted to touch it, see if it felt different from the rest of her blondish hair underneath. It wasn't attractive but I figured that was the goal, to make herself less pretty, and it was working. There was also a tiny earring in her nose that I'd initially mistaken for a pimple.

"I'm trying to find my granddaughter a gift and think I've picked out too many things. I'm not sure. It seems like it might be too much."

"Let's see what you've got so far," she said, taking the bag from my hand.

"I already got her a dress and some books, too."

She squatted and pulled out the boxes of animals along with

a light-up jump rope, a pack of glitter markers, some mermaid stickers, and a hair accessory/makeup combo kit. "I see she likes sparkly things."

"Don't all girls like sparkly things? And when they get older they like them even more."

"Okaaay," she said, ignoring my observation. "So this seems like a lot of different stuff. Let's streamline a bit." She pointed out that I had two Glittering Gardens when I only needed one because it hatched all of the animals. "You know what? How about you let me do this. How much do you want to spend?"

"I don't know—sixty or seventy dollars. But I don't want to look cheap. I can spend more."

"This'll only take a second," she said, and I watched her backside until she was out of sight. Her hair was the swingy kind, or she did something with her head as she walked that made it swing. When she came back, she handed me a different bag with different tissue paper and much less stuff in it. Then she told me to take the price tags off and wrap each individual item.

"You're very helpful," I said. "Thank you."

"I volunteer at an old folks' home on weekends."

Was she calling me old? I supposed I wasn't young but I wasn't old, either. I took the bag from her and went over to the grocery section, watched myself walk along in the freezer cases, which projected a clear image in the glass. Turned out I was old and also quite fat, fatter than I had ever been, which was unfortunate. I wasn't going to cut my food in half, though. I wasn't going to do anything so rash as that. I picked up some coffee and bologna and toilet paper and then set everything on the floor and went to get a cart.

I stopped at some point to eat a hot dog and managed to get ketchup on my pants. Then I purchased a bag of popcorn. I was stalling and knew I was stalling but I felt glued to the plastic chair. I didn't want to see Ellen, didn't want to be in the same room with her. I didn't want to hear about her boyfriend, *Rick*, or imagine the two of them hiking or whatever the hell they liked to do when they weren't screwing people out of money that wasn't theirs. I hoped they got lost in the woods. Perhaps he'd even managed to get her in the water—she must have a nice pool at that luxury beachfront condo. Why had I agreed to go? I should've said I had plans and would bring Laurel's present over another time. I shoveled the popcorn into my mouth, pieces falling everywhere. Someone would have to clean up after me and I felt sorry about it but my sloppiness also guaranteed that that person would have a job tomorrow and the day after that. Slobs served a purpose. I wouldn't be convinced we didn't.

When the bag was empty, I pushed the cart out of the store without paying, not realizing I hadn't paid until I was home and everything had been unloaded and put away. I would have to go back. I called instead and told the manager what I'd gotten and asked if I could mail him a check, but no, he didn't like the sound of that at all, so I had to gather everything up and put it in the car and return to the store, haul it inside.

I was irritated at that point and said something I shouldn't have said to the girl checking me out even though it wasn't her fault. Then I went back home, put everything away again, and changed pants. I was exhausted and the party was well under way at that point but my stomach hurt so I sat on the toilet for a while, talking to Layla, apologizing to her even though I was a good dog owner. In order to back up my claim, I made a list of everything I'd done for her that day: taken her on two walks, cooked an egg and waited for it to cool before putting it on her bowl of expensive dry food made especially for dogs of her size and age, replaced yesterday's water with fresh water. She had taken two poops and somewhere north of five pisses. I'd petted her in bed that morning and here I was on the toilet while she sniffed my pants, tried to get a few good licks on my legs as I moved them from side to side.

By the time I arrived at Maxine's, the party was over.

Ellen answered the door.

"Hello, Lou," she said. She looked fine—she looked good, even—a bit thinner and wearing a flowy shirt I didn't recognize, but the same ole Ellen. "You brought your dog with you, I see. That's strange."

"Is it? Everyone loves dogs. Even Hitler loved dogs."

She backed into the house, telling me I'd missed the party. Her lip all curled up in disgust. I wished I'd seen her sooner. If I'd had my doubts about the end of our marriage, I'd only needed to see her for a moment to be reminded. And why'd she have to be so nasty to me? There was no reason for her to be nasty anymore. I stopped myself from saying anything else, which was difficult, but I was going to be the bigger person.

Laurel came hurtling at me and got me around the leg. I touched her springy hair and she looked up at me with such joy as I passed her the bag. Craig shook my hand, Maxine kissed my cheek.

"I'm sorry I'm late," I said. "I had some issues."

"We're just glad you're here now, Dad," Maxine said.

"You're lucky you missed it," Craig said. "One of the kids

had an accident and we spent half the party disinfecting. It was a real mess."

"I had some trouble earlier, as well," I said. "It's why I was delayed."

"You probably used the bathroom, though," he said, and I assured him I had.

"I don't know why you feel compelled to tell people things like that," Ellen said. "It's gross." She gave me a haughty look as she moved about the room, picking up discarded plates and cups. "No one wants to hear about that."

"You're not my wife anymore—"

"It's gross," she repeated.

"—so you can keep your opinions to yourself." It was unfortunate that I'd spent so much time thinking about her in the early years of our marriage, and those biscuits—why had I been stuck on those damn biscuits?—when whatever good things we'd had were memories best forgotten.

"Do you want ice cream with your cake?" Maxine asked.

"Sure do," I said, and she put a big scoop on a generous slice and I sat in what had to be Craig's chair because it was the only comfortable one in the room while Laurel tried to decide between playing with Layla and opening my present. She sat and then stood, jumped up and down, took the dog's face in her hands and planted a good one on her nose. She squealed. Plopped down on the floor. It was dizzying to watch but entertaining enough for a short time.

"Take it easy, Laurie," Craig said, sitting next to her. I noticed him holding one of his knees. Perhaps we might talk about our knees sometime.

"Laurie," I said, "now that's a cute name."

"*Dad*," Maxine said, and I shoved a piece of cake into my mouth as Craig helped Laurel dig through the bag. I hadn't taken the price tags off or wrapped each of the individual items in tissue paper but she didn't mind. I'd bought her one Glittering Garden, which was the right number of Glittering Gardens, and two of the eggs that you put in the garden to hatch. And there was also the jump rope. She pumped it above her head and sprang to her feet to try it out, but she wasn't very good. On her third attempt to get the rope past her feet, she knocked Ellen's drink out of her hand—what looked to be white wine—and it spilled all over her pants.

"I didn't consider the liability of a jump rope," I said.

Ellen looked more upset than she should've so they must have been new, and expensive, purchased via the generosity of my dead father. I hoped all her future pants got ketchup on them.

Craig said he wished Laurel would go ahead and break everything, be done with it already. Laurel, it seemed, was a real klutz. And just when had Craig become so likeable? What a nice guy. I'd have to mention it to Maxine the next time I saw her, what a great guy he was, how much his personality had improved. What had I ever held against him? I realized it was as simple as he hadn't seemed to like me enough, hadn't gone out of his way to make me feel like he gave a shit when I had raised the woman who would become his wife, but I hadn't gone out of my way, either. In fact, I had ignored him. Called him the wrong name. Why would he have extended me courtesies after such insults?

Ellen left after that, didn't look at me as she walked out the door and got into a car that was not a dark blue Buick Regal but a silver SUV, and then it was the four of us.

"Do you want another piece of cake?" Maxine asked. "Or some pizza? It's cold but I can heat it up."

"Another piece of cake might be nice, but a small one this time. And no ice cream. I'm gonna be like Frank and start watching my weight."

"Why would he be watching his weight?" she asked. "He's not even fat."

"That's what I said. Who knows with Frank, though, he's a man of mystery."

She laughed and said Frank was the least mysterious man she'd ever known. I left it at that, didn't want to out him. Laurel was getting the hang of the jump rope by that point, counting out Mississippis, which pleased me. Even in Mississippi the children counted Mississippis—we had the river and the measurement of seconds. We had a lot of other stuff, too, stuff that others would never know about because they only wanted to rehash the bad things.

Craig excused himself while Maxine messed around in the kitchen, leaving Laurel and me alone. She climbed into my lap and I told her some things I knew: that she could get blue hair if she wanted, but she shouldn't do it just to be ugly, that dogs were excellent company, much better than people, though they didn't live all that long and were prone to running away. And they had poor gag reflexes, though that was maybe anecdotal. I told her that cakes were more delicious when other people made them, as was most everything else. I tried to think of other things I knew, advice she might find useful.

"What are you telling her in there?" Maxine called.

"I'm giving her life advice."

"Oh no," she said. "Don't do that! Don't listen to him, Laurel!"

"What? I give good advice. I'm a fount of wisdom."

Laurel scooted to the floor and I got down there with her, watched her set up the eggs and run back and forth to her room to grab other mechanical toys to show me how they worked. They didn't seem any more advanced than the toys of fifty years ago; so far as I could tell, they just sped directly into walls and spun their wheels.

"Rainbow eyes!" she yelled, and the eggs split: one and then the other, twins in each. One of them sang and the other danced. They shifted their heads and made strange sounds and Laurel clapped and squealed. It was every girl's dream to have a twin, a replica of herself to admire, while also imagining herself better.

"I have more presents for you," I said. "I nearly forgot." I went back out to my car and brought in the books and the dress.

"This is too much, Dad," Maxine said. "You didn't have to get her all this stuff. It's really too much."

"I spared you the oven. I considered it but decided to save you from buying all those mixes."

Another hour passed and I remained on the floor, unwilling to take the dog and return to the house. I imagined it there, how quiet and dark. Closed up. Craig had returned and Maxine was done in the kitchen so the three of us watched Laurel play. She was wearing the dress I'd bought for her over her other dress and was pleased to be wearing two of them. She yelled at her animals to be good, to stop being so bad, pausing every once in a while to pet Layla roughly or yank her ears. Layla was a good sport about it, seemed to enjoy it even.

"I've been thinking about putting the house on the market—get out from under the house, as they say. What would you think about that?" I asked Maxine.

"That would be fine with me. I never liked that house," she said.

"Because it has bad memories for you?"

"No. It doesn't have bad memories—I had a good childhood. The house is just dark and the ceilings are low. It feels cramped. It needs to be updated."

"You had a good childhood?"

"Of course I had a good childhood, Dad. Y'all were great parents. You did your best."

These were different things, being great parents and having done our best but I decided to focus on the former.

"Would you get out of Biloxi?" Craig asked.

I told them the plan, which I now realized was the plan, and not a dream or an idea. The rest of my life, and who knew how long that was, would be mine: I would sell everything, all of which meant absolutely nothing, and buy a luxury RV—or at least a very nice one—and the dog and I would hit the road. I asked if they'd be interested in coming along on one of my trips, perhaps in the summer. We'd drive to the tip of Florida and see the Everglades, over all of those bridges and that blue, blue water. Beaches would be much prettier than we were used to, the water clear and clean. We could drive to the Grand Canyon, across Nevada and Utah, Montana and Idaho and Wyoming. Craig nodded, seeming to like the idea of it. Probably he was thinking of his own escape. Maxine said that sounded nice in the way that people tell you future plans that are unlikely to happen sound nice.

"I'm really going to do it," I said, because I knew how to keep my word, or I'd known at one time and would find that man again. I felt the fear and excitement of an unknown life in which terrible and wonderful things would happen, knowing that there was no other way to spend my remaining years. Being terrified was far better than the nothingness of a life spent in a chair, surrounded by the to-go boxes from someone else's leftovers.

It was getting late and Craig told Laurel to give me a kiss. I expected her to yell that she wasn't ready for bed, but she stood and walked over to me, kissed my cheek with her sticky lips.

"I love you," she said, though no one had told her to say that.

"I love you, too."

Maxine and I smiled at each other as Craig took her to her room, leaving the two of us alone. It was easier to talk to her with Craig there, with Laurel yelling at her toys or reminding me how much she liked chicken nuggets. I wanted to ask my daughter about her childhood again, if we'd actually been good parents, had done a decent job of things. She had said it, though, and I would leave it at that. Parents probably always thought they'd messed it up, could have done better, done more. It was the struggle and worry of having brought another person into the world and then giving them the freedom to figure things out on their own. If nothing else, Ellen and I had done the second part well. Maxine was a good person, a good mother and wife. She had made a nice life for herself.

"I almost got Laurel a dog, but thought you'd make me take it back," I said. "And then I'd probably've kept it and Layla's plenty for me. Plus y'all have all those cats—where *are* the cats?"

"They hide when we have people over," she said. "And there's only two of them. We don't have, like, a dozen cats."

"That's right. Penny and Ginger," I said, impressed with myself for recalling their names. "One of them was waking you up early to eat. Is it still doing that?"

"Ginger's an early riser. I can't believe you remembered their names."

"I'm a good listener."

"No, you're not, Dad."

"Okay, you're right, but I'm trying to be a better listener." Then I told her Layla and I were also early risers and I needed to get her home, take her for one last spin around the block.

She walked me outside and we stood in the driveway.

"Laurel sure does love her chicken nuggets," I said.

"I know! And I don't even let her eat them that often. I have no idea why she insists on broadcasting it all over town." She hugged me and said she hoped I'd come back soon, and it sounded like she meant it. I'd intended to say something nice to my daughter—about how happy they seemed or how proud I was of her. I could do it some other time, though. It wasn't like it was the last time I'd ever see them.

I sat in the car with the windows down, Layla patiently beside me as I watched the lights in their house go off and others turn on. I wanted to pause my life, remember everything about this moment. The chill in the air indicating the arrival of a new season at last, the feel of whatever substance Laurel had transferred to my cheek, and Maxine's house, behind the doors and windows of which my daughter and her family prepared for bed. They were my family, too, and had been all along. Everything going forward was up to me. I could continue down the road I'd been on. I knew exactly what that road held. It wouldn't offer me any surprises and I had never liked surprises, or this was the story I'd told myself all these years, but the story could change. It already had.

ACKNOWLEDGMENTS

THANKS TO the following:

Melissa Ginsburg and Lee Durkee, faithful readers

Katie Henderson Adams, Gina Iaquinta, and Liveright Publishing Company

Sam Stoloff, Matt McGowan, and Frances Goldin Literary Agency

The original team: Matt, Nick, Betsy, Mom and Dad + Lucky Tucker

And the Mississippi Gulf Coast, where I spent an irrecoverable year of my life walking the beaches, cruising Hwy 90, waiting for alligators to move, cashing hail-damage checks, and eating all of the oysters. Shout-out to Vincent Scarpa for going miles and miles out of his way to eat burgers with me. That was nice.